CHILD OF ANOTHER KIND

STEVEN DECKER

STEVEN DECKER

CHILD OF ANOTHER KIND

Quotes of scripture are from the World English Bible.

ISBN 979-8-9873940-0-7 (print)
ISBN 979-8-9873940-1-4 (eBook)

Library of Congress Control Number: 2022921992

Book Cover by Damonza
Interior design and formatting by Sabrina Milazzo

First edition 2023

Visit the author's website at www.stevendecker.com
Published by TIER Books LLC

TIER

For Diane

Novels by Steven Decker

Distant Finish

The Time Chain Series:
Time Chain
The Balance of Time
Addicted to Time

The Another Kind Series:
Child of Another Kind
Earth of Another Kind
Gods of Another Kind
Genesis of Another Kind

Walking Into Dreams

PART 1

Cynthia and Maddie

Chapter 1

Cynthia

My daughter and I shared everything, but I never understood what she actually was until I died trying to protect her. Some labeled Maddie as "difficult" or "disruptive," even "dangerous," but our time together was precious to me, a gift from God cut short by the ignorance of others. Maddie helped me see the truth on more than one occasion, and she even saved my life once.

The whole thing was my fault; I should never have let that man into our home. I remember a morning rain was just ending, ushering in a beautiful spring day. The year was 1990. As we sat at the kitchen table together, Maddie in her booster seat beside me and the "bad man" (Maddie's words, not mine) across from us, I could tell she was agitated.

Even as an infant, she'd cry when certain people held her yet coo and smile when others did the same. I suspected something was different about her even then, and as time went by I learned more, but not everything, until after my life on Earth ended. Even now, after all that's happened, my only regret about adopting Maddie is not being with her anymore. The troubles we had weren't so different from those of any parent and child, except in cases when her "abilities" took center stage, like they did on the morning of the bad man.

While sitting at the kitchen table, both Maddie and I could see out through the window above the sink, but Mr. Turner couldn't, because his back was facing the window. A rainbow pierced the sky and curled into the green mountains, but nature's tranquility outside seemed to have no effect on Maddie's frame of mind inside. She was still as a statue, glaring at the man across the table with her pale blue, saucer-like eyes. Her delicate, blond hair was frozen in place, draped over her bony shoulders, and her mouth was closed but turned down. As I watched her narrow her eyes, a thought bloomed in my mind.

He's a bad man, Mama, came the thought, somehow manifesting itself into the voice of my little Maddie.

I felt my face flash red and hoped Mr. Turner didn't notice. And it wasn't from embarrassment that I blushed, I'll tell you that. It was because at that moment, I realized I'd made a mistake letting him into the house. I didn't find out until some years later *how* Maddie could do things such as projecting her voice into people's minds and knowing their memories, but the one thing I was certain of, on that glorious and frightening morning, was that my daughter was always right about people. All it took for her was a long look into their eyes, and she'd been doing plenty of that since the man had sat down. By now, she knew the truth of who he really was.

He'd come to the door of our modest home with pamphlets in hand, describing the mission of his church, asking if he could come in for a brief conversation. I was a Christian too, and even though my denomination wasn't the same as the one this misguided soul had claimed to represent, I rarely passed up an opportunity to explore how one faith differs from another. It mattered little to me whether I was called Protestant, Catholic, or whatever. My view was that all Christians sought the same thing—eternal salvation—and I was continually perplexed that our differences in how to achieve this could lead, in some cases, to extreme prejudices against one another. I myself was not a party to such hate, because I knew in my heart that it ran counter to the most basic teachings of our Lord.

But now I was on high alert, wondering if my time to ascend to heaven had arrived. More importantly, though, I knew I wasn't about to let that man harm Maddie before I went. She'd been given to me by the grace of God, and I believed my service to Him was inextricably linked to this special child. I would never want to harm another human being, even one as damaged as the man in front of me, but I needed to act quickly if I was to have any chance of protecting my daughter.

"Would you like some coffee, Mr. Turner?" I asked, rising up and moving around the kitchen table to the counter beside the sink. I glanced out the window at the stunning rainbow hanging in the clear blue sky, hovering over the Appalachians like a halo over the head of an angel, and I resolved to do what was necessary to ensure that my family could enjoy views like this for years to come. My back was now to his back, and I was worried he might turn his head and discover what I was up to.

"No thank you, Mrs. Pace," he said, his voice calm. When he spoke, I noticed for the first time that, unlike Maddie and myself, he had no Southern accent. He must not have been from anywhere near our peaceful town of Asheville.

"I think I'll have some," I said, reaching for a cup with my right hand while quietly opening a drawer with my left. I slipped my hand into the drawer and withdrew the tiny canister, quickly pushing it into the pocket of my slacks, attempting to act casual while I poured the coffee. Then I returned to the other side of the table, set the cup down, and sat. Steam rose from the coffee, and I could smell the staleness of it—I'd made it hours ago—as I dropped my left hand below the surface of the table and slowly removed the pepper spray from my pocket, all the while engaging the man with my friendly smile and innocent eyes.

He was very plain-looking—average height and weight, neatly cropped brown hair, wearing a white short-sleeved shirt and khaki pants—but when I dared to look directly into his eyes, it was hard to say what color they were. They were very dark, and they didn't seem as moist and shiny as most people's eyes, almost like they'd been painted in matte onto his pale face and weren't really alive.

When I looked at Maddie, I saw her emotions boiling over. I reached over with my free hand to calm her, but she could no longer contain herself.

"You should go away!" she screamed at the man.

I squeezed Maddie's arm, urging her to restrain herself.

"Now, now, honey. Mr. Turner is just here to spread the word of his church. I'm sorry, sir. She's only four. Sometimes she doesn't realize what she's saying." I widened my smile, trying to convince him not to harm us with an expression that I hoped would veil the urgent beating of my heart.

Maddie had explained to me, many times, that she didn't understand why the thoughts flooded her mind every time she met a new person, but they came, and they were not always pleasant. I wondered what gruesome memories she'd dredged from this imposter's mind, but I couldn't ask her right then. I was watching him as closely as she was.

He sat there smiling, seeming not at all concerned about what she'd said. Slowly, he lowered his hand below the surface of the table, then brought it back up, holding a gun. Placing hand and gun calmly on the table, he addressed me.

"I'm not here to hurt you, Mrs. Pace. I just need whatever cash you have and a few of your most valuable possessions."

"He's lying!" screamed Maddie. "He wants to hurt us, Mama!"

I felt my eyes grow wide, sensing the moment of truth had arrived. A determination built inside me, slowing the beating of my heart. I became calm because I had to.

"Mr. Turner," I pleaded. "You can't really mean to hurt us."

The man stood, leaving the gun lying on the table, then picked up the pouch he'd brought in with him. I admit I was thinking about trying to reach across the table and take the gun, but I suppose that was easy for him to figure out.

"I wouldn't do that, Mrs. Pace," he said, and even though he said it calmly, as my eyes moved up to his, I saw hatred in them.

Not taking his gaze off me, he unzipped the pouch and removed some duct tape.

"We'll just need to quiet the little girl, and then we can get on with this," he said. "You just stay where you are, Mrs. Pace."

He extended his free arm to retrieve the gun, but before he reached it, I shot up from my seat and blasted him with the pepper spray. He let out a howl and recoiled, dropping the duct tape and bringing both hands to his eyes. I lunged across the table and snatched the gun, then pushed myself back up and pointed it at him, unsure what I would do if he tried to come at us.

"I've got the gun pointed at you right now, Mr. Turner!" I screamed. "Don't move!"

But he did move, in the direction of the door to the living room. Mr. Turner stumbled through the opening and found his way to the front door, where he ran outside and nearly fell down the steps. As he hurtled away along the sidewalk in our quiet suburban neighborhood, frantically rubbing at his face, I stepped out onto the front porch and spotted a neighbor across the street, working in her yard.

"Get his license plate number, Margie!" I shouted. "He needs to be stopped!"

I ran back into the house as Mr. Turner's car screeched away. By the time the 911 operator answered the phone, Margie had entered our home. I gave the make and model of the car to the operator, then handed the phone to Margie, who recited the license plate number. I gave them a description of the man as well, and explained that I had his gun and the other things he'd brought into our home. The operator told me a patrol car would be dispatched to our residence and an APB would be issued to pursue the man.

After I hung up, I went to my daughter, who was still sitting at the kitchen table.

"He was a bad man," she said, frowning, nearly in tears. "He hasn't been to church since he was a little boy. And he likes to hurt people! He does it all the time!"

I picked her up out of her booster seat and held her tightly, patting her back in an attempt to calm her.

"But how do you know that?" I asked, not at all doubting the truth of her knowledge, just continuously curious as to how a child of four could be both blessed and cursed with such abilities. She'd always been advanced—talking by the age of nine months, reading by the time she was three and a half—but these other things she did with her mind were astounding.

Maddie shook her head from side to side, speaking in her sweet, quiet Southern voice.

"I don't know, Mama. I don't know."

Chapter 2

Maddie

Everyone on Earth knows there's no love as strong as a mother's love. I experienced this from the perspective of a daughter. I was an only child. My mother was Cynthia Pace. I write from a place quite distant from her now, but my memories are clear. I remember the good, and the bad, and the … end.

I always thought my mother was a beautiful woman. She had such depth, such soul—and she was pretty too. Certainly a lot prettier than me. She had wavy, auburn hair, fair skin, and a good shape to her body. I, on the other hand, had that stringy blond hair, pale skin, and eyes that looked like an owl's in a head that seemed too big for my thin and gangly body. Even as a toddler, I would never be called cute unless someone was lying. But I felt my mother's love, always, and it has carried me through a difficult life. Even now, separated from her by unfathomable circumstances, I feel that love. It lifts me up in times of sorrow, and as I write these words, I feel such grief, but also hope. Hope that I might find her again.

On that day when the bad man came to our house, I was only four. But even then, my abilities were showing themselves, and they did a service for Mom and me on that day. She was so brave she would have died to protect me, and years later, she proved it. But it was on the day of the bad man that I first witnessed that fierce, animal love, unknown to me until I saw it in her. Even then, I wondered if I had something like that in myself. That pureness, that profound caring for another. I believed I did. I would die for my mother, just as she would for me, and even though I've been told by others that I'm not like her, that I'm not human at all, I know in my heart that I am. She taught me. She showed me, every day of her life, what it is to be good.

On the day of the bad man, I was just a little girl in her booster seat, scared because of what I'd learned when I entered his mind. The man was a rapist and a killer. That was why he was there. I didn't even know what rape was back then, but I knew it was bad, and I knew killing was even worse. He wasn't there for money, although he would have taken that too if he could have. But his primary motivation was to fulfill his own sick need to harm others, to make himself feel more powerful by taking advantage of those who couldn't protect themselves. He was wrong about us, though. A tiny thought transmission from me to Mom was all it took. The bad man didn't stand a chance after that, because he was trying to take us from one another, and she knew it. End of story, for him. But not for me and my mom. Not yet.

Chapter 3

Cynthia

Fall 1992

"Good morning, Mrs. Pace," said Principal Banes. "Thank you for coming in."

I took a seat in front of her desk. It was 8:30 a.m. The meeting time had allowed me to drop Maddie off at class and go straight to the principal's office.

"Thank you, Mrs. Banes," I said. "I'm glad to be here."

The principal was a thrifty-looking woman in her mid-fifties, with close-cropped gray hair, wearing a charcoal suit and a white blouse. She sat back in her chair, turning her mouth down in a frown.

"I'm sorry for the circumstances, Mrs. Pace."

"Please, call me Cynthia," I said, trying my best to give her an endearing smile. But that didn't seem to warm the chilly atmosphere in the room at all.

"I think under the circumstances we should keep this formal, Mrs. Pace. This is a serious matter that will require definitive follow-up actions."

I'd been called into her office due to Maddie's "behavior issues." Maddie had entered the first grade at Hickory Forest

Elementary school in early September and was now six weeks into her first term. Already in trouble, apparently, and it didn't take a rocket scientist to guess why. Nevertheless, I feigned ignorance.

"Can you tell me, specifically, what these behavior issues with Maddie involve?" I asked.

"Certainly," said Principal Banes. "It's basically a self-control issue. Madison has been accusing certain other students of poor conduct, both in and out of school."

"Can you give me some details?"

"Yes. For example, she accused Jayden Fox of killing a squirrel with a BB gun. She accused Melissa Davenport of shoplifting. And she accused Terrence Dorn of lying to his mother about what he'd been doing during his playday with Billy Ralston. She claimed they'd put dog feces in a bag and dropped it on a neighbor's porch, set the bag on fire, then rang the doorbell and ran away."

"Was that the extent of it?" I asked, implying with my tone that these seemed to be trivial matters, simply a child voicing her opinion.

"Why no, actually. She's having at least one outburst per day, usually in the mornings when class has just started."

"Can I ask you if the things she's accusing people of are actually true?" I asked, raising my eyebrows in a challenging display.

Principal Banes was having none of that. "That's irrelevant," she said. "Madison's *outbursts* are what we're here to discuss, Mrs. Pace."

"Yes, Mrs. Banes, I understand. But can you indulge me, please? Are you finding that Maddie's accusations are true, or false?"

The principal sighed, seeming reluctant to verify what I knew with certainty already.

"From what we've been able to piece together, yes, Madison's accusations are basically true," she said. "But these outbursts are very upsetting to the class, especially to the children who are being accused. If we can't get this under control, we're going to have to place Maddie in a special education group, and if that doesn't work, she'll have to be moved to a special school for children with behavioral issues."

"Or we could homeschool her," I retorted.

"Yes, of course, that's an option. Do you have the credentials for that, and the time, Mrs. Pace?"

Other than my volunteer work for the church, which was substantial, I was a full-time homemaker. But since Maddie had started school, I was becoming a little bored with my life. I'd been planning on accepting a job at the church, replacing the former administrator when she retired at the end of the year, but I'd have to wait before deciding on that until this matter was resolved—or wasn't.

"I have the time," I responded. "And if I need to obtain some kind of certification, I'll be able to do that."

"That may end up being the best option then, unless we can correct her behavior so she can remain here at Hickory Forest. But why don't you speak to her first and see if we can get her to stop confronting others about matters that are not her business?"

"Yes, of course. I'll speak with her. We've been dealing with this issue since she was about two years old. We adopted Maddie when she was an infant. The adoption agency didn't have much information on her, so we don't know her family background, although they said they'd conducted a genetic test of some sort and found her gene pool to be 'Slavic.' So they think she might have come from somewhere like Russia."

"Does Madison know she's adopted, Mrs. Pace?"

"Of course," I responded. I mean, wasn't it obvious to the woman? We couldn't have kept that knowledge from her even if we wanted to.

"I see," said Principal Banes, a tone of disapproval in her voice. She really didn't seem to understand, or care, what a tremendously unique situation this was.

"Has the school psychologist met with Maddie?" I asked.

"Not yet. Would you like him to?"

"Yes, I would. We've been considering having her seen privately, but anything you can learn here might be helpful."

"Very well, Mrs. Pace. We'll have you sign a permission form and make that happen. In the meantime, please speak to Madison. She's a very bright little girl, already a candidate for skipping a grade, but with behavior like we've seen so far, her progress could be severely curtailed rather than advanced."

"Has the school considered the exceptional aspects of Maddie's condition?" I inquired, still feeling like the woman was missing the point here. "I mean, she can literally look at someone and know their past. Don't you think that's extraordinary?"

"If it's real, yes. But exploring something like that is not within the scope of a public school's capabilities. If you feel Maddie has a special ability, I would suggest you have someone evaluate her privately."

"Is a psychologist the right place to start?"

"It's as good as any, I would imagine."

"Well, since your school psychologist is going to see her, can he share his findings with me and my husband?"

"Yes, that's standard protocol. Our psychologist is Dr. Bertram Rand. You should be aware, though, that his emphasis will be on correcting the inappropriate behavior, as opposed to exploring Madison's purported special ability."

She still wasn't getting it.

"I understand, Mrs. Banes. But I'm not sure he'll have a choice."

Chapter 4

Maddie

As I look back on my childhood all these years later, I try to remember what it felt like then, to be different. I remember knowing I wasn't the same as other children but not understanding why. And because I was so young, I didn't comprehend that being different in the *ways* I was different was something to be kept secret. I learned that quickly, however, prodded into understanding by meetings with unfortunate results, such as the one with Dr. Rand in October of 1992.

I gazed directly into Dr. Rand's squinting brown eyes, and my mind whirled. Images from his past appeared. I was somewhat stunned, and completely confused. Why would such a man even be allowed to be near children? I distinctly remember feeling the irony of him being employed to help them. Yes, I was six, and one must wonder how a child of six could feel anything like irony at all. But there were many things I could feel that no six-year-old had done before. At least that was what I thought for many years, until I met others who were like me.

At the time, I didn't understand exactly what a doctor like Dr. Rand actually did. He didn't check my temperature or feel my pulse. He just stared at me. My mom had explained that Dr. Rand's job was finding out why people did the things they did, and then helping them to stop doing things that were considered to be bad. This confused me further, because I didn't understand what that had to do with me. I'd done nothing wrong. My mother had also warned me to avoid confronting Dr. Rand with his past, no matter what I saw when I met him.

He was a tiny man, much smaller than my father, with precisely clipped brown hair and a puffy, cratered face.

"So, Madison, how are you today?" he said. His voice was smooth and melodic, in stark contrast to his hideous appearance.

"Fine, thank you," I replied.

"What would you like to talk about today, Madison?"

"I don't know."

"Can we talk about what's been happening in class?"

"All right."

"Can you tell me what you feel when you talk to the other children about things you think they've done?"

"I feel angry."

"Why is that, Madison?"

"Because they shouldn't do bad things! People should only do good things. That's what my mom and dad say, and I believe them."

As I spoke those words, the thought crossed my mind that it was more than my parents' guidance that made me feel that way. I didn't know the word at the time, but later I would come to realize that my belief in "good," and my disdain for "bad," was something innate. It was so deeply imbued in my being that as a younger person, I simply couldn't control my vehemence when I encountered a person I knew to be bad. Like Dr. Rand, for example.

The psychologist sat back in his chair and clasped his hands, resting them on his lap.

"Why, yes," he said. "It's always good to do good things. Do you think you're doing a good thing when you interrupt the class to challenge the other children, Madison?"

"I think so," I peeped, but uncertainty had crept into my voice.

"But hasn't your teacher, and your mom, explained to you that interrupting is not a good thing?"

"Yes."

"So why do you do it?"

I pressed my lips together, turning them down into a frown, and latched on to a strand of hair between my thumb and forefinger, twisting it between my fingers.

"People shouldn't do bad things!" I retorted.

"Very true," said Dr. Rand. "But if interrupting the class is a bad thing, then why do you do it?"

I was becoming angry with this doctor. I didn't understand why a man like that would be allowed to tell kids what to do. I tried my best to avoid confronting him, like my mother said, but it was very hard.

"I want to go home!" I yelled.

"Why is that?" he asked, his voice so pleasant that it made me sick. "Don't you want to stay in this school, Madison?"

"I like the school," I said, almost pleading, but then things began to unravel inside me. "But I don't like you!"

"Why is that?" His voice was so calm that it was infuriating. At that moment, I could no longer contain my anger.

"Because you're a bad man!"

"What would make you say that, Madison? I'm only trying to help you." Again the calm voice, so inconsistent with who this terrible man really was.

"You look at pictures of kids with no clothes on!" I asserted.

Dr. Rand's eyes widened, and his splotchy face boiled red, at first with embarrassment, then with anger. He quickly recovered.

"I'm sorry you think that," he said, his voice just a bit less tranquil, a little more urgent, as if he were orchestrating a fire drill for a class of children. "I can see you believe this, but you are very wrong. I only want to help children like yourself. Clearly, though, you're uncomfortable here, so why don't you run along back to class? Maybe we'll talk about this more next time."

Relieved, I jumped up out of my seat and rushed out of the room.

The next day, I was asked to leave the school. I was only six, but I was certain it was Dr. Rand's doing. The world was becoming a very puzzling place for me. I didn't understand why bad people were allowed to tell good people what to do. What kind of world would allow that to happen?

Chapter 5

Cynthia

Spring 1998

I was nervous as I sat across from the psychologist who'd been working with Maddie for the past six years. Amelia Branch was a handsome, intelligent woman in her mid-thirties, with medium-length, wavy dark hair and an angular face. Her hobby was competing in triathlons, and her physique, while on the thinner side, was unsurprisingly muscular. She had a PhD in psychology but didn't want us to call her Dr. Branch; in fact, she insisted that we call her Amy. I suppose it was part of her approach with patients, to help them open up with her.

Whatever the case, Amy was not only a talented psychologist, she was a good person—which Maddie had confirmed many times—and I was grateful she'd waived her fee after her first consultation with us. Maddie's ability to see people's pasts had become apparent during that first meeting, as she recited things from Amy's life that should have been unknown to her. The doctor was moved by the profound implications this "ability" carried with it, not the least of which was the potential for substantial damage to the child's own psyche from the things she saw in others' pasts, as well as social rejection from those whom she shared her "readings" with.

Amy had strongly recommended homeschooling for Maddie, and I'd been managing that to the best of my abilities. But my daughter's powerful mind had quickly surpassed my own knowledge base. I had a degree from the local community college in religious studies, which didn't make me a scholar by any stretch of the imagination. On the positive side, Maddie could easily assimilate the materials by herself, and was already studying at the level of a high school senior honors student, even though she was only twelve years old.

Other than homeschooling, the first order of business for Amy had been to help Maddie understand that her readings of other people's pasts should *not* be shared with anyone except for her and myself. I reinforced this at home, unfortunately with no help from Maddie's father, who was now out of our lives completely. When Maddie was seven years old, she revealed to me that my husband had been having an affair—and that it wasn't the first one. Maddie hadn't figured out until that age that this was wrong, so she hadn't brought it up. Of course, I immediately divorced him, and apparently he was so uncomfortable with Maddie's abilities going forward that he granted full custody to me, coupled with generous child support. Even though he was Maddie's adoptive father, he went to court to terminate any parental rights, formally ending his relationship with both his daughter and me. It seemed he had no interest in sharing his memories with us going forward.

I kept David's last name, primarily because Maddie and I were going through a traumatic time when he left, and I didn't need to add to her confusion by changing my name. After we got back on steady ground, I guess I kept "Pace" just because it was easier that way. I certainly had no desire to ever rekindle my relationship with David; he was history that would not repeat itself.

Today's meeting had been requested by Amy. I knew something major was coming because of the urgency of her request. She'd told me she needed to see me "as soon as possible," and thus the anxiety I was currently feeling.

"I have to tell you, Amy," I said, "I'm very nervous about this meeting."

She pressed her lips together, an expression of regret coupled with resolve on her face.

"I'm sorry, Cynthia," she said, "but things are changing with Maddie. I really think I've reached the point where I'm no longer qualified to treat her."

My heart rate increased as Amy delivered the blow, but I leaned forward, not yet ready to give up.

"But why?" I asked. "Maddie adores you, and you've come so far with her. She rarely confronts people anymore about her readings of their pasts. Yes, she shares them with me, when she feels it's important, but she saved my life once by doing that, and I'm not going to encourage her to stop talking to me. She's getting to that age where kids clam up with their parents. And she's doing so well with her schoolwork! What happened to cause this change of heart?"

"It's not really a change of heart. I treasure my time with Maddie. But, you see, her intellectual development isn't the only thing that's accelerating. So are her special abilities."

"How so?" I asked.

"Maddie's experiences with other people's memories are becoming more detailed. More intimate. I think she's actually started living out some of these events, in her mind. And that adds another layer of complexity to her emotional state, because now she's feeling emotions from a number of different people, not just herself."

"I see," I said. "But how is that related to ending her treatment?"

Amy folded her hands, then carried on.

"First, I don't seem to be able to stop her from doing it. Frankly, I'm not sure if it *can* be stopped, but I know *I'm* not making any progress. Secondly, and this is the primary issue—Maddie has now started … well, she's started to erase some of my own memories."

"My goodness!" I exclaimed. "That's terrifying. Can you give me an example?"

"I can give you one, but of course I'm not sure if there are others, because obviously I wouldn't remember them. But there's one situation where it became clear what's going on. My mother died when I was nine years old. Of course I still remember my mother, but one day, when I was thinking of her, I couldn't remember *how* she died. I asked my husband if I'd ever told him how it happened, and he explained that it was a long, drawn-out, horribly painful battle with cancer. But I remembered nothing about it, nor did I feel the trauma and grief that should accompany a memory like that, until my husband explained it all to me again."

"Do you think she's trying to erase painful memories?" I asked.

"Possibly. Has it happened to you? You spend more time with her than anyone."

"I don't think so. But how can I be sure?"

"You can't. That's the problem."

"Have you discussed what's happening in your mind with her?"

"Yes, of course. She claims she doesn't know she's doing it. Well, let me clarify that. She says she knows it's happening, but she doesn't seem to be able to control it. And I simply cannot risk this going any further while trying to figure out how to get her to establish control over it."

"Is there another kind of specialist she could see?" I asked.

"I've given a lot of thought to that," said Amy. "There's no question in my mind that Maddie has some kind of telepathic abilities. And they're two-directional—she can extract information from people's minds, and she can plant information as well, like she does when she communicates with you sometimes."

I thought about the times when thoughts from Maddie just popped into my mind. It was a rare occurrence, usually in emergencies, like that time years earlier when she warned me about the troubled soul who called himself Mr. Turner. He was in prison now, put away for life for unspeakable crimes, and I prayed often that he would be healed. That message from Maddie had definitely saved our lives. To my knowledge, she'd never communicated with anyone other than myself in that way.

"Telepathy is studied by parapsychologists," said Amy, "but that's a controversial field. It's not considered to be 'real' science, at least in medical circles. As such, there's no doubt that if Maddie saw a parapsychologist, you'd be put under tremendous pressure to allow them to publish this outrageously spectacular case. They'd guarantee anonymity, but it would be hard for them to ensure that, because they'd want to share this information with as many colleagues as possible. This would lead to an endless stream of requests for further study of Maddie, and I'm certain that would *not* be healthy for her. Even worse, the government would probably hear of it and get involved, and who knows where that would lead."

"So what should we do?" I asked, hoping Amy wouldn't just leave us to fend for ourselves.

Then she explained her plan to me, and a speck of light appeared at the end of the dark tunnel I'd begun to envision in my mind.

"I think you should see a neurologist as a first step," she said. "They'll be able to determine if there's a physiological basis for what's going on with Maddie. They'll do things like MRIs and EEGs, which are perfectly safe and won't harm her. It might go nowhere, but it might reveal something important. If they *do* find something, though, they might be able to figure out a way to help us control what Maddie's doing."

"You mean like drugs?" I asked, frightened at the prospect of Maddie becoming dependent on medicine for the rest of her life, pills that might turn her into a completely different person.

"I don't know, Cynthia. But neither of us is going to allow the treatment to be worse than the cure, right?"

"Correct," I said, feeling better, almost optimistic. "Do you have someone in mind?"

"Yes, I do. My husband, Tom, is a neurologist. I've referred a few patients to him before, for purely medical reasons, but obviously I trust him. By working with him, I can stay involved in the case without actually having to see Maddie in ongoing sessions. If we're lucky, maybe Tom can figure out a way to control her abilities that would allow me to resume our therapy."

Amy's recommendation felt like a drink of fresh water after a hot day in the sun, but it was only fair to warn her about the potential consequences.

"But wouldn't your husband be worried about Maddie erasing some of his own memories?" I asked.

"I'm pretty sure Maddie doesn't do that until she knows the person very well, and for a long period of time," said Amy. "Plus, Tom is confident he can come up with something fairly quickly to limit Maddie's intrusions into other people's minds. He knows there's a risk, but frankly, he seems really fired up about meeting Maddie and trying to help her."

I can't tell you how excited I was to hear all of this, after beginning the meeting with Amy feeling as if we would be losing the anchor that held both Maddie and me in place, but since Amy would be passing the ball to her husband, it was only fair to make sure she understood what that could mean, for her.

"Amy, you realize that my marriage was ended because of a reading Maddie did on my ex-husband, right?" I asked.

"Yes, I'm aware of that," she replied. "And I've thought about those kind of ramifications. I trust Tom, and most importantly, I want the best for Maddie, and for you. I'm sure you understand that her abilities would be of interest to an endless number of entities, including government agencies like the FBI, the CIA, the military, the police—not to mention the private sector. By allowing Tom to evaluate Maddie, we can ensure that we keep things under wraps, for as long as possible."

This last comment got me worrying again. Just when I thought we had a plan that might help us take a great leap forward with Maddie, now the implication was that no matter what we did, it wouldn't last.

"What do you mean 'as long as possible,' Amy?"

"Cynthia, the power we're talking about here is undeniable. I know how badly you want Maddie to lead a normal life, but as you've already experienced, that may not be possible."

"Yes, I know," I admitted. "She's gotten much better about keeping her knowledge of others to herself, but whenever she gets close to a new friend, she ends up sharing things with them that inevitably end the friendship. And she sees so much *bad* when she reads people's thoughts. It can't be healthy for her to experience that."

"I understand fully," said Amy. "But even if her gift was kept secret from others, the fact remains that she knows what she knows. Somehow, she has to live with that—and so do you. The question is, how? I can honestly say I don't know the answer to that, although I've tried my best to help her, and you, to manage it."

"And you've helped us so much, Amy. I just don't know what we'll do without you."

"Well, there's still hope I can resume the therapy, if Tom comes up with some answers."

"Yes, that would be great!"

"Still," she said, "even if we get things back on track, there's only so much any of us can do to help Maddie."

"So what are you saying?" I asked, my optimism about the future eroding further.

"I'm saying that in the long term, neither you nor I can determine where this will lead. In the end, it will be Maddie who decides. For now, we can keep it quiet. But she's growing up, Cynthia, and soon she'll want to make decisions on her own. By working with Tom, we may be able to help her better understand her differences, while at the same time maintaining absolute confidentiality on the subject. I'll offer the case to him, based on his agreement never to publish any of his findings. I couldn't do that with anyone but him."

"All right, let's do it," I said, still shaken by the precarious nature of what Maddie and I were facing. I had hoped that as she got older, things would get easier. Maybe they still would, but Amy had made it clear that soon, Maddie's destiny would be more in her hands than in mine. I just didn't realize how quickly that was going to happen.

Chapter 6

Maddie

When I met Dr. Tom Branch for the first time, I did what I always did when I met a new person: I entered his mind and tried to find out if I could trust him or not. There was one memory in particular that surfaced that told me all I needed to know about him. It was something that happened to him in December of 1980, while he was still in high school. I'll tell it to you as an outside observer, rather than as Tom Branch himself. You see, when I experience memories from someone for the first time, I read them just as the owner of the memories does, and consequently I feel what they feel. But in order to get their emotions out of my head, I always try to relive the memory from the outside. This way, I don't get confused about who I am, and who they are. Anyway, here's my story of that memory:

Seventeen-year-old Tom Branch was pulling his biology book out of his locker when he heard the altercation down the hall. He looked up and saw a gargantuan boy slamming an innocent kid up against a locker. The aggressor was Justin

Pugh, the nose tackle for the football team and the heavyweight for the wrestling team. The other one, average-sized, was Timothy Beecher, captain of the chess team and very likely the next valedictorian of Parson Hills High School.

Like Timothy, Tom was a senior. Justin was a junior, but he was the biggest person in the school at over three hundred pounds, and also the most notorious bully. Tom was the captain of the wrestling team, so he and Justin knew each other well, though Tom wrestled in the 167 weight class. His off-season weight was around 180, but since the season had started, he'd been cutting, and was down to around 170 at the moment. The next match wasn't for almost a week, so he'd lose the three pounds of water weight a couple of days before the match.

Tom threw his biology book back into his locker and slammed it shut, then rushed over to intervene in the mismatch. By the time he arrived, Timothy was already on the floor, and Justin was about to deliver a kick to his ribs. Tom had no choice. He threw himself into Justin with all he had, and was somehow able to move him a few feet away from Timothy. The nose tackle's sheer density caused Tom to bounce back, and both remained upright. The smaller chess captain scrambled away, but now the confrontation was between Justin and Tom.

"What are you doing, man?" yelled Tom. "You could kill that kid!"

"So now I get to kill you instead!" Justin screamed, lumbering forward, on the attack.

"I'm sure you could do that," Tom said, trying to put a reasonable tone into his voice while at the same time squatting into a wrestler's stance, knees bent and arms loose and at his sides.

"Oh, so you want to wrestle then, Captain Tom?"

"I don't want to, Justin. I'd rather you just settle down and go on with your day."

"Oh, I'm goin' on with my day, all right," said Justin, charging at Tom with his arms extended.

Tom ducked under the massive arms and slid down into a single-leg takedown. He scooped up Justin's huge right leg, raised up, and swept his left at Justin's left. The massive boy fell backward, hard, his head impacting the floor with an audible crack. Tom let go and stepped back, waiting to see what happened next.

Justin moved to get up, shaking the cobwebs from his head, but just then the head football coach and the head wrestling coach came running down the hall. Coach Raines restrained Justin, and Coach Gable wrestled Tom into submission.

"That's it, boys," said Coach Raines. "This nonsense is over."

"For now," Justin mumbled, and snarled in Tom's direction.

"If you want to stay in this school, and on the team, I suggest you think that statement over," said Coach Gable. "Now let's get to the principal's office and figure this out."

When I finished that memory for the first time, I was really happy.

Wow! I thought. *That was scary! But Dr. Branch is a good person. That's obvious. And brave. But most importantly, I can trust him.*

Bullying like what happened in Dr. Branch's memory happens all the time. I've read about it in newspapers, and magazines and books. It even happened to me during my short-lived first grade experience, and on a few occasions afterward. What rarely happens in real-life bullying, though, is a third party stepping up and defending the person who's being bullied. Yet Tom Branch did. He risked his own well-being to help someone who couldn't help themselves, and in a very real way, the doctor was doing exactly the same thing with me.

"You with us, Maddie?" he asked.

"Yes, sir," I responded, coming back to the present after my visit to 1980 through the mind of the man in front of me.

"Okay, good. It seemed like you were drifting off for a minute. Do you need me to go over that again?"

"No, sir. I think I understand. The first phase will be an MRI, short for magnetic resonance imaging. The next test will depend on what the MRI shows, but it could be an EEG, an Electroencephalogram, or it might be an fMRI, functional magnetic resonance imaging, which can detect the location of brain activity. There are other test methodologies that might be considered, depending on the results of the other tests."

Dr. Branch, Amy, and my mom all raised their eyebrows, looking shocked at the details I'd just recited. Probably some of it hadn't been spoken about, so I guess I'd gleaned that from his memories. He, meanwhile, seemed interested in how I'd come up with that information.

"Maddie, if I might ask, how did you learn about all of those tests? I didn't really go into that level of detail when I was explaining the plan."

"Uh, I'm not sure," I lied. "I just knew it."

I suppose I should have just confessed the truth. I mean, all three of them knew about my condition. That was what we were there to discuss, after all. But it had been drilled into me for so many years to keep my "abilities" secret that my knee-jerk reaction was to avoid the subject completely, even when interacting with people who already knew about it.

"Maddie," said Amy, her voice calm and soothing as always. "It's okay if you don't know how you learned this information, but in the past, you've told me you knew how you learned certain things, and it's fine to tell us if you *do* actually know how the information came to you. We don't mind at all."

"Well," I said, "I probably learned it from Dr. Branch. I was actually learning quite a few things about him, and that was probably some of it."

"We understand," said Amy. "No problem."

"But it kind of *is* a problem, isn't it?" I said. "That's why we're doing all these tests. Because I'm different. And not in a good way, right?"

"Nothing we can't deal with," said Dr. Branch, sounding confident and upbeat.

I remember thinking at the time that it was good to have one more positive voice on my side. Now there were three: Mom, Amy, and Dr. Tom Branch. I liked him from the start.

Chapter 7

Maddie

After all the tests were done, we gathered in Dr. Branch's office to discuss the results. He would lead the meeting, but he made it clear that each of us—my mom, Amy, and especially me—could ask questions or make comments as we saw fit.

Dr. Branch was a triathlete, like Amy, and in great shape. I would've guessed he was about thirty-five years old (well, I knew he was), and he was bald. He could have had a full head of hair, but he preferred the bald look. Despite his lanky frame, he was kind of muscular too, like Amy. Maybe that was what all highly competitive triathletes looked like, and they were definitely successful triathletes. Both were ranked in the top ten in the world in their age group. They only competed as amateurs, so there were a lot of pros that could beat them, but they qualified every year for the World Championships in Hawaii, the one they referred to as "Kona," always with great respect and awe in their voices.

They were a good couple, and both were salt-of-the-earth kind of people, always wanting to help others. They seemed to especially want to help me. I kind of already knew what the results of my tests were, but it was polite to let Dr. Branch explain it to Amy and my mom.

"So there *is* a mass in Maddie's brain," he said.

"Oh my," said Mom, raising her hand to her mouth. "Is it a tumor?"

"No," said the doctor. "It's something I've never seen before. Something I don't think anyone has seen before."

"My brain is different, Mom," I said, with impatience and maybe a little embarrassment.

Amy stepped in, playing the role of moderator.

"Why don't we let Tom explain what's going on to your mother, okay Maddie?"

"Sure," I said, anxious to get on with things.

Her husband continued.

"The mass is in the center of Maddie's brain, just above the choroid plexus and ventricles. It's surrounded by the cerebrum, which is the largest part of the brain. If you'll take a look at the screen to the right of my desk, I'll bring it up."

The screen filled with an image of my brain. Dr. Branch reached over to the screen and used the forefinger of his left hand to point at the mass, drawing a circle around it without touching the screen.

"You can see that it's spherical, and around six centimeters in diameter, which is about the size of a racquetball."

"What is it?" my mom asked, her eyes wide and a look of horror on her face.

"Well," said Dr. Branch, "that's what we started to explore with the next battery of tests. First, we performed a functional MRI. We placed a video screen into the tunnel with Maddie, a few inches above her face. Then we put images of people onto the screen. If the image was someone Maddie knew, such as you, Amy or myself, the mass in the center of her brain lit up with activity. When we showed people she didn't know, the mass would flash on, but then quickly shut down."

My mom looked a little confused. "So what does that mean?"

"The hypothesis is that the area of Maddie's brain that's different, the spherical mass right in the brain's center, allows her to access other people's memories, but it's also where she stores that information. When we showed her someone she knew, the area lit up because she was accessing the stored memories from that person. When we showed her a picture of someone she didn't, the area lit up briefly, trying to access the memories of the individual, but since there were no stored memories to be found, the area shut down."

Now my mom seemed to understand, and her confusion shifted to concern. "How did this happen to Maddie?" she asked.

"We can speculate on that," he said with a shrug. "But before we do, let me tell you what we did in the last round of testing. If you'll look at the screen, you'll see another brain. This brain is normal and doesn't contain the central mass we found in Maddie's brain."

"Whose is it?" my mom asked.

"It's mine," said Dr. Branch. "Maddie and I switched places. I went into the MRI tube and she stayed outside, but where she could see me. Since there's two-way communication capability through the audio system in the MRI, she and I could talk. While the machine was reading my brain, I told Maddie I had a secret that I'd just discovered that morning. Immediately following that, the area of my brain that stores short-term memories lit up. Since there wasn't actually a secret, it was unlikely the activity in that area was initiated by me. It would have been initiated by Maddie, looking to find the secret.

"Next, I told her I had a secret from my childhood that I had never told anyone about. And sure enough, the area of my brain that stores long-term memories, which is different from where short-term memories are stored, lit up like a Christmas tree. Again, we assume that it was Maddie, trying to find the secret."

"What does all of this mean, though?" Mom asked, clearly quite distressed. "How could this have happened to Maddie?"

"Well," he said, "you're familiar with Darwin's theory of evolution, aren't you, Ms. Pace?"

"Yes, I am," she said, somewhat sternly. "But to the degree this theory conflicts with my religious beliefs, I choose not to believe it."

My mom was pretty religious. I'm not sure why she never pushed it on me, but it was probably because she knew taking me to church with her, or putting me in Sunday School, would just cause more problems for us. The fact is, I had a full understanding of her beliefs anyway, because of my abilities, and we'd discussed it several times. She knew I wasn't buying in to the Christian way of life, no matter if I went to church or not. It just didn't make sense to me, and she seemed to accept that. Still, she went to church every Sunday, always scrambling to find a babysitter for me that I hadn't upset before. For a religious person, I found Mom to be fairly open-minded, but she always seemed to find a way to give religious meaning to things that happened. I was okay with that—I mean, who was I to say she wasn't right, even if it didn't all add up for me?

"That's fine," said the doctor. "But indulge me for a moment, okay?"

"Sure," she said, but she pursed her lips as if preparing to hear something distasteful.

"Darwin's theory speculates that over long periods of time, mutations occur in all living things. Individuals may by chance develop subtle differences from their peers. Sometimes, these differences give them an advantage versus the rest of their species, and these dominant individuals pass the advantage on to their offspring. Ultimately, more and more individuals with the advantage survive, until the advantage becomes the norm and the species advances."

"I understand," said my mom. "And you're saying that's what's going on with Maddie? She has some kind of a mutation that gives her an advantage versus other humans?"

"I wish it were that simple," he said. "First, we can't truly say that the difference Maddie has really gives her an advantage in our society. I mean, after all, you've had to homeschool her and isolate her from others just to keep things from being too disruptive in the groups that a normal child would operate in."

"Tom," said Amy, "I think we should phrase that differently. After all, Maddie is here, and she's acutely aware that she's different, but our objective from the beginning has been to help her gain control over the unique processes she possesses, with the ultimate goal of allowing her to reenter society in a more complete and fulfilling way. Your phrasing implies that Maddie's condition will never allow this to happen, and I don't believe that's true."

I loved Amy. She always made me feel better.

"My apologies, to all," he said, nodding at his wife. "I too believe we can help Maddie control this … this gift, and in so doing, it would indeed allow her to have advantages that no others have. So from a Darwinian point of view, Maddie is potentially the next evolution of the human species. What's confusing is that it's a huge biological jump, not the incremental advancement that is more consistent with Darwin's theory."

"What about God?" asked Mom.

Here she goes again, I thought.

"What do you mean?" he asked.

"What if we say this is the work of God, not a Darwinian mutation?"

"We can say that, because Maddie's 'brain within her brain' is such a radical advancement in human biology, it really *is* hard to accept that it happened according to normal Darwinian Natural Selection. So your hypothesis is as good as any, perhaps the best one we have at this point." The doctor gave her an appraising look. "When it comes down to it, I have no firm explanation of how this happened."

"That's good enough for me," said my mom. "I always put my faith in God when things can't be explained."

"But what about me?" I interjected. "What about my feelings? What about my explanation?"

"Do you have an explanation?" Amy asked.

"Not yet," I said. "But if I can uncover everyone else's past, I *have* to believe I can uncover mine. Can you three help me do that?"

"But you were just an infant when you were taken on by the adoption agency," my mom pointed out. "How could you remember anything before that?"

"I can't, but maybe the adoption agency wasn't telling you everything. I'm suggesting we do some good old-fashioned detective work, and that should be a lot more productive if I use my abilities while we're there."

The three adults nodded, warming to my idea. Dr. Branch had a suggestion.

"Detective work involves going out in the world and asking questions," he said. "Why don't we come up with a way to make it easier for you to do that? There will be times when you'll want to use your power to read people's pasts, but there will also be times when it'll be a distraction to you."

I nodded, warming up to him even more. "That could be useful. My mind gets so preoccupied by other people's past lives that it's hard to concentrate on anything else. What are you thinking, Doctor?"

"I have some ideas," he said. "It'll involve some more testing and some trial and error, but I think we've got a good shot at a solution. And if I'm right, it will help all of us, not just you."

Chapter 8

Maddie

After all of the follow-up testing was complete, Mom took me to meet with Dr. Branch. Amy couldn't be at the meeting because she had to see other patients that day. I knew he'd been working on some kind of glasses for me, and I knew why, but as a twelve-year-old who already thought of herself as unattractive, the idea of wearing glasses wasn't very appealing to me.

"Try these on," said Dr. Branch, handing me the pair.

"But I don't need glasses," I said, resisting.

"That's quite true," he responded. "In fact, your vision is better than literally anyone I've ever heard of. It measured at 20/5, which is comparable to the sight of an eagle. From twenty feet away, you can see all the details that most of us can only see from five feet away."

"So why the glasses?" my mom asked.

"Our additional testing verified that Maddie's eyes play a critical role in her memory reading. Her eyes seem to have an ability to bore into another person's mind. We believe she goes in through the eyes of the other person, but we aren't certain about that."

"Does that mean that if someone closed their eyes, she wouldn't be able to read their memories?" asked Mom.

"I don't think so. Which is why we aren't certain about how exactly her eyes get into another person's mind. We tested her ability on me, with my eyes open and closed, and she could access my mind either way, although with a slight reduction in clarity of recall when my eyes were closed. We'll study it further. But back to your original question—these glasses aren't for sight correction. They're designed to deter Maddie's ability to read memories. The lenses have been infused with lead and barium, the same as what's done with glass in X-ray rooms to protect the technicians from radiation."

"Hmmm," my mom murmured.

"So let's get on with it, if we have to," I said, still resistant to wearing glasses but getting a little more excited about what it might mean if they actually worked.

Dr. Branch handed me the glasses, and I put them on.

"How do we determine if they work?" asked my mom.

"I'll just ask Maddie the right question," he said. "Maddie, what did I have for breakfast this morning?"

"Yogurt with fresh blueberries, whole wheat toast with butter, a glass of orange juice, and a cup of black coffee," I said. "But I already knew that before you gave me the glasses."

"All right, I have another idea," he said. "I'm going to leave the room and go do something. I'll be right back."

The doctor left the room, leaving Mom and I alone together.

"I'd prefer not to wear glasses," I said. "But I realize that if they work, I can start to have a more normal life, and so can you."

"Yes," she said. "It could be a big help. Then all we'll have to figure out is how you can go to college as a thirteen-year-old."

Frankly, I wasn't at all sure that I wanted to go to college. I mean, I was twelve. And even though I understood it could help me get a job when I grew up, I was much more interested in just having a normal life, and college at the age of thirteen was about as far from normal as you could get. But my mom wanted me to, and I knew it would be easy anyway, so I didn't fight her on it.

"I don't mind living at home while I go to college, Mom. UNC-Asheville would be fine."

"I know you could do well at any college, honey, but you're right—something like that might be the best solution, until you get a little older."

"Well," I said, letting out a deep breath, not wanting to think about college at the moment, "let's hope they work, I guess."

Dr. Branch returned to the room.

"All right," he said. "You should try to access my short-term memory center to see if you can find out what I just did."

We all went quiet as I attempted to read the doctor's memory from the past five minutes. Around thirty seconds passed, and I had processed no incoming memories. The feeling when I had the glasses on was a little awkward at first. They didn't block my vision, but they did block my mind from doing things it could do when I wasn't wearing the glasses. It's hard to explain, but my eyes and brain are linked in a way that's beyond what other people experience. When I look at a person when I'm not wearing the glasses, I know them, intimately, almost immediately, and if I keep looking at them, I can keep track of what they're thinking by accessing their short-term memories. No matter if the person is good or bad, I still have a feeling of control, because I don't have to guess what's on their mind, or in their past. With the glasses on, though, I feel vulnerable, because I know a lot less about what's going on with the people around me. It was going to take some getting used to.

The others were waiting for me to say something, so I reported to them what they were all hoping to hear.

"Nothing," I said. "I can't read your memories."

"Now take the glasses off," he said.

I removed the glasses, holding them in my hand and looking directly at him. Now my world was back. I was in control again—I could go inside Dr. Branch's mind and extract the information I needed. I suppose for most people, this flood of information from another person's mind would be disturbing, but in my case, it was like coming home after a long trip abroad. I was glad to be home, and Dr. Branch's little secret was a secret no longer.

"You went to your office and called Amy, but she wasn't there, so you left a message."

"Yes, that was it," he said. "I didn't expect Amy to answer because she's seeing patients today, but it was something to do, and I think we just proved that the glasses work!"

"Yay!" I yelled, feeling excited, not even thinking anymore about how I looked in the glasses.

"Double yay!" My mom matched my enthusiasm.

The doctor smiled. "Triple yay!"

It was an important moment, for all of us. The glasses could help me lead a more normal life. I'd have to resist the temptation to take them off from time to time, especially when I was feeling uncomfortable about the people around me, but I'd deal with that whenever it arose. The upside was that I didn't have to read people's memories unless I wanted to, and that would help me have more friends, and would also allow my mind to have some peace when I was around other people, with no memories intruding on my consciousness. The glasses would help in the other direction too, with people like my mom, and Amy and Dr. Branch, who knew what I could do and didn't want or need me constantly in their heads.

"So where do we go from here?" My mom addressed her question to Dr. Branch, but I couldn't help myself and interrupted.

"I'd like to visit the adoption agency who placed me with you, if it's okay."

"That's fine, honey," she said. "But don't get your hopes up. They knew almost nothing about your past when we adopted you."

"That's all right. I won't wear the glasses while we're in there to make sure they're telling us all they know. And if we come up empty, we can cross that off our list and try something else."

Chapter 9

Maddie

The trip to the adoption agency didn't last long. Mom and I drove downtown at around ten in the morning, found a place to park, then walked along Patton Avenue toward the building where the adoption agency was located. Downtown Asheville was really nice in those days. It was loaded with trendy restaurants and shops and had an artsy-craftsy kind of feel. Nestled in the Appalachian Mountains in western North Carolina, it was a gem of a town. If you went downtown during one of the festivals you'd encounter crowds of people, but most days it was pretty laid back, as it was on the first day of our detective work.

The adoption agency was on the second floor of an old four-story townhouse that had been converted to offices, a trend in that section of the city. Lawyers, accountants, and investment companies populated the area, with a smattering of other small businesses.

I was wearing my glasses during the drive and the walk, to keep my mind clear, but I took them off as we climbed the stairs. Arriving on the second floor, we located the door of Child Power Adoption. We entered and saw a few chairs in a waiting area and a reception desk right in front of us. A woman in her mid-fifties sat behind the desk. Her gray hair was tied back in a bun, and she wore a yellow summer dress, bright like her smile as she saw us come in.

"Welcome to Child Power," she said, in a classic Southern accent. "How may I help you two ladies?" I always got a kick out of it when someone called me a lady. I mean, I know people were just trying to be polite, but I was a gangly twelve-year-old who rarely went out in the world. I guess hearing myself called that gave me hope that it might one day be true.

While my mom informed the receptionist about our appointment with Mrs. Williams, I took the opportunity to scan her memories. Her name was Edwina Hotchkins, and she'd been born and raised in the Asheville area, was married, and had three children. She was a Southern Baptist and went to church every Sunday. The feeling I got was that she was a good person, trying her best to do good on this earth and make her way to heaven in the end. She hadn't been employed here when I was adopted, however, so there was no information about that in her memories.

"Very well then," said Mrs. Hotchkins. "I'll just let Mrs. Williams know y'all are here."

She picked up the phone, and within one minute, a door to an inner office opened. A black woman in her late forties peered out, a wide smile on her pretty face.

"Well, now," she said. "Please come in, Mrs. Pace! It's been a long time."

She opened the door wide, and we entered. Mrs. Williams shook my mom's hand warmly, then turned to me.

"And this must be Madison! Oh my, what a tall thing you've become!"

She approached me and hugged me as if I were a long-lost child of her own. I just kind of stood there and took it, but my mind was working on hers even then. By the time we sat down, I knew the whole story. I let Mrs. Williams explain it to my mom. The story was that I'd been dropped off twelve years ago at the fire station, a few blocks from here, and that no one had seen the person, or people, who did it. The chief of the station had called Child Power, and I'd been temporarily placed in a foster home until I was adopted by the Pace family. And this was the truth, at least as far as Mrs. Williams was concerned.

"Well then," said my mother. "I guess we should go to the fire station."

"You are certainly welcome to," said the jovial woman. "The chief is still there. Most of these firefighters stay at the same post for their entire careers. And what a wonderful retirement package when they retire. They certainly have earned it!"

The small talk came to a quick close, and we said our goodbyes. I put the glasses back on as we left the office. After a five-minute walk, we found the fire station. I was wondering if we'd have to go upstairs to the room where the men slept, and if there really *was* a pole they slid down when the siren screeched to alert them about a fire. Instead, it was just a bland office, and behind it was an open door, revealing a hallway that looked like it led to the bunk room.

The man at the desk was the chief of the station. We introduced ourselves, and he stood and shook our hands, introducing himself as Captain Weeks. He was of medium height, with neatly combed, dark hair and a bit of a potbelly.

"How may I help you?" he asked, addressing my mom.

"My daughter Maddie here was dropped off at your station when she was a baby, twelve years ago," she said. "I believe you were involved in that. Do you remember?"

"Yes, ma'am, I do indeed remember that," he said, leaning back in his chair. "She was a cute little baby, but that's about all I recall."

"We're trying to find out more about the person, or persons, who dropped Maddie off." Just then, I remembered I still had my glasses on, so I removed them, holding them in my hand as Captain Weeks responded.

"Didn't the adoption agency tell you there was no one here in the office when the baby was left?" he asked. "She was just wrapped in a blanket, nestled in one of the chairs over there. I found her when I came out front from the bunk room." He glanced at some comfortable-looking seating arranged in front of a TV on the wall. "Still got those same chairs."

While Captain Weeks and my mom talked, with no information forthcoming, I scanned his memories and saw that he appeared to be telling the truth. But there was something different about the way his long-term memories were organized. It was the same thing I'd noticed before, in Amy's mind, after I'd involuntarily removed her memories of her mother's death. It was like there was a gap in there, a folder that had been removed from a file cabinet and never returned.

Someone, someone like me, might have removed his memory of the incident. Feeling a bit exhilarated, I thought of a way I might capitalize on this newly acquired information.

"Captain Weeks," I said. "Are any of the men who were on duty that day here?"

The chief put his hand on his chin and narrowed his eyes, thinking. Then he nodded his head.

"I remember Lieutenant Bradford was just bringing one of the trucks back from a call. But when he came in from the garage, I'd already found the baby—I mean, found *you*—so he probably knows less than I do."

"Can we speak with him, please?"

He brought Lieutenant Bradford out from the bunk room and explained who I was to him. The lieutenant was a slender man in his late forties, with a kind, narrow face and honest eyes.

"Well, it's good to see our station helped, in our own small way, to make such a beautiful young lady," he said, in a thick Southern accent.

I rolled my eyes, knowing he was patronizing me, because beautiful I was not.

"Thank you, sir," I said, blushing a little in spite of myself.

"How can I help you, young lady?" he asked.

"I was wondering if you saw anyone leaving the station when you were pulling the fire truck back in that day?"

While Lieutenant Bradford raised his head toward the ceiling, obviously thinking back, I took the opportunity to bore into his mind. It was helpful that my question had him thinking about that moment, and even though the memory didn't surface for him, it did for me.

"No, I'm sorry," he said. "I don't remember anything."

After we had thanked the captain and the lieutenant for their time, we left the station. As we walked toward the restaurant for our next meeting, the glasses back on my head, my mom took my hand.

"I'm sorry we didn't uncover anything, dear," she said, a slight frown on her face.

I squeezed her hand and gave her the good news.

"Oh but we did, Mom! The lieutenant didn't remember, but I found the memory. A tall, slender man, with straight blond hair like mine, was walking away from the station when Lieutenant Bradford pulled his fire truck into the station. And I think the blond-haired man has the same powers I do, because he wiped the memory of the drop-off from Captain Weeks's mind. But he must not have done it to Lieutenant Bradford, because that memory is still there!"

Chapter 10

Maddie

Our euphoria from learning there might be others out there like myself didn't last long. We'd scheduled a lunch meeting downtown with Dr. Branch and Amy to bring them up to date on our findings, and headed directly there after our meeting at the fire station.

The restaurant was petite but uncrowded, so we could talk without fear of being overheard. Still wearing my glasses, which we'd all agreed should be standard protocol for all our meetings with both Dr. Branch and Amy, I quickly brought them up to date on what we'd discovered. I was a little surprised that neither of them seemed to share in my excitement—in fact, they appeared to be having the opposite reaction. They wore sad faces and looked anxious. I couldn't get a reading on what was bothering them due to the glasses, so I simply asked.

"Is something wrong? You both seem a little down."

They looked at each other, as if they needed to check in before proceeding, but then Amy spoke.

"Both our offices were broken into last night," she said.

"Oh my!" said my mom. "Were things stolen? Was there vandalism?"

"In both cases, only one thing was taken."

"What?" asked Mom, but even without my ability to read their memories, I could guess.

"Your files on me, right?"

Amy and Dr. Branch nodded. My mom put her hand to her mouth and drew in a sharp breath.

"Oh no," was all she said. The implications were obvious. We all sat quietly, waiting for someone to break the ice. Then Dr. Branch put words to it.

"It seems Maddie's abilities have come to the attention of someone," he said. "Someone who wants to know more."

"And now they know everything," Mom said, frowning.

"Yes." The doctor shook his head, looking equally distressed.

"What should we do?" she asked.

Once again, husband and wife glanced at one another. Amy gave a quick nod, and Dr. Branch spoke.

"These people are willing to break the law to gather information on Maddie," he said. "That's not a good sign."

My mom nodded. "It's frightening."

"Yes," said Dr. Branch, twisting his hands together, "and we have no idea who they are. They could be private contractors working for some ruthless corporation, or they could be part of an organized crime group, or maybe even part of a government group that's willing and able to break laws in the name of national security or some such malarkey."

"So what should we do? Go to the police?" she asked.

"We already have," he said. "We also suggested they pay a visit to your home, to see if it's also been raided. The police are waiting for you there."

"Did they go in?" asked my mom.

"I don't know, but they're there. Amy and I think you should go meet them, right away."

"Yes, of course." Mom was already making a move to go, but Dr. Branch reached out a hand and gently took hold of her wrist.

"Ms. Pace," he said. "We don't think you should stay there, for a while, until this matter gets sorted out."

"But where can we go?" she asked, settling back into her seat.

"Amy and I have a second home up in the mountains. We go there on weekends, to train and to relax. It's quite remote, but it has running water and electricity. We know you don't have a mobile phone, but the house has a hard line. We think it would be a good place for you two to go, until we can figure things out."

"But why do we have to leave? With the police involved, we should be fine."

My mom was always an optimist, but sometimes it led to naivete, and this seemed like one of those times. I suppose she didn't process information the same way I did, which led me to think of "worst-case scenarios" more often than not, but in this case it was pretty obvious that if people were willing to break into offices and steal confidential files, they weren't going to be deterred by the involvement of the local police. Luckily, Amy seemed to agree with my logic.

"That's probably true," said Amy. "But once these people read our files, they'll know conclusively about all of Maddie's abilities. And they'll want to learn more. About her. We don't know what lengths they might go to."

"You mean kidnap her?" My mother almost shrieked the words. Other people in the restaurant looked up from their tables.

Dr. Branch reached over and squeezed her wrist again.

"Please," he said quietly, "we should discuss this further, but calmly."

We talked things through. My mother agreed to return to our home, meet with the police, pack some things, and go to the house in the mountains. Dr. Branch and Amy gave her the keys and instructions on how to get there. As we were leaving, my mom took both of them by the hand, speaking in a soft voice.

"I don't know what might happen," she said. "But you two, especially *you*, Amy, know Maddie better than anyone. I've made no arrangements for her care in the event something should happen to me, and my ex-husband has relinquished all his parental rights regarding Maddie. I don't want her to become a ward of the state if … if …"

"I understand," said Amy. "But what about family? Do you have any siblings? Parents?"

"My parents are gone," she said. "I have a sister who lives in Colorado, but she's not comfortable around Maddie, because of—well, you know."

Amy looked at Dr. Branch, pressing her lips together, then back at my mom.

"We'll do everything we can to help Maddie, of course," she said. "But Tom and I have never discussed this, never had any thought of the possibility. I'm sure you'll be fine, anyway."

"Will you please discuss it, then?"

I didn't know why she was so insistent on it. It was a subject I'd never even considered, and now that it was being discussed, I was very uncomfortable with the implications.

"Yes, of course," said Amy. "And we'll call you later to speak further. We'll check on you daily."

"Thank you," said my mom.

I must admit that my mother's sense of urgency about my care in the event something happened to her rattled me. Yes, my mind was advanced, and could process information much more rapidly than normal people, but I was still only twelve years old, and was perhaps more emotionally retarded than most due to my lack of socialization. So it scared me. I took off my glasses and looked at my mother, trying to understand what was driving her thinking, but there was nothing specific. Just a kind of primal fear, something very deep in her. Later, I would understand more fully how deep and enduring the love of a mother for her child can be, but at that time, I just knew she felt something coming, something dangerous.

Chapter 11

Cynthia

We met the police at our house and took them in. They saw no sign of forced entry through the front or back door, or through any of the windows. After walking through the whole place, we told them we didn't see anything missing either. They said they would file a report and start doing random drive-bys to check on things. We told them we would be leaving town for a few days, and they said that was a good idea, then left. It was reassuring to know that our home hadn't been broken into, but I was still concerned about the break-ins at Tom's and Amy's offices.

When the police had gone, we packed our things and drove north, up Interstate 26. After about twenty miles, we exited the highway at the quiet town of Mars Hill. We passed through the town, and then the two-lane road started winding, threading deeper into the mountainous forest. Next, we turned right and wound our way up a narrow canyon road for several miles.

The road surface was roughly paved, and tall trees encroached on it from both sides. Every now and then, we passed houses, none of them fancy, and they were separated by long distances, suggesting each homeowner owned a large tract of the hilly, tree-covered landscape. We eventually came to a mailbox on the right with the house number we were looking for, turned up the gravel-and-dirt driveway, and drove slowly onward, deeper into the forest. The driveway was straight, not too steep, and after a few hundred yards we saw a pleasant-looking A-frame off to the right. A large gravel parking area allowed us to drive up beside the house.

The entrance was in the basement. Inside, I could see a set of stairs across the unfinished room, which was full of exercise equipment that Amy and Dr. Branch must have used for their training. We carried our bags up and found ourselves in the main living area. It was all one room and had the feel of a studio apartment, with the kitchen on one side, an adjacent dining area, and then a large living space with a couch and some chairs. There was no television. A bathroom sat at the rear, and there was a deck in the front overlooking a small pond. Maddie went out on the deck, and not long after that, she screamed.

"Oh no!" she shrieked. "Snakes!"

I rushed out on the deck and looked down at the pond. I'd lived in the rural South my entire life, so I wasn't at all surprised to see several fat, gray snakes sunning themselves on the banks of the pond.

"They're just water snakes, honey," I said. "They can't really hurt you. But there are likely other kinds, mostly Copperheads, and maybe a few rattlers, that are poisonous, so we'll have to be careful when we're outside."

"But what if they come into the house?" she cried.

"I don't think they will. Really. But if they did, the basement is where they'd be, so just keep an eye out when you're going through there. Come on, let's go back inside and settle in."

Another set of stairs took us up to an area with two bedrooms, separated by a hallway and another bathroom. I took the front bedroom, and Maddie took the back. After we unpacked, we drove into town to buy some groceries, then returned to make dinner.

While we were cooking, the phone rang. Maddie ran to answer it.

"Hello?" she said.

It was Amy. They spoke for a while—mostly about snakes, it seemed. Then Maddie looked up at me.

"Amy wants to speak with you, Mom." As she handed me the phone, she said, "Amy hasn't seen any poisonous snakes, and she says they have an organic vegetable garden out back."

"Great," I replied. "Can you keep an eye on the pasta, honey? I think it's almost ready."

"Sure."

Maddie walked over to the kitchen. While Amy and I talked, I watched my self-sufficient daughter work. She kept an eye on the pasta, and when it was ready, she found a strainer in the cupboard and some oven mitts in a drawer, drained the noodles, and put them back in the pot. Then she poured the spaghetti sauce over the top of the pasta and mixed it together.

After Amy had fully updated me, I joined Maddie at the dining room table. She'd already set it and was dolloping out the food as I sat down. She wasn't wearing her glasses, so I knew she could have found out what was going on by reading my memories, but I was happy to give her the good news.

"Amy and Tom would love to become your guardians if something were to happen to me. They're going to contact an attorney and get some papers drawn up for me to sign. They'll bring them up here to us next week."

"Okay, good," she said, kind of meekly. I reached over and took her hand.

"It's all right, honey. I'm sure we'll both be fine, but it's the prudent thing to make sure you'll be taken care of in case I'm ever hit by a bus."

Maddie frowned, obviously not wanting to think about such a morose subject any further.

"Hey," I said, "after dinner, why don't we go out and check out the vegetable garden, before it gets dark? There might be some really good stuff for us to eat out there."

"What about the snakes?" she asked.

"Well, we're here, right? So we might as well learn to live here. After all, we're in charge of our lives, not the snakes."

As I said this, the irony of my statement hit me. As things stood, we were hiding from some human snakes and really weren't in charge of our lives at all. I wasn't worried about myself because I was destined to go wherever God took me, but I worried how Maddie would fare if I were taken from her. She was very independent in her own way, spending hours alone learning about everything under the sun, but she was still so young, and helpless in the way that all young people are. She needed me, and I needed her, but it seemed that forces beyond our control were conspiring to break us apart.

Chapter 12

Maddie

They came for me the next morning. Mom and I were up in the garden picking vegetables when we heard a car coming up the driveway. The garden was about a hundred yards from the house, nestled behind a thicket of trees that limited the view of it from the parking area. We approached the trees and peered out. An odd-looking van of some kind pulled up and stopped beside my mom's Subaru. It had a boxy look and a military green color, perhaps inconspicuous on a base but not here in western North Carolina.

Two massive men got out, both wearing gray polo shirts and Khaki pants. They looked like football players. One of them knocked on the basement door. He waited a minute or so, then he opened the door and went in. The other stepped back and began looking around. His gaze came toward the thicket of trees we were hiding behind. We slowly stepped back.

"We should go farther into the woods," my mom whispered, taking my hand as she turned to head away from the house.

The garden was in a flat, narrow depression, with heavily forested hills on each side. The flat land extended back a ways, and we followed a deer path for several hundred yards until we came to a barbed wire fence that marked the property line. An open field lay on the other side, which didn't seem like a good option if we wanted to stay hidden. Our choices were to either follow the fence line up the hill to the left or up the hill to the right. My mom chose left.

There was no path, but the underbrush was sparser near the fence. We encountered some briars and both got some scratches, but we kept moving up as fast as we could. I was so scared of the men that I didn't have time to worry about snakes. About halfway up the hill, we heard the crack of a stick down below, as if someone had stepped on it. We assumed it was the men following us, so we quickened our pace. When we reached the top of the hill, we stopped to listen. It sounded like the men were about halfway up behind us.

"If we go left here, we can follow the ridge to the road," said my mom.

She pulled my hand and we rushed forward. The going at the top of the ridge wasn't bad. There was very little underbrush, and the trees seemed less densely grouped than on the way up. We were almost running now, and making good time. After a few hundred more yards, we came to the end of the ridge. Unfortunately, it ended in a cliff. About fifty feet below, we could see the road snaking its way up the canyon. The men were closing in behind us.

"What do we do?" I asked.

My mom pressed her lips together. "Do you see that ledge down there?" she asked.

I looked down and saw a ledge about ten feet below us, and my mom told me her plan.

"If we can get down there, we might be able to hide below it, where they can't see us. And even if we can't get below it, they won't be able to reach us. Eventually, a car will drive by, and we can scream for help before they figure out a way to capture us."

I thought about this. Mom was thirty-seven years old, and I'd never known her to be athletic. I myself was twelve and had never participated in sports due to my issues. I wondered if we could make it down there safely.

She saw my hesitancy. "Maddie, I wouldn't ask you to do this unless I thought both of our lives depended on it."

"You think they want to kill us?" I asked, incredulous.

"No," she said. "I think they want to separate us, forever. And I'd rather die than let that happen. Please, we'll go together. Side by side. There looks to be an easy way right here."

My mom got down on all fours, crawled over the edge, and grabbed the top of the cliff, easing her way down. She waited for me to come with her.

"See," she said, "we can do it!"

I looked back at the ridge and thought I could see the men, so I slipped over. The adrenaline must have been pumping hard at that point, because I found the climbing quite easy. My mom was doing okay as well.

"Come on," she whispered. "There's a little rock outcropping below the ledge. Once we reach the ledge, it should be easy to get to, and then we can stand on it and they won't be able to see us. The ledge will block their view."

I saw what my mom was talking about and continued down. I was surprised at how agile and strong I was, and the ease of the descent enabled me to reach the ledge before my mom did. But when I stepped onto it, I felt it give a little and realized it wasn't stable. I opened my mouth to warn her at literally the same time she put her foot down. The extra weight caused it to buckle. The ledge gave way, and both of us fell.

Something came over me at that point that I'd never felt before. It wasn't fear. It was rage. I pushed myself away from the side of the cliff, out into the air, and plummeted down toward the road below. I didn't think about dying. Instead, I distinctly remember strength pouring into my legs as I accelerated toward the ground, forty feet below. Things seemed to be moving very slowly during the fall, and I had more than enough time to position myself to land on my feet. My knees compressed when my feet hit the road, but I hardly felt it. My mom wasn't so lucky.

She landed on her back and didn't move. I straightened up, completely fine, but looking down at her I saw a pool of blood streaming from her inert body. I knelt down beside her, my heart pounding, unsure what to do. Reaching over, I touched my hand to her cheek, trying to pour whatever power was inside me into her. She opened her eyes a little and looked at me.

"I love you, Maddie," she said. Her voice was weak and ragged, as if she could barely breathe.

"I love you, Mom! You're going to be okay. I'll go get help!"

"I don't want to leave you, honey," she wheezed. "But you'll be okay. Amy and Dr. Branch will take care of you. Now run! Run up the road and go to the nearest house for help."

"No, Mom! I won't leave you."

I could see the light fading from her eyes, and I realized death was coming to her.

"I'll watch over you from heaven," was the last thing she said to me. And then I felt something. It was apart from me, not of my own mind. I was still touching my mother's cheek when an electric shock passed through it, and then it was gone.

Then she died. I had the distinct impression that the surge had originated in her, and I wondered briefly, hoped actually, that what I'd felt was her soul going to heaven. I wasn't a believer, but she was, and she so very much deserved to go to a place where good souls went. That thought passed quickly out of my mind, though, because other feelings took hold of me.

The strength I had felt just a moment before drained out of me faster than a tub emptying of water. I collapsed onto my mother's dead body and held her tightly, waves of anguish passing through me. I heard myself sobbing hysterically. This was the one person in my life who I depended on for everything. Not only my physical well-being, but my emotional strength as well. I was an outcast in this world, and the only thing that kept me going was her. And now she was gone.

The sadness and horror coursing within me began to change once again, replaced by that unfamiliar anger I'd experienced before. I felt the unearthly strength returning. I pushed my hands under my mom's body and lifted her up, standing with her in my arms as if I were holding a blanket, warm and soft. I began walking down the road toward our driveway, but then I heard a noise up above, at the top of the cliff. It sounded like sharp pop. I felt a sting in my upper arm, and looked down to see a dart sticking out. Turning my gaze back up, I saw one of the men with a rifle.

In a matter of seconds, I felt light-headed. I knelt in the road and gently laid my mother down. Then I fell forward onto her and lost consciousness.

Chapter 13

Cynthia

When I woke, I was sitting in lush, green grass, on a hillside overlooking a bay. There were a few homes below, around halfway up the hill, all white, and out in the water I could see a boat with a white sail leisurely making its way across the calm water. The sky was blue, with just a smattering of clouds ambling slowly along the horizon. The air was warm, maybe in the mid-seventies. I was wearing a comfortable robe of white linen and felt nothing underneath. There was a narrow path coming up the hill from the area of the homes, and I could see a woman with long, dark hair making her way up it, heading toward me. She was still a good distance away, so I had time to think.

My first thought was to recognize that I had a physical body. This was inconsistent with my belief that my soul would be sent to an intermediate place, to wait, in the company of God, for the Second Coming of Christ. It was very clear in my mind that I was not supposed to have a body while I was in the intermediate place waiting for the Second Coming. I was supposed to be a soul only, in full connection with God. But

I *had* a body. The second problem was that I did not feel the presence of God, and I should have, if I were in heaven.

I considered the possibility that I might be in Purgatory, the intermediate place espoused by the Catholic religion, but my memory of that faith was that in Purgatory there is also no body, and the pain experienced during the trials there is a spiritual pain. I felt no pain of any sort, physical or emotional. On the contrary, I was quite relaxed and felt good.

As I sat there on that peaceful hillside, I had only vague memories of my last moments on Earth. I remembered there was an accident, but I couldn't recall if I'd been alone or if someone had been with me. I was also confused as to where I was at that moment since it was inconsistent with the teachings of my faith. Then I remembered, from my time on Earth, that I was open-minded regarding Christianity. I believed that all Christian religions were merely interpretations of the Bible, and that the details might not be as concrete as professed by any given denomination. Some people I knew were adamant that the specific teachings of their particular faith were the absolute, unalterable truth, but my faith in God wasn't weighed down by such dogma. So in spite of my misgivings at that moment, I held out hope that wherever I was, it was part of my path to eternal salvation. Perhaps the young woman climbing toward me could help me understand.

She had dark skin and looked to be of Persian or Arab descent. This didn't disturb me, because Christianity was still present in such places, even though the Muslim religion was the dominant one there. And she could have been a naturally born American for all I knew. She was tall and slender and moved gracefully up the hill, and when she reached me I saw that she had blue eyes, which I wouldn't have expected. Her clothes were also a surprise. She was wearing jeans and a white T-shirt, not a robe of white linen, like me. As she approached, she smiled, revealing white teeth that were perfectly aligned. She looked to be around twenty years old.

"Hello, Cynthia," she said. "Welcome. I am Aya."

Her voice was gentle, but accented, as if she did come from one of those Middle Eastern countries. I wanted to ask her questions, of course, but I hadn't forgotten my manners since I'd died. I stood and extended my hand, and we shook.

"Very nice to meet you, Aya," I said. "Thank you for coming up the hill to greet me."

"It is my pleasure," she said, still smiling. "I always do so when new people arrive. It is my job."

Now the urge to find out more overwhelmed my sense of propriety.

"Aya, would you mind telling me exactly where I have arrived?" I asked.

"This place is known as World 2A," she said. "And it really is a very nice place." She gave me a reassuring smile as she said this.

"How did I get here?" I asked.

"I do not know, exactly. We all arrived in the same way you did. Sitting on this beautiful hillside, looking out at the sea, wearing the white robes."

Robes of white linen were what I had expected to be wearing when I got to heaven, but apparently they were optional here, wherever this was.

"Why aren't you wearing the robes now?" I asked.

"The robes are what we wear during the final stages of the preparation process," she said. "After that, we can choose other clothing."

"What is the preparation process?" I asked, wondering if she could be talking about preparing for the Second Coming.

"Cynthia, that is not to be explained at this time. Later, you will learn."

"How long have you been here?" I asked, frustrated at the vagueness of virtually all of Aya's answers.

"I do not know."

"How can you not know?" I asked, perplexed.

"Time is different here."

"Different? How so?"

"That will be explained to you, later. We don't really think of time here on World 2A."

I seemed to be gaining no enlightenment about what kind of place this was or how I'd gotten here, so I decided to take a different approach.

"All right," I said. "Can you tell me how you came to be here?"

"I was killed."

"I'm very sorry that happened to you," I said, and I meant it. "Do you remember what year you were killed, Aya?"

"Yes," she replied. "It was 1978."

"And I died in 1998, so you must have been here for twenty years. Yet you look so young. How is that possible?"

"Many things are possible here that could never happen on Earth," she said. "This is a wonderful place."

Aya's enthusiasm caused a surge of hope to well up inside me. Perhaps this could be heaven after all.

"Do you know how long we will be here?" I asked, hoping she would answer that we would return to Earth upon the Second Coming of Christ. Instead, she paused, a look of realization dawning on her face.

"Are you a Christian?" she asked, tilting her head to the side.

"Of course," I said. "Aren't you?"

"Actually, I'm an atheist," she answered. "Many of us here are. We don't get many Christians coming through, at least since I've been here."

"But how did you get here if you're a non-believer?" I asked.

Aya pressed her lips together, a look of concern passing across her face. "It is not for me to explain these things to you," she said, her tone conciliatory.

"Of course not," I said. "It will be God himself who shares with me all the glory of heaven."

Aya frowned. "The man who will explain things to you is known as the Teacher," she said. "He has asked me to bring you directly to him, which is not what normally happens. So perhaps he will tell you things the rest of us have not heard. You should know it is very rare for any of us to meet with the Teacher. Some come here and never meet with him. You must be very special." She offered a comforting smile as she said this, but below it, I detected something else. Was it envy?

I wondered if it was possible this "Teacher" could be God. Even though Aya had called him a man, it was common knowledge that God had created man in his own image, so I suppose it was possible, although I was skeptical. Based on what I'd experienced so far, so unlike what I had expected, I very much doubted I was in heaven, and thought it highly unlikely this Teacher was God.

"Please, follow me," said Aya. She reached out and took my hand, helping me to stand. "I will take you to the dwelling that has been prepared for you," she said. "Then I will escort you to the Teacher."

Chapter 14

Maddie

I'd heard the expression about living in glass houses, but I never expected to actually be doing that. Yet when I woke up, feeling groggy and with a headache, I found myself inside a glass cube of sorts. It was about the size of a hotel room, except the ceiling was higher. I was lying on a single bed. Beside the bed was a dresser, and off in one corner was a room with darkened sides that I guessed was the bathroom. There was also a table with a chair in the center of the space. I noticed my special glasses were sitting on the table, but I hadn't been wearing them when the men shot me. They must have gotten them from the A-frame.

Then I remembered my mom was dead, and grief poured through me like a sickness, but that was soon supplanted by a molten anger. The rage flowing in my veins caused the unnatural strength to return. I could feel it in my muscles, like they were filling with raw power, and I wondered if I could break out of the glass house. Finally, my mind returned and took charge of things. I needed to understand more about where I was before I could try to get away.

Sitting up in the bed, I threw my legs over the side, making contact with a soft rubber floor of some kind. Looking out through the clear glass, I counted five more of these "houses." They were lined up in two rows, with three houses per row, all contained within a much larger room, perhaps the size of a gymnasium, which appeared to be constructed of metal. There were lights in the high ceiling, but there were no windows, only a set of double doors off to one side.

I saw people in two of the houses nearest to my own. One of them was a boy who looked to be about my age. He was dressed in an orange jumpsuit. I looked down at my clothing and saw that I was wearing one as well. The boy was sitting in a chair at a table that mirrored the ones in my cube. He looked like me. His hair wasn't as long as mine, although it was longer than most boys' hair that I had seen.

He was looking over at me, a dull expression on his face, like he was tired, or maybe drugged. In the other occupied house, an old woman was standing very close to the glass wall nearest to me, staring with intense brown eyes. She had black skin and was short and stocky, with curly gray hair cut close to her scalp, and was wearing the same jumpsuit we were. She was much older, probably around seventy, though I couldn't tell for sure.

While the boy seemed to be in some kind of stupor, the woman waved at me, trying to get my attention. I waved back to let her know that I saw her. With my exceptionally powerful vision, I could see her face clearly even from twenty feet away. She began moving her lips, mouthing words to me. I concentrated, trying to ascertain through the fog in my own brain what she was saying. She pointed at herself with one hand, mouthing the word "I." She followed that with "am," then "like," then "you" as she pointed at me. I nodded to show her that I understood.

Suddenly, the glass wall the woman was standing beside began to darken. Within five seconds, it had turned completely black, and I could no longer see her. But I had learned quite a bit already. First, if the woman was like me, she could project her thoughts telepathically. It was something I'd been able to do since I was about three years old, but I learned quickly that it made people uncomfortable, so I only did it with my mom, and even with her not that often. Yet, something was preventing her from doing so with me, otherwise she wouldn't have had to mouth the words. So the glass that our houses were made from was probably that same kind that Dr. Branch had used to make my glasses. It blocked radiation and apparently also the telepathic abilities that we, and perhaps the boy as well, possessed.

It was also obvious that we were being observed by some hidden cameras that I had yet to identify. The glass wall in the woman's house had been darkened so that we could no longer communicate. The best news of the day was confirmation that there were others like me, just as I had hoped when I extracted the memory from Lieutenant Bradford at the fire station. I didn't know exactly why this information was so comforting. The hurt of my mother dying was still there, of course, and I suspected it always would be. Plus, I was being held prisoner by unknown captors, as were the other two that were like me. But knowing I wasn't alone—not some singular freak with no one else on Earth that was anything like me—helped me begin to cope with the loss of my mother. Here were people, relatives of a sort, who might be able to help me in ways my mother never could, simply because she wasn't like me.

As I considered these things, still quite groggy, I saw one of the double doors open. The two men in polo shirts entered the large room, closing the door behind them. I couldn't hear the doors when they closed, so the glass houses had to also be soundproof to some degree.

The men approached my house. As I looked where they were heading, I saw the outline of a door for the first time in one of the walls. There were hinges and a strong lock embedded in the thick glass, with a handle on the outside. When the men arrived, one of them pulled some handcuffs from his pocket, and the other removed what looked like a remote control. He pushed a button, and the lock on the door disengaged.

At that moment, the overwhelming urge to escape poured into me. The memory of landing on my feet after a forty-foot fall and hardly feeling it led me to believe I had the strength to overpower these men. Luckily, a sliver of reason entered my mind. It grew and spread, asking questions about what was on the other side of the double doors, where the building was located, and if I really stood any chance of escaping without this knowledge. For most of my life, I'd been trained by my mom and by Amy to control my emotions, to let reason prevail and do the sensible thing. To stay quiet when the urge to scream was surging through me. Now was not the time to escape—a completely different approach than physical strength was called for. Patience. Cooperation. Trust.

The man with the handcuffs entered the house and approached the bed I was sitting on.

"Stand up and turn around, Madison," he said. "You should know, before you consider trying anything, that the remote control my colleague is holding does more than unlock doors. We'll stun you if you try anything foolish."

I stood up and turned around.

"Put your arms behind your back," he said.

I did as I was told, and the man put the handcuffs on me, then turned me around and led me toward the door of my house.

"Where are we going?" I asked.

"To have a little talk," he said, escorting me by pushing my elbow, out through the door of my house and toward the double doors they'd entered through.

Chapter 15

Cynthia

As we walked down the hill toward the buildings below, my mind whirled. I was confused about where I was. I still held out hope that this could be heaven, but at the same time I wondered what it would mean if it wasn't.

Aya took my hand, as if she could feel the turmoil within me. Her touch was gentle, comforting.

"Where are you from, Aya?" I asked.

"I am from Lebanon," she answered.

"Is it too personal for me to ask how you were killed?"

"I died in an explosion, from a bomb."

"Where did the bomb come from?"

"I don't know," she said. "It does not matter."

"Why doesn't it matter?" I asked, intrigued as to what her answer would be, and she didn't hesitate to give one.

"Because I hate no one," she said. "That is why I am here."

We continued on down the path in silence and soon reached the enclave of dwellings. There were four of them. Three were single-story white stucco cottages with slate roofs. The final building was the same style, just larger and two-stories tall.

Aya led me to one of the cottages. "This is your dwelling," she said, opening the unlocked door.

The inside of the cottage was a single room, neat and tidy. It struck me as odd that there was no bed, but one corner was finished off with walls, probably the bathroom. The kitchen sat along another wall, with a refrigerator, a stove and oven, a sink, and some counters with cupboards above and below.

"We have running water here," said Aya.

"Good." I noticed I was beginning to get hungry. "Do we eat?" I asked.

"Yes," said Aya, smiling. "These bodies will never get sick and can live forever, but they need fuel to function properly. I'm sure you are hungry, but your meeting with the Teacher must happen now. I will take you to town to get food and clothing when you return. Please follow me."

We walked out and continued down the hill toward the water. Soon, we came to a simple wooden dock, and as I looked out at the bay, I saw the sailboat I'd seen earlier approaching. The sail folded down as we walked out onto the dock. Aya reached out, grabbed a rope, and threw it to the man on the boat when it came up alongside. He quickly secured the rope to a cleat on the deck, then stood, gazing at me.

He had straight blond hair that stretched far down his back, and he towered over me. He was wearing a long white robe, tied at the waist, similar to the one I was wearing, and looked to be around forty years old. The moment I saw him, something clicked in my mind, and it began to clear.

The first distinct memory I had was Maddie's description of the man who had dropped her off at the fire station when she was a baby. Apart from his clothes, the man in front of me fit that description. That tidbit of information from my prior life was followed by a flood of memories. The way I had died returned in vivid detail, and with it the knowledge that my precious Maddie may have been abducted. With all of these conflicting emotions swirling throughout me, I knew in my heart that this was not heaven, because if it were, I would be feeling completely exhilarated, with no worries whatsoever. Instead, my entire being was filled with dread for my child.

"I am the Teacher," said the man. "Please, come aboard with me. We will talk."

Reeling from the memory dump, I stepped precariously off the dock and onto the boat. The Teacher untied the rope from the cleat and tossed it back onto the dock. As he pushed the boat away, he looked up at Aya.

She nodded back at him, smiled and waved goodbye to me, then folded her hands behind her back, remaining on the dock. It appeared she would be waiting for my return.

The Teacher pulled another rope, and the sail went up and caught the wind. He tied the rope down, then went to the back of the boat and took hold of a handle that appeared to be for steering. We turned out into the bay. The water was completely calm, almost like glass, and the peaceful sound of the boat slicing through it, with the wind on my face, helped me to settle down.

"Please, sit," said the Teacher, patting the bench that ran along the sides of the boat.

I approached him and sat adjacent to him.

"I realize you have many questions," he said. "I will answer some, but others will have to wait, if you are not ready to hear the answers. Please, ask your questions now."

"Where am I?" I asked.

"You are in a place called World 2A, as Aya explained. There are exactly one hundred humans living here, and you are now one of them."

A total of a hundred souls was less than I would have expected, but the Bible *did* say "Few are those who find it." I was afraid to ask the question that needed asking, but I worked my way toward it.

"But where is here?" I asked. "Is it a long way from Earth?"

"By our standards, no, it is not. But we are unseen by the people there."

"You mean, like a parallel universe? Something like that?"

"It might be too soon to explain all of that to you, Cynthia. It's not overly complicated, but where we are is not really relevant. Why is that so important to you?"

Since the Teacher had asked the question, I thought I'd just put everything on the table, and if I didn't get the answer I wanted, I would at least be able to move on and deal with it.

"The teachings of the Bible are that heaven is a parallel universe, unseen by the people of Earth. Is this heaven?"

"Not in a biblical sense, no," he said. "But World 2A is a very nice place to be. And you are one of the lucky few who have come here."

But what about God? I thought to myself, hesitant to ask the Teacher. *Where is He?*

The Teacher laughed. "God is not here," he said.

I realized then that the Teacher could read my thoughts, similar to how Maddie could read my memories. I was used to that, at least, and had nothing to hide anyway.

"So where is God?" I asked.

The Teacher drew in a deep breath, and exhaled slowly.

"We are not aware of where your God is, I'm afraid."

I became quiet at this revelation, disappointed but not surprised based on what I had seen and heard and felt thus far in my time on World 2A. I looked up to see where the boat was going. We'd left the bay and now seemed to be circling an island. There were fields of grain and vegetables and fruit trees covering much of the land, and I saw mountains in the distance.

"How big is World 2A?" I asked.

"World 2A is not actually a world as might be described in a dictionary," he said. "It's actually just this island we are sailing around. We call it a 'World' because it is completely self-sufficient, and it was very specifically designed for the people who come here."

"Do we ever get to leave?" I asked.

"Oh yes, you will leave this place, at the appropriate time," he said.

"How will that be determined?"

"I will decide what path is right for you after you have spent some time living and working here."

Well, I was getting more answers from the Teacher than I had from Aya. This isn't to say Aya wasn't a nice person. She just hadn't been able to tell me much, perhaps because she'd been instructed not to tell me or simply didn't know the answers. And even though I was getting a few answers, the number of questions I had was only growing.

"So there is more than one path I could take from here?" I asked.

"Yes," said the Teacher. "You will either be selected to move on to the World of the Makers, or you will not."

"Who are the Makers?"

"They are the beings who made this place," he said. "They have made many places similar to this throughout the universe."

"Are the Makers God?" I asked, not quite willing to give up on my hope that God was nearby, but the Teacher quickly dashed that possibility.

He shook his head. "Not the God you are thinking of."

This statement caused me to reconsider things a little. It was clear this was not heaven, but the words also revealed that the Teacher knew a lot more about me than I did about him. It also appeared that I had been brought here for some purpose. Something to do with the beings the Teacher had called the Makers. If they didn't find me useful, perhaps they would let me go, so I could move on to where I was supposed to be.

"And what does it mean if I'm not selected to go to the Makers?"

"Cynthia, first, please know that your presence here does not mean the teachings of your faith are wrong. We do not disavow that possibility. For you, that could very well come later, after your time here is done. Or it might not. We simply do not know."

"But you *do* know this is not heaven," I said, not to reopen a subject that had been thoroughly disavowed by the Teacher, but simply to segue to my next line of questioning.

"Yes, we know that," he responded.

"Then how did I get here?"

"We send beings to Earth, beings called Imprints. Their purpose is to identify humans that are right for World 2A, and to mark them, so we can track them and bring them here at the time of their deaths."

"So how was *I* identified?" I asked, although an understanding was creeping into my conscious mind.

"Of course, it was the one you call Maddie who marked you as a person worthy of coming to World 2A."

Chapter 16

Maddie

I found it interesting that the men who were escorting me hadn't taken measures to protect their minds from me. My captors were clearly aware of my abilities, but they weren't wearing any kind of protective gear on their heads, and they hadn't asked me to wear my glasses. So I took the opportunity to take a look inside the minds of the two men wearing polo shirts, and considering the sparse information I obtained from them, it became obvious why they hadn't protected themselves.

They were contractors, and didn't know very much at all that was useful. There was a little, though. Their employer was the Department of Defense. Their assignment was to go where they were told and capture whoever they'd been instructed to apprehend, in this case, me. They weren't the ones who'd stolen Amy's and Dr. Branch's files, but they'd been briefed on the information in the files.

I was the second subject these two had captured. The boy in the glass house next to mine was the other. The old woman had apparently been taken by someone else, since she'd been here longer than either of them had been employed in their current capacity. I also learned that the boy had been seized in Grand Rapids, Michigan and that we were currently located in a facility inside a military base in rural Nevada.

They also had information about my mother's body. It had traveled with us the entire way here. The men had driven to a private airfield and put me in the passenger area of the plane, storing my mother's body in the hold. The jet had flown directly to the special military base where we were now. Her body had been cremated, so no one would ever know what happened to her. While I wanted to hate the men in the polo shirts, they had both bowed their heads during the cremation. One of them had said the words, "May her soul go to the place her faith promised her, and be at peace," and then together with the other man, "Amen." This made me feel better about them, even though they didn't seem to be treating me with the same respect they had shown my mother. They were tight up against me, and each gripped one of my arms, which seemed unnecessary considering my hands were cuffed behind my back. Their grip was overly tight and causing me some discomfort.

After a brief walk down a hallway, they escorted me into a room. It was like a conference room, except there was a clear glass wall running down the center of it. Obviously, whoever I was going to meet with cared little about the knowledge I'd extracted from the men, but they weren't going to leak anything from their own mind into mine. There was a table and chair on my side of the wall. One of the men told me to sit, then the two left the room.

On the other side of the glass was a similar table and chair. A door on that side opened, and a woman came in. Shoulder-length dark hair, dark pantsuit, not heavy, not thin. Very average looking. I suppose she could have been pretty if she'd wanted to, but she wore no makeup and didn't seem to care whether she looked pretty or not. She sat down, opened a folder she'd brought with her, stared at it for a moment, then looked up at me.

"Hello, Maddie," she said. Her voice was being broadcast to me through a speaker in the ceiling on my side of the room. "My name is Dr. Lemare. How are you feeling?"

I saw no reason to resist answering, so I spoke the truth. "I have a headache, I'm heartbroken over the death of my mother, and I'm very hungry."

"What kind of food do you like?" she asked.

"I like pasta, mostly. And veggies."

"We'll rustle up something for you then," she said with a friendly tone. "While we're waiting for that, I'll brief you on what we think we know. You are welcome to provide clarification or ask questions as we go along. There are no rules, except that violence of any kind will not be permitted."

"Why do you think I might be violent?" I asked, genuinely curious, although this question reminded me of the exceptional strength I'd displayed during the fall from the cliff and when I'd carried my mom's body down the road. Dr. Lemare was quick to answer my question.

"Because both the others have been violent," she said.

"You mean the people in the glass cages back there?" I asked, a little sarcasm in my voice.

"Yes, them. But Maddie, you must realize we wouldn't be going to all this trouble if you and they were simply 'people.' You may or may not know it, but all indications are that you and your colleagues are not from Earth, and you're *not* human."

I took that statement like a punch to the gut, but I didn't show it. Something inside me was telling me to maintain my composure, that my well-being depended to a large degree on that. But I had to say something, since she seemed to be waiting for me to react.

"I can see how you might think that," I said.

"Actually, we *know* that," she replied. "The boy knows nothing, but the old woman knows a lot. Her story is quite an amazing one."

"Why won't you let her tell it to me?" I asked, remembering the darkening of the glass when the old woman was trying to communicate with me.

"It's for security purposes," she said. "We can't have the inmates conspiring to make an escape."

"Dr. Lemare, I'm only twelve years old, but I'm fairly well educated for my age. And it seems to me that you have no legal basis for capturing and detaining me and those other people."

"On the contrary, Maddie, we have every right to detain you, since you are not people, and therefore have no rights whatsoever. So let me tell you what's going to happen next. We're going to verify that your brain matches those of your colleagues, and when we do that, we'll know for certain you are not one of us. At that point, the questioning will begin."

The door to my side of the room opened, and one of the gray polo shirts brought in a tray of food and a bottle of water. He placed the tray on my table and departed.

"Enjoy your food," said Dr. Lemare. "I'll speak to you later." She got up and left her side of the room.

Chapter 17

Cynthia

The sailboat continued circling the island, rounding the bend to the other side. We sailed a little farther out into the ocean for some reason, and I thought I caught a glimpse of another island.

"Is that another island I see out there?" I asked.

"Yes," said the Teacher.

"Are there any people there?"

"Yes."

"Are they part of the hundred souls you brought here?"

"They are part of a different group of one hundred humans," he said. "The island out there is known as World 2B."

"What's the difference between World 2A and World 2B?" I asked.

"It's too soon to discuss that. But I assure you that the people there are very different than the people on World 2A. In time, I will tell you how they are different, and why they are there, and why you are here."

"Very well," I said, not pushing the matter, even though I really wanted more answers.

The sailboat had turned back toward shore. We were approaching a modest port of some kind, where three fishing boats were docked. Cranes lifted the catch from the boats and placed it onto the beds of compact trucks. I detected very little noise coming from the docks and wondered if the boats and cranes and vehicles were electric. I wanted to ask about that, but I had more important questions at the moment, and as the boat turned parallel to the shore to continue its path around the island, I kept them coming.

"My daughter, Maddie," I said. "She's not from Earth?"

"No, she's not," said the Teacher.

"Where is she from?"

"She was made here. She's what we call an Imprint, and is similar to me, although I have certain other 'abilities' she does not."

"You say 'made.' What does that mean?"

"One of the things we do here on World 2A is produce living things. We use technology that was given to us by the Makers to do this. We have growing facilities where this takes place. There is a facility to grow the Imprints, and also one to grow the human bodies. The Human House is the larger building near the dwelling you will be living in during your adjustment period."

I took in this information, but it only led to more questions. I tried to remember what it felt like to be me, living in my body on Earth. I hadn't yet seen myself in a mirror here on World 2A, so I didn't know if I looked different or not. I felt my nose and cheeks, looked down at my arms, and could detect very little difference from my former self, although my muscles seemed tighter and my skin might have looked younger.

"Was this body, the one I'm in now, made here?" I asked.

"Yes," he said. "At the Human House."

"But how?"

"The Imprint who marked you, the one you call Maddie, is able to do much more than what you and Dr. Branch and Amy were able to learn. The aspects of her abilities that you uncovered sketched only rough outlines of what actually goes on when she bores into a person. Yes, she gathers their memories, and this allows for an evaluation process to take place within her subconscious mind, where a person is categorized, and rated. People like you are marked as candidates for World 2A. Others are marked for World 2B, and most are not marked at all."

Although the information the Teacher was imparting was relatively basic, it was hard for me to process, because it was simply not what I wanted to hear. What I wanted was a clear description of how this World 2A was a part of my path to God in heaven, but I wasn't getting that. I forced myself to stay focused.

"What does this marking entail?" I asked.

The Teacher continued on, and I noticed that he remained very calm, almost seeming bored as he inundated me with information. It was as if he'd done this many times before.

"The Imprint creates a signaling device in your brain that allows us to track you for the rest of your life. It's not a physical device. It's simply an arrangement of neurons from your own brain that can communicate with us, to let us know if you continue to demonstrate all the characteristics we are seeking for residence on World 2A. It also alerts us when you are about to die."

"What happens at the time of death?"

"If there's an opening here on World 2A at the time of death, and you are at the top of the list of candidates, the Essence of who you are is captured, microseconds before death occurs. Your Essence is then transferred from Earth to World 2A, and stored here.

"You mean the soul, right?" I asked. "You move the soul to World 2A."

"We do not use the word 'soul' here," said the Teacher. "But you may use the word, if you wish to."

"Why don't you?" I asked, intrigued.

"Because we are unaware of its existence," he said. "All living things have an Essence, which we can capture, but we have no knowledge of, or experience with, the soul, as it is described in your Bible."

"I assure you, it is there," I said.

"As you say," he said. "But the reality is that you are not exactly the same as you were, on Earth."

"How am I different?"

"The first difference is your body. At the time of your death on Earth, we begin growing your new body, using highly detailed genetic mapping, which is supplied by the Imprints at the time of your marking. But we make perfections, things like straightening your teeth and making you immune to disease."

"How long does it take to grow the body?"

"Not long," he said. "You will learn that time is unimportant here on World 2A. We speak of it primarily when referencing events on Earth."

"Do I look the same as I did on Earth?"

"You look younger, and more perfect," he said. "You were twenty-seven years old when Maddie marked you, so that is how old you look now."

"Does Maddie know her origin? Her purpose? She always said she didn't."

"Before I explain that, Cynthia, let me first tell you what real science is. It is trial and error. Your scientists on Earth have known this for some time, and it is true. So even though the science of the Makers is far, far more advanced than science on Earth, it is still science. Mistakes are made."

"Are you implying Maddie is a mistake?" I asked, offended.

"Maddie is a new generation of Imprint. For many thousands of years, our Imprints were sent to Earth as fully grown adults, with knowledge of their origin and purpose, and with specific instructions never to reveal this to humans. They quietly inserted themselves into human society and fulfilled their assignment, growing old and dying just as humans do. Throughout the millennia, a limited number of them were discovered due to ... problems they developed. Most of those were jailed or killed. A few were burned as witches. But there was never any definitive proof they weren't human. As human technology advanced, however, humans eventually developed a means of uncovering the physical differences of the Imprint brain. As I said, from time to time, an Imprint has a problem and is captured. We have ways of helping them escape before revealing their true origin, but not long ago an Imprint was captured and hidden in a way where we could not find her.

"That is when we knew a different approach was needed. Maddie is part of an experiment where we placed the Imprints on Earth as infants, with no inherent knowledge of who they really were or what their true purpose was. We did program in a basic understanding of good and bad, to help them avoid people who might harm them as they got older, but that was the extent of our preparation with this batch of imprints. Our idea was to begin communicating with them when they reached puberty, so they would get answers to the questions that needed answering. But that experiment needs programming enhancements, because the power of the Imprint mind is too great to leave untethered for that long, without guidance. A few of this new generation of Imprints, including Maddie, have been discovered and captured. Their captors will learn nothing from them, except that they are not human, but it's still unproductive to have them taken out of service. So an entirely different approach is needed, and is now being implemented."

I didn't fully understand all that the Teacher was telling me. My mind was never one for science, or the scientific method. All I knew was that I loved my daughter, and wanted to know more about her heritage and her current situation.

"Were you the one who dropped Maddie off at the fire station?" I asked.

"Yes, that is part of my role," he said.

"Who were the people who captured Maddie?"

"They are from your government. Some well-hidden department that is responsible for investigating alien life-forms in the name of national security. They have learned enough about the abilities of the Imprints to hide them from us, so we are not able to find them. But we will keep looking, I assure you."

"How did Maddie survive that fall? I remember she seemed unharmed, and then I, uh, died."

"All Imprints have exceptional strength. The tissues that form their bodies are of a more advanced biology than normal human tissues. Maddie was unaware of this strength because she knew nothing of who she really was, but she used it to save herself. We program the Imprints we send to Earth so that their extraordinary physical power does not appear unless the Imprint experiences a very high amount of emotional distress. Your death was obviously the catalyst that helped Maddie discover this power."

Discussing Maddie, especially her experience at the time of my death, was very painful to me. I shook my head to clear it of the emotions I was feeling, and looked up to see the Teacher staring at me, his face stoic. That brought me back to the moment. We were on the sailboat, cruising along on the peaceful water, and I used this to slow my heartbeat and get my mind back on track.

I thought about raising Maddie for the first twelve years of her life. I had no memory of her ever exhibiting abnormal strength, but I also couldn't think of a circumstance where she would have needed to use it. We never worked in the yard together, I never asked her to help move the furniture, and the household chores that were her responsibility didn't require anything other than normal exertion. And maybe none of these things would summon the physical strength anyway, because apparently she needed an extremely traumatic experience to bring it on. That wasn't to say she hadn't had trauma in her life, but no doubt my death was far more traumatic than anything else she'd experienced. Then I wondered about myself. I knew the body I was in wasn't original, but was it stronger?

"What about the humans here? Are their bodies made from the same tissues as the Imprints?"

"Yes, but that's only for the sake of efficiency. The humans here have very little use for the extra strength their bodies possess. Perhaps it helps the fisherman or the farmers to a limited degree, but no harm is done by giving it to them."

So I was stronger than I had been on Earth. Funny that I hadn't noticed anything, but I'd only just arrived. I couldn't deny that I felt great energy, at least. Trying not to be conspicuous in front of the Teacher, I felt my body in places that had gotten a little soft, and found that they were no longer soft at all. Tight as a drum, actually.

The Teacher must have noticed.

"Yes, Cynthia," he said. "Your new body has been made more perfect in addition to being made stronger. Your teeth are perfectly straight, and your muscles are perfectly formed. You have virtually no body fat, except in places that are meant to be that way."

I felt myself blush and tried to get off the subjects of humans, specifically myself.

"Why do the Imprints need extra strength?" I asked.

"The Imprints here on World 2A, which you will encounter from time to time, sometimes perform certain kinds of manual labor, such as digging or chopping trees or breaking rocks to make a path, and the extra strength helps in those cases. The ones on Earth don't really need it, but I suppose it comes in handy from time to time, as it did for Maddie."

Now that the subject had swung back around to Maddie, I was compelled to lobby on her behalf.

"I'm worried about my daughter, Teacher. She's been captured and she doesn't even know who she is!"

But the Teacher didn't seem moved by my display of emotion.

"Perhaps she will learn from her captors who she is, or from the others who've been taken, but it's impossible to know with certainty what she will learn, or what will happen to her. My suspicion, however, is that Maddie will figure it out, regardless of whatever precautions the humans take."

While the Teacher's words indicated no inclination to intervene on Maddie's behalf, his confidence in her actually buoyed my own a bit.

"She's the smartest person I've ever met," I said.

"That's because she's not a person, Cynthia."

I didn't like it when the Teacher made that comment, but I stayed quiet and continued to absorb all this information, noting that the boat was rounding the last bend and heading back to the bay where we had started. I assumed that meant this session was coming to an end, so I tried to prioritize my questions.

"You said my 'Essence' was brought here," I said. "To me, this is confirmation there really *is* a soul, just as the Bible described. I'm alive now because my soul will live forever."

"Not exactly," said the Teacher. "Your Bible says that the soul is of divine origin, created by God and infused into the human body. But that is not the way it works."

"How do you think it works?" I asked, giving him the opportunity to speak his mind, while knowing in advance his answer would be wrong.

"Your universe is composed of a nearly unlimited number of suns and planets, and contains living beings of many, many different kinds. All of them have evolved over time from random combinations of molecules and planetary conditions, just as humans evolved on Earth. We are able to capture the Essence of these beings, just as we can capture yours, at the time of death. Your Bible says the soul is unique to your people, but it is not, if indeed what we call Essence is the same thing you call the soul."

"But that's my point!" I exclaimed. "The soul is more than this Essence you speak of, because it contains a part of God himself in it."

"As you say," he said. "We do not prohibit you from believing this here on World 2A."

I wasn't frustrated, because I'd encountered many skeptics on Earth who denied the existence of God, and the soul, just as the Teacher was denying it—or more to the point, ignoring it. What I couldn't figure out was why I was here. Why were these Makers gathering human Essences here?

"Teacher," I said, "if you have no interest, or belief, in the human soul, why do you gather us here? What is so special about us, humans, that makes you bring our Essence here to World 2A?"

"The Makers have projects like this one all over your universe, Cynthia. This is just one of them. But there are things about humans they find to be unique, and interesting. To help you understand, please allow me to continue your astronomy lesson."

I nodded my head, and the Teacher continued.

"Your universe is vast, Cynthia. Your galaxy alone—the one you call the Milky Way—has 100 billion suns, with planets revolving around many of them. And there are 100 billion more galaxies like the Milky Way that are part of your universe. All of this is known by humans, but there is more, which you do not know. There are actually billions of other universes beyond your own. All of these universes combined we refer to as the Megaverse, in your language. Humans will never reach the other universes. They may never even reach any of the stars in your own galaxy, other than the one you call Sol. But the Makers can reach all of it. Every star and every planet in every universe, because they live outside of the space of all of these universes, including yours. The space of the Makers surrounds all of the space occupied by universes like your own. The Makers have the ability to move around and through these universes with ease. Imagine that your universe is a sphere—which it is, by the way. An ever-expanding sphere, but a sphere nonetheless. The Makers can see this sphere, and they can enter it anywhere they choose to. The Makers have encountered countless numbers of intelligent beings throughout your universe, and other ones. What is special about humans is not the thing you call the soul. It is that humans exhibit a range of emotions that is more diverse than what the Makers have encountered in other intelligent species. It is the variety of emotions in your species that is of interest to them."

"That *is* interesting," I said. "But that doesn't preclude God existing, on a plane above and beyond wherever these Makers of yours live. Because they most certainly are not God, if they aren't even aware of the existence of the human soul."

"The Makers are not God, at least not as you think of him," said the Teacher. "And I have already told you that neither the Makers, nor I myself, deny the existence of your God. We simply have found no evidence of his existence."

"The evidence is inside me! In my heart. In my soul."

"As you say," said the Teacher. "This belief is permitted here. And you seem to clearly understand this is not heaven, at least not the heaven described in your Bible. So I think you will be fine here on World 2A."

"I go where the Lord takes me," I said, a tinge of defiance in my voice. "I'm here, so that is where He must want me to be."

I knew in my heart that the words I spoke were the truth, not just an attempt to defend my position. This was what I believed, and whatever this experience on World 2A would entail, I knew it was not the end for me. It was also refreshing that the Teacher was making no attempt to talk me out of it.

"This is fine, Cynthia," he said. "In fact, it is good and healthy that even now, your faith remains with you."

"Thank you, Teacher," I said. It felt good that he was encouraging me to keep the faith while I was here. But I had one more question. "Where is the World of the Makers?" I asked.

"Perhaps you will meet them one day," said the Teacher. "If you are selected."

"Selected to do what?"

"It's not time to discuss that," he said. "I would only say this. If things go as planned, there's a very good chance you will go to the Makers. They are quite intrigued by you."

"Why?" I asked.

"Cynthia," said the Teacher, shaking his head from side to side, "you've only just arrived. My judgment is that you've heard enough, for now. Further discussion of the Makers will have to wait for another session."

Chapter 18

Maddie

When I went for the MRI, the technician asked me if I needed to be sedated or if I was going to cooperate. I said I would cooperate, although the two gray polo shirts stayed in the area to make sure of it. When the imaging was complete, I was returned to the divided conference room. Dr. Lemare was on the other side of the glass, waiting for me. As soon as I sat down, she spoke.

"As suspected, the MRI confirms you're one of them."

"One of what?" I asked. I wanted to learn as much as I could about who I really was.

"Your origin is not of this Earth, based on what we've learned from the old woman. I know more, but I don't want to influence you prior to the next phase. Maddie, we're assuming you're like the boy and know nothing about who or what you are, or your purpose here, but we have to go through the proper procedures to verify that."

"What does it involve?" I asked.

"We have a choice between hypnosis and a truth serum. We were forced to use the truth serum on the boy and the old woman because they're not cooperative. With *you*, assuming I'm correct, we'll be able to conduct the hypnosis, and skip the truth serum. It can have really nasty side effects, and you don't want to go through that unless you have to."

"How long will the hypnosis take?" I asked.

"Typically, about one hour," she replied. "It depends on how easily you go into a hypnotic state. And I should tell you that if the hypnosis doesn't work, we'll have to use the truth serum."

The urge to escape was rising in me, but I tamped it down and reminded myself that now was not the time, that cooperation was called for at this juncture.

"Fine," I said. "Let's get started."

"Okay," she said. "I'm a qualified hypnotist, so let's begin. Please listen carefully to my voice, Maddie, and look at the metronome I have just placed on my table."

I watched the hand on the device click resolutely back and forth, back and forth, its repetitive ticking coming into my ears through the speakers.

"Now please try to relax," she said. "Just watch the metronome and listen to my voice ..."

"Very well," said Dr. Lemare. "That revealed nothing, as I suspected. Since you're cooperating, over the coming days and weeks, we would like begin testing your abilities, to gain a better understand of your species."

"That's fine," I said, feeling that cooperating was still very much in my best interest. In fact, I decided to test that hypothesis. "Actually, Dr. Lemare, I want to learn as much as I can about myself too. And it seems the old woman is the best source of information. What is her name, by the way? Would it be possible for me to speak with her?"

The doctor shook her head.

"I'm afraid not," she said, apparently not even willing to tell me the woman's name. "First of all, she would more than likely communicate with you telepathically, and we cannot allow that. She's very devious, quite intent on escaping, actually. She's tried several times and would undoubtedly want to involve you in her next plot. I'm sorry."

Thinking about this, I could understand Dr. Lemare's position, so I took a different approach.

"That's reasonable," I said. "Would it be possible, then, for you to tell me what *you've* learned from her?"

"That would be highly irregular," she said, but I could sense that she was considering it.

"Dr. Lemare," I told her, "I'll very likely spend the rest of my life here. To be honest, my prospects out in the real world aren't very good anyway. I'm a twelve-year-old with no parents and no designated guardians. I have very few social skills, I'm ugly, and not likely to be adopted by a good family, if at all. So being here isn't such a bad option from my perspective, especially if we can make it a cooperative arrangement. I propose that you study me as much as you want, but if I could have books to read and things to keep me busy, it would be a lot more productive, for both of us. Also, the more I know about my history, the more helpful I can be. Does that make any sense at all?"

Dr. Lemare sat back in her chair. For the first time, she seemed to be softening, as if I'd broken through her professional barrier and reached her on a personal level. I assumed she was a psychologist of some kind, which meant, presumably, that she wanted to help people. Perhaps I wasn't a person to her, but her posture was saying otherwise.

"Let me speak with my superiors, okay, Maddie? I'll see what we can do."

"Thank you, Doctor. In the meantime, I'm ready to do any testing you need."

Chapter 19

Cynthia

Aya was waiting at the dock when we returned from our trip around the island. As before, she threw the rope to the Teacher and he lashed it to the cleat. I stepped off the boat, and he followed.

"We will meet again, soon," he said. "There is still much for you to learn, and challenges for you to face. Please be patient."

"I will," I said, wondering what kind of challenges he was referring to.

Aya took me by the hand, and we walked back up the hill together, while the Teacher stayed on the dock.

"We'll walk to town now," she said. "To get you some food, provisions, and clothing."

"Very well," I said, still feeling overwhelmed and confused, not to mention terribly sad. I missed my poor Maddie. It didn't matter at all to me that he'd said she wasn't human. She was my daughter, period.

"The Teacher has given me permission to speak freely with you," Aya said after a minute of silence. "Perhaps I can answer more of your questions."

"When did he give you permission?" I asked. "I didn't hear him speak to you at all."

"The Teacher sometimes speaks to us directly, without his physical voice," she said.

"You mean telepathy, right?"

"Yes."

I looked back to the docks, to see if the Teacher was following us or going back out on his boat, but I didn't see him.

"Where did he go?" I asked.

"I do not know," said Aya. "The Teacher goes many places. Mostly he stays here on World 2A, but he also goes to Earth, and to see the Makers, and other places, I think, but this is not for us to know or care about. Each of us has our own responsibilities."

"And what will my responsibilities be?"

"I can answer that!" she said, and her face lit up as if she was excited to be helpful. "The Teacher has given you your first work assignment."

"Oh, really. What will I be doing?"

"You will work at the Imprint House," she said.

"Where they make the beings who go to Earth to find souls worth saving?" I asked, sarcasm in my voice. But Aya had an answer that surprised me.

"Yes," she said, brightening. "We like to call them Angels, for that very reason."

"Angels have many responsibilities," I said. "Saving souls is just one of them. And according to the Teacher, there's no such thing as a soul."

"As you say," said Aya. "You do not have to call them Angels if it makes you uncomfortable."

"When will I start work?" I asked, hoping I could get something to eat first.

"We will have some food in town and get you some clothes, if you wish, and then I can walk you over to the Imprint House."

"But won't it be getting dark soon?" I asked.

"No, it will not," said Aya. "It is always daylight here."

I looked up at the sky. It was still wonderfully bright and blue, with a few peaceful clouds floating here and there, but I saw no sun.

"Where is the sun?" I asked.

"I do not know," said Aya. "I have never seen a sun, or a moon, or stars, since I've been here."

"Well, that's different," I said. "Maybe the planets in this universe don't revolve around a sun."

"Perhaps," said Aya.

"When do people sleep?" I asked.

"We do not sleep," said Aya. "These bodies do not require it. All they need is food to provide them with energy. Sleep is not needed."

Of course—that was why there was no bed in the cottage where I'd be staying.

"Well, that's a new one too," I said. "So do we just work all the time? Twenty-four seven?"

"We work as much as the Teacher asks us to. Some people work more than others, but I do not know why. The Teacher will signal you when to start and when to stop."

"And what do we do when we're not working?" I asked.

"Many things," she said. "I will show you when we have time."

I had no idea how long it took us to reach the town, but it seemed as if no time at all had passed. I took a look around. There were three restaurants, a grocery store, a clothing store, a bookstore, and what looked like a wine bar. No banks, no post office, no hardware store, no town hall, no cars, no parking meters. I followed Aya into one of the restaurants, with a sign that said "Restaurant 1."

We sat down at a table. The others were empty. A waitress came up to us, and when I looked up at her, I nearly fainted, because she looked like what I hoped Maddie would look like when she grew up. The woman was young, about eighteen years old, and she was tall, with long blond hair, blue eyes, fair skin, and a shapely body. She was truly beautiful, just as I'd hoped my little Maddie would become one day.

"Is everything okay?" Aya asked.

I regained my senses and settled down.

"Yes, of course. I'll have an unsweetened iced tea if you have it, miss." I didn't look at the waitress as I spoke, afraid it might send me into another bout of frantic nostalgia.

The woman nodded. Aya ordered lemonade, and the waitress left the table. I noticed she hadn't given us a menu.

"Do they have menus here?" I asked.

"They're not needed," said Aya. "This restaurant serves pasta and vegetables. Restaurant 2 serves fish, vegetables, and rice, and Restaurant 3 serves fruit and vegetables, including potatoes. All three restaurants serve bread."

"So no meat, other than fish?" I asked.

"That's correct," she said. "There are no animals here, other than the fish in the sea."

"That's fine with me," I said. "I've been a pescatarian for many years."

"Yes," said Aya, "that is the case with many of us who come here. And for those who ate the meat of land animals back on Earth, they easily adjust. Food is not a source of pleasure here. Only fuel to give us the energy we need."

"Wasn't that a wine bar I saw outside?" I asked. "If the food gives no pleasure, then why should the wine?"

"The wine helps some to lighten their spirits," she said.

I frowned. "But for others, it's a weakness, and causes them to make reckless decisions."

"I myself do not drink, but I go there sometimes with people who do. I have never seen anyone abuse the privilege of drinking the wine grown and made here by our farmers."

I wasn't a big drinker, but I had wine from time to time, and did enjoy the taste of some, and the lightness a glass or two could provide. Perhaps I'd try the wine bar and see if what Aya had said was true.

The waitress brought the drinks, and the food, and we began to eat. And yes, the eating was a different experience than it had been on Earth. I could taste the food, but as it made contact with my taste buds, and as I chewed it and swallowed it, I experienced no feeling of satisfaction. I would eat until my stomach told me I was full, and then I would stop. It really was like filling a car up with gas. Just a chore that had to be done. But I had many more questions, and took the time to ask a few.

"What jobs are there here on World 2A?" I asked. "I know I've been assigned to the Imprint House, but what other jobs are there?"

"Imprints staff the retail establishments and restaurants and also handle most of the construction and maintenance work. The humans are fisherman, farmers, Imprint House workers, Human House workers, and Monitoring Station workers," she said. "Normally, the new people are given jobs in fishing or farming first and have to work their way up before they get a job at Imprint House or Human House. The Teacher must feel you are special to give you such an assignment as your first job. There is only one job more prestigious than that—the Monitoring Station."

"What happens there?" I asked.

"The station has two functions. One is to monitor the Imprints on Earth. The other is to monitor the humans they have marked. When death comes to a marked human, their Essence is captured and brought here, if there is an opening."

The Monitoring Station sounded very intriguing, and I wondered if I could earn a chance to work there, for selfish reasons—I wanted to know where my daughter was and what she was doing. But there would be time to figure that out, time to learn more about this new world, so I kept my questions focused for the moment.

"Did the Teacher say anything about *me*, to you?" I asked.

"Yes, of course," she said. "After your boat trip, he said you being Christian is not going to be an issue."

"Why would it be an issue in the first place?" I asked.

"Some of the Christians who've come here before did not adjust well. They have a preconceived notion about life after death, and World 2A does not fit their definition as perfectly as they would like. So they become bitter and lose their right to be here."

"What happens to them?" I asked.

"They continue the journey that began with their death on Earth," she said.

"But where is that?" I asked.

She shrugged. "I don't know."

I couldn't tell if Aya was avoiding the truth about this or truly didn't know, but I didn't press her on it. I knew where I'd be heading when I left this place but until that time came I wanted to learn as much as I could to try to help Maddie back on Earth.

"The Teacher said something about the Makers," I said. "That I might meet them one day. What can you tell me about them?"

"The Makers are the ones who founded World 2A. They created the Imprints and the human bodies we inhabit. They created all the technology we use."

"I noticed the boats and cranes and trucks don't make much noise, like they're electric. Where do they get their power?"

"Fusion power runs everything here," said Aya. "Each boat, each vehicle, each shop or restaurant, each dwelling, each facility has its own fusion power plant. Some are quite tiny, others are larger—it just depends on how much power is needed."

"Fusion power is only a theory on Earth," I said.

"Yes, but here it is real. The Makers provided it."

"How do you qualify to meet the Makers?" I asked.

"I do not know," she said. "If I did, I would have already gone to them. But as you pointed out, I have been here for twenty years and I am still here. Many people have come and gone during my time on World 2A, but not me. They keep me here—I suppose because I am good at what I do, but maybe not good enough to go to the Makers, and not flawed enough to continue on."

"So everyone either goes to the Makers, or they 'continue on.' Is that it?"

"Yes, that is the way of things here."

We finished our food and left. I noticed we hadn't paid for the meal.

"Why didn't we pay?" I asked.

"There is no need for money here," said Aya. "Everyone works. Everyone takes only what they need."

"I see," I said. "I kind of like that."

Next we went to get me some clothes. I had seen only a few people on the streets, but none of them were wearing the white robe, so I felt I should change into something more "normal." I picked out some underwear, a few bras, three pairs of jeans, three cotton shirts with collars and buttons, a few T-shirts, and some socks and shoes. Aya suggested I get a swim suit, telling me there were many great places to swim around the island. I chose a one-piece that was my size, and while I was doing it, Aya went somewhere else in the store and came back with a daypack, which made sense, since it appeared the primary mode of transportation on World 2A was walking. I changed in the changing room, and we left. Again, we didn't pay. In fact, I saw no one working in the store the entire time we were there.

As I thought about it, I realized that calling all of these places "stores" was probably inaccurate, because a store is a place where merchandise is sold, and there was no money here on World 2A. But it really didn't matter. It was just easier to call them by the closest equivalent, so that was what I continued to do.

After the clothing store, we went to the grocery store. Aya suggested I buy only a few things since there was plenty of time to shop for food in a world where no one ever slept, and the restaurants were always open anyway. She said she'd take my clothing and provisions to my house since she lived in that area too. Then she escorted me to the Imprint House, and we said our goodbyes.

"After you finish work, I can show you some of the things we do when we aren't working," said Aya. "I will take you to my favorite place!"

"Oh, great," I said, trying to be positive but feeling very nervous about going to the Imprint House. "Sorry to ask again, but how will I know when I'm done working?"

"You will know," she said. Then she hugged me, kissed me once on each cheek, and left.

Chapter 20

Maddie

Over the next few weeks, I willingly participated in all the tests Dr. Lemare had planned for me. Several of them were the same as what I'd already gone through with Dr. Branch, but there were also strength tests. And from the looks on the faces of the two polo shirts while I lifted exceptionally large amounts of weight, or climbed a rope to the ceiling with ease, I was a lot stronger than they were. If only I'd known that before my mom and I had decided to run from them, I might have been able to stop them without her losing her life.

There was also a whole new series of tests where I was placed in a room with a person and asked to report what I'd learned about them after they'd been removed from the room. Dr. Lemare would ask me to go over any memories I'd extracted that seemed particularly important to me, and she always ended the questioning about a particular subject by asking me if I felt the individual in question was a good or a bad person.

I found this interesting, because it reminded me of the way my mind had always worked, even though I had never really placed any particular importance on it. The fact was that I'd always made a judgment on people I'd "read" as to whether they were good, bad, or something in between. This led me to believe that Dr. Lemare was familiar with this "judgment" process and was trying to learn more about it.

As the days went by, my cooperative attitude was paying off. The doctor granted most of my requests for books, as well as paper and a pen. I enjoyed writing, so I decided to keep a journal about all that had happened to me. When I was writing, time moved much more quickly. I wondered how my two brethren could stand it with literally nothing to do, since they'd been awarded no special privileges like myself. The boy would glare at me from time to time, as if angry that I was receiving special treatment. The woman, on the other hand, always smiled at me, often waving to say hello. I wondered if she felt I still might be useful to her, maybe even more so now that I had gained some level of trust from our captors.

One day, at the end of a session with Dr. Lemare in the divided conference room, a smile came onto her face.

"I have good news for you, Maddie," she said.

"I'm being released!" I joked.

She laughed along with me. The doctor and I had developed a productive working relationship, and I felt she was slowly gaining a genuine affection for me. If I was honest with myself, I was starting to feel affection for her as well. Then she gave me the good news.

"Because of your exceptionally cooperative attitude, Maddie, my superiors have granted me permission to speak with you about your … background."

This *was* good news.

"That's great!" I said. "I've spent most of my life wondering who I was, and now, hopefully, I'll find out."

"I'll tell you what I've been authorized to reveal," she explained. "And I think it will be meaningful to you. Although, I must warn you, you may also find it quite shocking."

A wave of panic surged through me, but I settled down. Staying calm was the best way to keep her talking.

"Please, Dr. Lemare. Tell me what you can."

"Very well," she said. "First, as we've discussed, our testing has proven, without a doubt, that you are not human. You understand that, right?"

"I understand that I'm different, for sure. Very different. But my emotions are the same as everyone else's, so I *feel* quite human. I assume you're giving me a purely biological assessment, meaning that if me and my kind were to be classified as a species, we wouldn't fit into the homo sapiens group. Is that what you're saying?"

"Essentially, yes," she responded.

"And why is that important?"

"Because it gives credence to the idea that you are from somewhere other than Earth, Maddie. It's simply impossible that you and the others of your kind could have developed naturally, and independently of one another, on this planet. You need to understand that before we proceed further."

I didn't want to believe her, but it was hard, if not impossible, to refute the logic. But I wanted to learn more, and that made it much easier to agree with her.

"I understand," I said. "It's just hard to accept, emotionally."

"I sympathize with you," she said, and I believed she truly meant it. "Are you okay with me continuing on?"

"Definitely."

"Very well," she said. "First, there is one huge caveat that applies to everything I'm about to tell you. You see, that woman is our sole source of information, and she is absolutely, 100 percent insane. She was a normal seventy-two-year-old-woman who had led a normal life, with a normal job and plenty of friends. She had no family, and that was a bit odd, but nothing that would bring her to our attention. Then, suddenly, without provocation, she began confronting people and accusing them of committing crimes and ethical breaches, even going to the police with her accusations. Eventually, it was discovered that everything she was reporting was accurate, but there was no explanation as to how she'd obtained the information. She was sent for testing, and here we are. She's violent, often incoherent, and has an uncontrollable desire to escape, but she has a story to tell, and we've heard it."

Part of the woman's saga sounded a lot like my own, except I'd been doing it since I was a toddler, and she hadn't started accusing people of things until her seventies. Regardless, her brain was like mine, and her abilities were like mine, so when she mouthed the words "I am like you," on that first day, she was telling the truth. I wanted to hear more.

"All right," I said. "I'll take that into consideration, but I'd like to hear what she had to say. As much of it as you are permitted to tell me, please."

"Very well," said Dr. Lemare. "It's our understanding that you and your colleagues were, uh, born on another planet. It's unclear where this planet is, because the woman didn't really know, but there's been some speculation by our scientists that it may not be part of the universe in which we live."

"You mean like, another reality?" I said.

"Yes," she said, "something like that. We really have no idea. We only know what she's told us, and she says she came here from another planet. Her description of the transfer itself was that it was instantaneous, like stepping from one room to another, and that's what led to the speculation about an alternate reality. But it's purely speculation, nothing more."

"Did she come by herself?" I asked.

"Apparently not. She mentioned a powerful being, someone who was in charge of the 'Imprints'—which is what your species is called—brought her here."

"Did she say what he looked like? You must have asked her that, right?"

"Yes, of course," said Dr. Lemare. "She said he was tall and thin and had long, blond hair."

Like the man who dropped me at the fire station.

I nodded my head while considering what I'd learned so far, and while some of it was hard to accept, it answered literally every question about who I was and why I could do the things I did. My inclination was to run with it and keep asking questions.

"Is there any knowledge, from the old woman, of who my birth parents were?" I asked.

Dr. Lemare hesitated, and I prepared myself for the worst.

"From what we can tell, you don't actually have parents," she said. "It appears that your kind, which are called 'Imprints' on your world as I mentioned, are made in a laboratory."

"You mean like test tube babies?"

"Sort of. We don't have much information on that, but the Imprint creation process seems to be more of a manufacturing process than the traditional sperm and egg fertilization that occurs with humans."

This revelation was another gut punch, but I was getting what I wanted—answers—so I carried on.

"Does the place I come from have a name?" I asked.

"The woman said she'd been told it was called 'World 2A.' But she knew very little about what it was like since she came here directly from the growing facility where she was made." Dr. Lemare paused, a more tender, less professional expression taking over her face. "I'm sorry, Maddie. I know all of this must be hard to hear."

The doctor clearly understood my feelings. I'd been raised as a human, but now I'd just been told I was actually a manufactured product. I was stunned and hurt, but also aware that she was doing her best to lighten the load. And it helped. It felt good to have someone care for me again, even if it was only a little bit.

"Yes," I said. "Thank you. I wonder why it's called World 2A?"

"I have some information on that, too," she said, brightening. "But I want to caution you, Maddie, that the information I'm conveying is simply what she's told us. Some of it we can explore further, as we've been doing in our testing with you. But some of it, most of it actually, is beyond the realm of our science here on Earth. To be honest, there's quite a bit of skepticism throughout my department regarding the veracity of this information. It's just too incredible to simply accept as fact."

"That's fine," I said. "I want to know. I need to know."

"This place, World 2A, is supposedly a place where a specific kind of human is sent, and given a new life. The Imprints are here to identify and gather that kind of person."

"Are the people themselves actually removed from Earth?"

"Not their bodies," she said. "She referred to something she called their *Essence*. She said the Essence is captured at the time of a person's death."

Well, that was interesting. It seemed like my mother was right about life after death. I wondered what else she was right about.

"What kind of people are the Imprints looking for?" I asked. "I mean, I realize I'm supposed to be one of these beings, but even if I am, I still have no idea of what I've been instructed, or programmed, to do."

"Empathetic people," she responded.

Now that was *really* interesting. Empathetic people were generally good people, and good people went to heaven, according to my mom.

"So is this other world … heaven?" I asked, hardly believing I was asking that question.

"Not in a biblical sense," she said. "But if what that woman claims is true, there *is* life after death for the souls that go there, because they are given bodies. Human bodies."

"But why?" I asked. "Why are they doing this? Why am *I* doing this?"

"She didn't know why. She just knew what her assignment was. And there's more, I'm afraid."

I took a deep breath, wondering what could possibly be coming next.

"There's also another kind of person that the Imprints gather," she said.

"What kind?" I asked, afraid of what the answer might be.

"She used the word 'selfish,' but further probing suggests that it's more defined than that. What they seek is the polar opposite of the purely empathetic person, which to us would mean highly narcissistic people."

For some reason, when Dr. Lemare said this, my mind whirled back to the encounter with the bad man when I was four years old. If there ever was an example of a narcissistic soul in its worse form, he was it. And then I thought of my mother. After it was all over on that day, I read her memories, and the most profound thing I learned was that she actually felt sorry for him. She grieved that his soul had become so misguided, so corrupted. In short, her primary emotion from that encounter was empathy. Empathy for the bad man. And then it hit me. I was an Imprint. My mother was a highly empathetic person. Also, there was that current of energy that emerged from her at the time of her death. For me, the logic was irrefutable. My mother was still alive.

PART 2

Cynthia

Chapter 21

The Imprint House was just outside of town. It was a long, rectangular building, constructed of concrete blocks that had been painted white. I went into the building, entering a foyer of some kind. It seemed to have no use and was barren of furniture, as if nothing happened there. A woman entered from the other side of the room who appeared to be of Asian descent. She had a grin on her round face and spoke to me in what I thought was Chinese, maybe Mandarin, but the amazing thing was that my mind somehow translated her words as if she were speaking to me in English.

"Welcome," she said, bowing slightly. "My name is Wang Li. Please call me Wang Li." An incredulous look came onto her face, as if she wondered if I got the joke. "There's no need for formality here, except in following procedures," she continued. "One mistake and you're gone!" Wang Li smiled again, another joke, or at least I hoped it was.

"I am Cynthia," I said, bowing slightly rather than extending my hand. I had no idea what proper protocol was when meeting Chinese people.

"Yes, I know, dummy. Why do you think I met you at the front door?" Wang Li seemed to be overdoing it a little bit, but I was encouraged that joking was permitted here. Aya and the Teacher were so serious, but this woman didn't seem to care what people thought of her. It was actually quite refreshing.

Wang Li was of medium height, with shoulder-length, straight, silky dark hair and a round face. She looked to be about forty years old and had a very high energy level.

"Okay, Cynthia," she said. "I'll give you the five-cent tour." She turned around and opened one side of the double door she'd used to come into the room. "Please, follow me," she said, the mischievous smile never leaving her lively face.

She walked through the door, and it swung shut behind her, then swung back at me—it would have hit me if I hadn't reached out to steady its swing. It seemed manners weren't high on Wang Li's priority list. I pushed the door open and went through. I found myself in a room with shelves built into the left wall. The shelves were stocked with white, cubical boxes, about twelve inches on each side.

"This is Department 1," she said. "The Raw Materials department."

One of the blond Imprint women was sitting at a table that faced the wall of boxes. She looked the same as the waitress from the restaurant.

"Here is the raw material which is used for making Imprints," said Wang Li, reaching out and patting one of the boxes. "These days, we make twelve-pound Imprints, which is a baby about two months old. On the shelf we have different models, both male and female. There are four Caucasoid models, three Negroid models, and three Mongoloid models. That's White, Black and Asian, if you don't like science.

You ever hear someone say all Blacks look alike, or all Asians look alike?'" she asked.

"Well, yes," I said, a little embarrassed. "But of course, that's not true."

"Of course it's not true, dummy! You think all us Asians look alike?"

"No, not at all. I said it's not true." I found myself getting a little defensive, and then I remembered, Wang Li was a jokester. Right on time, a wide smile formed on her face.

"Actually," she said, "I told the Teacher there are a lot more than three kinds of Asians, but he said that was enough for 'our purposes.'" She emphasized the words "our purposes" with a tone that suggested disdain for the Teacher, or the Makers, or both. But knowing already the kind of person she was, I assumed she was just kidding.

"Next is Department 2," she said, exiting through a door in the center of the next wall.

I followed, waiting for the door to stop swinging, then entered the room. This room was a little longer than the first one. It contained ten long boxes the size and shape of coffins, five on each side wall of the room. I assumed these were machines of some kind, because they were made of stainless steel and had a control panel on one of the narrow sides. The machines had full-length lids, which allowed them to be opened and closed, also like a coffin. One of the blond, female Imprints was beside one of the open machines, pouring a gray powder from a plastic bag into it. An empty box from Department 1 sat open on the floor. The plastic bag of powder must have come from there.

When she finished pouring the powder into the machine, the woman closed the lid and pushed a button on the control panel. Then she picked up the bag and box and deposited them in a trash receptacle before sitting back down at a table in the center of the room. I couldn't hear any noise from the machine, or from any of the machines in the room.

"Now that mix will bake until ready," said Wang Li.

"How long will that take?" I asked.

"I don't know," she said. "It will be done when it's done, like this one over here."

She walked over to one of the machines on the other side of the room and opened its lid. The Imprint rushed over and pulled out an object that was shaped like a miniature blimp. It was about twenty inches long and maybe ten inches in diameter at its center. It was a gray color, and seemed to wobble in the hands of the technician, as if it were filled with jelly or something liquid. The technician hurried out of the room through a door in the center of the far wall, presumably heading to Department 3.

Department 3 contained ten large, circular vats made of clear glass, five on each side of the room. I saw the technician from Department 2 lowering the mini-blimp into one of the vats. It sank below the surface and hung there, perfectly suspended in the golden liquid. I glanced around at the other vats and saw fetal bodies in various stages of development. A few of them looked fully formed. I must say that my first reaction was one of revulsion. I was stunned that I was witnessing the manufacturing of living things, especially since one of those living things had become my daughter.

While I watched in horror, one of the technicians went to a vat that contained a fully formed fetus, reached in, and pulled it out. She turned it upside down and grabbed its two legs in one hand, down by the feet, while still holding it over the vat. Liquid poured off the fetus and out of its mouth. The mouth was moving, as if trying to suck in air unsuccessfully. The technician smacked the fetus on the back with her free hand, and a final surge of liquid poured out of its mouth. The baby breathed and began to wail. The technician ran through the door into what was undoubtedly Department 4. Wang Li followed, and I rushed after her, glad to be out of that space.

Department 4 contained ten tables, five on each side. Each looked something like an operating table, but the surface was made of a soft, dark foam, with a depression in it that approximated the size and shape of the babies. The head area in particular was quite deep. The technician from Department 3 placed the new baby, a plumb little Black boy, onto one of the tables. The baby was still crying, but then the technician flipped a switch on the side of the bed and the baby immediately went to sleep. There were babies on two of the other tables, and the rest were empty. The two babies that had been there before the new one was brought in were lying very still on the beds, as if they too were in a state of deep sleep. All three babies' heads were bald, held securely in place by the foam depression that surrounded them. I didn't feel as much revulsion in Department 4, but I wasn't completely comfortable there either. I couldn't imagine working in either of these departments. If I did, World 2A would turn out to be my own personal version of Hell.

"This is the Programming department," said Wang Li. "Here the babies are given the programming they need to perform their jobs on Earth."

"I see," I said. "How long does the programming take?" I asked.

"I don't know," said Wang Li. "But not long, because the babies need to eat!"

She moved to leave the room, exiting through a door in the center of the far wall. I followed her to Department 5. Immediately upon entering, the cries of many babies reached my ears. I saw women of various ages and races moving around the room, caring for the babies. One was changing a diaper, while several were holding the babies, gently jostling them up and down, some feeding them from baby bottles while holding them.

"This is Department 5," said Wang Li. "Nurturing. This department is staffed completely by humans."

"And the other departments?" I asked. "Do humans work there as well?"

"No," said Wang Li. "Only Imprints work in the boring departments. Nurturing is most important department. We must prepare the babies for their trip to Earth by making them feel loved. Imprints cannot do this job."

"I see," I said, relieved I wouldn't have to work in any of those other departments.

"Here," she said. "Take this baby." Wang Li reached into a crib and pulled up an Asian child who was crying and handed it to me.

I took the baby and quickly checked under its diaper to see if it needed changing. It was a boy, and it was clean and dry under there.

"Where is the formula?" I asked.

"Over there, in the refrigerator," she said, waving her head toward it. "You can heat it in the microwave oven, over there. Just put the bottle in the oven and push the button. The machine knows how long to heat it."

I did as Wang Li instructed and then inserted the nipple of the bottle into the hungry baby's mouth. He latched on to it with enthusiasm and sucked happily, his eyes getting that peaceful look babies have when feeding. I remembered the time of Maddie's infancy fondly. I must admit that I was a natural at taking care of babies, and I loved doing it, so it seemed the Teacher knew me better than I gave him credit for. This would be a good place for me to work.

As I was feeding the baby, I looked up at the far wall of Department 5. There was a set of double doors in the center there, identical to the other ones in the building.

"Is there a Department 6?" I asked Wang Li.

Her eyes widened a bit, a flash of fear passing over her face.

"Yes," she said. "But that department's not for us."

"What is it?" I asked, wondering why she was tightening up so much.

"The Transfer Station," she said. "That's where the babies are sent to Earth. Only the Teacher goes in there. No humans go in there!"

"Why?" I asked.

"Because if you go in there, you don't come out!" she said.

"Why? Do you end up back on Earth?"

"No. Humans cannot use the Transfer Station."

"Where then?" I asked. "Where do you end up if you go in there?"

"Gone," she said, and from the tone of her voice, I knew she wasn't joking.

Chapter 22

I don't know how long I worked at the Imprint House before I received a thought message from the Teacher to stop, but I had enjoyed it thoroughly. I loved babies. I remember that in all the years I had taken care of Maddie, from infancy until she was well into her twelfth year, she'd never gotten sick, and I realized now what a blessing that had been. Wang Li told me the Imprints were impervious to disease, and this wasn't surprising, since Aya had already informed me that the humans on World 2A never got sick either.

I remember that while I was working, I kept looking over at the door to the Transfer Station. Wang Li had seemed frightened when I mentioned it, and she'd been adamant that we were *never* to go in there. I wanted to ask her if it was locked but was afraid it might cause her to think I was considering going in, which I wasn't. At least not yet.

My curiosity was quelled when the Teacher arrived. He was wearing a different kind of robe than before and also had on a headdress like the kind you saw men from Saudi Arabia wearing on television. He smiled at me as he passed by, but did not speak. He walked over to one of the cribs and reached into it, pulling a baby up into his arms. It was a Caucasian baby, but it had darker skin and hair than I did. Maybe it would be going to the Middle East, because of the way it looked, and the Teacher was dressed the way he was so he could discreetly deliver the baby.

I found myself wondering how the babies could grow hair so quickly after being born with no hair. But then I realized I didn't know how long the babies remained in Department 5 before going to the Transfer Station. I could have asked Wang Li, but she undoubtedly wouldn't know the answer. No one here seemed to think about time at all. I wondered if one day I would stop thinking about it as well, because I certainly hadn't stopped yet. And the predominant thought in my mind was how long I should wait before trying to get through that door to the Transfer Station.

Meanwhile, the Teacher approached it, pushed it open with his free hand, and left the room, baby in tow. Just then, a thought entered my mind, and I heard the Teacher's voice. *You may stop working now*, said the voice. *You have seen what you needed to see today, and now your first challenge should be apparent to you.*

What? I thought. *What challenge?*

You must never walk through that door, came his voice. *Now go, and give some thought to this challenge. Try to imagine all that it means.*

I said goodbye to all the workers in Department 5 and made my way out of the building. I was hoping for another way out, but I had to go back through all of the other departments to get to the exit. I hurried, and wanted to close my eyes when I went through Department 3, the one with the clear vats where the babies were grown. I held my eyes straight ahead, almost running, and got out of there as fast as I could.

Aya was waiting for me in the empty entrance foyer. She greeted me with a quick kiss to both cheeks, and I must confess, I was very happy to see her. She really was good at her job of making the new people feel comfortable here.

"How was work?" she asked.

"It was nice," I said. "I love babies."

"Are you hungry?"

I hadn't thought about being hungry when I was at the Imprint House, but now I felt famished.

"Yes," I said. "I'm so hungry I could eat a fish!"

"Then we must go to Restaurant 2!" she said with great enthusiasm.

We entered the restaurant, and I saw that a few of the tables were occupied. There were two women sitting at one, and a man and a woman at another. The man was the first human male I had seen on World 2A.

"So there are men here!" I whispered.

"Yes," said Aya. "There are a few. But only about 20 percent of the population is men."

"Why is that?" I asked.

"The Teacher says it is because human women are naturally more empathetic than human men, and that is the kind of people who are gathered here."

"Empathetic people," I said, thinking that sounded pretty good. It wasn't heaven, but it was nice to hear that all the people here would be deserving of heaven, if they would only embrace the Lord our Savior.

I ordered fish and vegetables, as did Aya. It came out quickly and looked tasty, and it was, but without the pleasure that should have come with it. It was a white fish, like cod, and I assumed it was a copy of that species, just as our bodies were copies. The vegetables were broccoli and carrots, steamed. While we were filling our tanks to give us energy for what came next, Aya informed me we were going to the mountains, to her favorite place. We finished up and began our journey, quickly leaving the town behind, walking on a road that was about as wide as a driveway. It was made of gravel and had two compacted depressions running along it that looked like they'd been made by cars.

"Are these tire tracks?" I asked.

"Yes," said Aya, "from the vehicles used by the maintenance and construction workers."

We continued down the road through fields of freely growing grass, with beautiful ponds sprinkled along the way. Eventually, the road surface began to climb, and trees claimed the sides of the road from the grass. There were maple, oak, beech, and ash from what I could tell, and up ahead, the mountains were covered mostly by evergreens, interspersed with groves of what might have been Aspen trees. The road became steeper and more winding, and after a while it turned into switchbacks. We'd walk across and up in one direction, then switch back to the other, and this allowed us to continue up the very steep mountainside. Finally, we made it to the top of a ridge.

The view in front of us was breathtaking. The road we were on curled down into a beautiful valley. The road looked as if it became more narrow as it descended, and sections of it were hidden by massive evergreen trees. As it went lower, the road approached a beautiful mountain lake, surrounded on all sides by hills and forest. I noticed the weather was the same as always: bright with blue skies and sporadic clouds floating along, pushed by the gentle breeze that we always felt on our faces and arms. The temperature was comfortable, like a spring day in Asheville. But no sun.

We both had water bottles in our daypacks, and we drank from them as we looked out at the spectacular mountainscape below and above us.

"Does it ever rain here?" I asked Aya.

"No, it does not," she said. "It is always like this."

"That fits with my vision of what heaven would be like," I said.

"Do you still think you will go to heaven?" she asked, a playfulness in her voice, but I thought I detected a note of sarcasm as well.

"Absolutely," I said. "When my work here is done."

"I wish you the best on that," she said. "Shall we proceed?"

We started down the gravel road and soon found ourselves traveling through a dense evergreen forest, the trees brushing up tightly against the sides of the road. Lower down, the gravel road became a footpath and the trail grew soft, padded with fallen brown pine needles. We passed by a bubbling brook, interspersed with clear pools that looked delicious for a quick swim, but soon the energetic gasps of the stream fell behind us. The forest was still and quiet, the only sounds our breathing and muffled footfalls. We instinctively refrained from conversation, reveling instead in the silent beauty of the woods. The pines were giving way to deciduous growth, and the brown needles on the path were soon left behind. The sound of our footsteps on the hard-packed earth was louder than before, and we came out of the spell nature had cast upon us.

"Where are we going?" I asked.

"To the lake that we saw from up above," she said. "We're nearly there."

We came out of the forest, and just below us I could see a beautiful sand beach. There were people on the beach and in the water, both men and women. I counted five men and three women, but with our arrival, the balance between the genders would be equalized. I noticed that everyone was young, in their late teens or early twenties, around the same age as Aya. A few of the young men seemed handsome, and I wondered, since this was Aya's favorite place, if she favored one of them.

"Is there a young man down there you're interested in?" I asked, blushing a little for being so forward.

Aya laughed out loud.

"You mean, like in a sexual way?" she asked.

"Well, no," I said, my embarrassment growing. "That would be for later, after you're married."

Still smiling, Aya answered me.

"There is no marriage on World 2A," she said. "And no sex either. The sexual attraction that people on Earth feel for one another has been programmed out of us."

Well, that was a bit of a shock—not because I'd been looking forward to meeting someone and getting married again, but because it just seemed … harsh. I mean, sexual attraction is such a big part of what being human is, and they had simply erased it.

Then I felt myself blushing further, because I remembered that the teachings of my faith said there would be no marriage and no sex in heaven, and I was ashamed that my natural impulsive reaction to the way things were on World 2A was hypocritical. Rather than feel guilty, though, I decided to use this as a learning experience, preparatory to my eventual rise to heaven. I tried to remember how it felt to be sexually attracted to someone back on Earth, and compare it to how I felt at this moment.

Right now, I was looking at the attractive young men, and I was saying to myself they were attractive, but I wasn't feeling anything. I was simply categorizing them, intellectually, based on standards I had followed on Earth. But there, these "standards" were biological impulses. I would feel them. And even though I would never act on them, because that was not the way of my beliefs, I had to admit that I still felt them. But now I did not, and it was okay. I wasn't at all frustrated, so I concluded that the absence of marriage and sex, here and in heaven, was a good thing. Still, I wondered what the logic was behind this choice by the Makers. Perhaps knowing the answer would provide some enlightenment on God's decision to take the same path in heaven.

"Why did they do that?" I asked.

"Empathy is all the Makers seek from us," she said. "Perhaps the Teacher can tell you why. I do not know. But it is obvious that biological attraction to one another is not part of their equation for empathy."

"Hmmm," I replied, and upon final reflection, I felt that the Makers and God had gotten this one right.

When we arrived at the beach, Aya introduced me to everyone. All the women were wearing bikinis, and the men had on those baggy trunks that are so popular back on Earth. Aya removed her T-shirt and shorts and was wearing a bikini underneath as well. I could see, intellectually, that she was a strikingly beautiful young woman, but now that I knew the truth of things regarding sexual attraction here on World 2A,

I noticed that not one person there even glanced Aya's way when she revealed her shapely body. I myself saw no need to remove my T-shirt, since there was no sun to tan our skin, and I wondered why everyone else had done so. But then I realized they did it to go swimming. They dove in the water from time to time, swam around, playing games and whatnot, and then would come out and let the air dry them off. No one seemed to have any towels.

One young man, named Jimmy, was different from the rest of us. He had Down syndrome. He was about the same age as the others and seemed very happy. It warmed my heart to see him so well accepted by everyone on the beach, just another one of the gang. I reflected that on Earth it didn't always work that way when people were different. That made me think of Maddie, and my heart sank. A desperate need to pray overwhelmed my senses, so I tapped Aya on the shoulder.

"Aya, I need to spend some time alone," I said. "Is there a nice place nearby I can go?"

Aya didn't hesitate.

"Yes, of course," she said. "If you go back up the path about a hundred meters, there is a narrow footpath on the right that will take you to a very quiet viewing point. There's a bench there—I think you'll love it."

I thanked Aya and went back up the path. Finding the footpath, I followed it through the trees until it emerged onto a flat section that overlooked the lake. I sat on the stone bench and looked down at the calm, dark water. Slowly, I turned my head up and took in the steep cliff that rose up hundreds of feet from the lake. For the first time, I noticed a sliver of water dropping all the way down from the top of the cliff into the water of the lake. A waterfall, unlike any I had ever seen before. Watching the water peacefully cascade down and down and down helped to calm my nerves, a great mindset for starting a prayer. I lowered my head, clasped my hands together, closed my eyes, and prayed.

My Lord in heaven. I am in a place I wonder if you can see. I believe in my heart that you can, because how could you send me somewhere you cannot see? It is actually quite beautiful here, and I suppose it could be heaven, if only you were here as well. But I do not feel your presence, my Lord, and I so very much need guidance on what to do. My daughter Maddie, the gift you gave me twelve years ago, is in trouble. I want to help her. There is a door in the place where I work. I believe it is a door that could take me back to Earth. I know my time on Earth ended, and that you must have sent me here for a reason yet unknown to me. So I ask for your guidance. Please, tell me why I am here. Or give me a sign as to what I should do. The people here are very nice, but because I do not feel your presence, I am very much alone. And not content. I am torn, between the desire to go back to help my Maddie, and the hope that you will soon provide counsel as to my purpose here. Please, dear Lord. Send me a sign. In the name of the Son, the Father, and the Holy Spirit, I ask for your help. Amen.

Chapter 23

Aya and I had returned to our dwellings when a message came to me from the Teacher.

Please come down to the dock below and meet me.

I can't explain why, but it seemed obvious I was to go at that moment. Nor can I explain why I gathered my daypack, grabbed a few pieces of fruit, and filled a water bottle from the sink, but I did. Then I left the dwelling and went down to the dock.

The Teacher was waiting for me there. He took my hand and helped me onto the boat, then jumped on, untied the rope, and pushed us off. I tried to think of what I had felt when my hand touched the Teacher's hand, and nothing popped into my mind. I experienced no electric shock or surge of power, no hot or cold sensations when our hands touched. It was just a hand, seemingly like any other human one might touch. Except he wasn't human, I reminded myself.

We sailed out of the bay and turned left, the same direction we had gone before. As we reached the turn to go around to the other side, I could see the mountains where I had been with Aya. They were beautiful, and I felt the urge to return to them soon. My prayer, however, remained unanswered for now.

As we got to the other side of the island, I noticed the Teacher did not turn left. He kept the boat going straight out to sea.

"Where are we going, Teacher?" I asked.

"We're paying a visit to World 2B."

I raised my eyebrows, wondering what this new adventure would bring.

"Is it normal for you to take new people to visit World 2B?" I asked.

"Not at all," he said. "No one from World 2A has ever been on World 2B."

Why me? I asked myself. And then I realized the Teacher had always plainly answered most of my questions. I was about to ask aloud, but he answered me before I could.

"Because I need your help," he said.

"What kind of help?"

"I need help trying to unravel why World 2B is the way it is. It's a very different place than World 2A, and much more challenging."

"What makes it challenging?" I asked.

"The people who are gathered there are a more … *challenging* kind of people."

"How so?"

"We will speak more of this during our visit," he said. "But before we arrive, I'd like to speak with you about something else. Will that be all right with you?"

I wondered what the Teacher would do if I refused, but I had no reason to. I found him to be a fascinating … being, and I enjoyed his company.

"Of course," I replied. "What would you like to discuss?"

"I would like to discuss the door."

The Teacher was looking directly into my eyes as he said this, and of course I knew what door he was referring to immediately. He was steering the boat but not looking where he was going, which was probably fine, but the intensity of his stare was a little frightening. His fine blond hair was blowing back behind his head, and his pale blue eyes bored into my own. He wasn't speaking, and he wasn't telepathizing, yet it was clear he was imploring me to be honest, not only with him, but with myself. I understood that if I purposely lied, he would know it, and there was no reason to do so anyway. What was important was for me to understand my true feelings about the door. What did I really want? And then I knew.

"I want to go through that door," I said.

All he said was, "Yes."

"What will happen to me if I go through that door?" I asked.

"What do you want to happen?"

"I want to find my daughter and make sure she's okay."

"Of course."

"But would I? If I went through that door?"

"It *might* be possible for you to go to Earth if you pass through that door," he said. "But when you get there, you will not find your daughter."

"How do you know this?" I asked.

"Because *we* cannot find her."

"But if we worked together, perhaps we could," I countered.

"Perhaps," he said. "What is important, however, is that you know what you want. You may not ever attain it, but your mind is clear. And this is the way we want it."

"Why?" I asked.

"That will be explained later," he said. "We are arriving at our destination."

I saw the island in the distance. We were still about a mile away, and it seemed to me there should be plenty of time left for the Teacher to answer my question. But I was a patient person, and I had the ear of the most powerful being on this planet, by all indications. I wanted to keep it that way. The Teacher was my pathway out of here, I hoped, and even though he knew my every thought, I wasn't worried about it. He and I were a good team. He was helping me sort out my own feelings, and in return, I hoped I could help him unravel some of his own confusion, about World 2B.

As we grew closer to the island, I saw fins in the water. A lot of them.

"Are those sharks?" I asked, frightened and not understanding their presence.

"Yes," he said.

"I haven't seen any sharks around our island. Why do I see them here?"

"They are needed here," he said. "The people of World 2B are a bit more … adventurous than the people of World 2A. And some of them are good swimmers. The sharks keep them close to shore. Very close."

"What about boats? Couldn't they just sail away if they wanted?"

"There are no boats here on World 2B. We found out early on that these people could not be trusted with boats."

"Where do they get their fish, then?"

"The fisherman of World 2A deliver the fish that are eaten here," he said.

"I thought you said I was the first person from World 2A to come here?"

"I said no one from World 2A has ever been *on* World 2B. The fishermen never step off their boats when they come here. It is forbidden."

Chapter 24

We entered a bay that looked exactly like the bay below my house on World 2A, and soon pulled alongside a dock that was a duplicate of the one there as well. I looked up and saw four white houses with slate roofs—three small, one larger. Above them was the beautiful hill of green grass, just like where I had entered World 2A.

"Is World 2B a duplicate of World 2A?" I asked.

The Teacher was tying the rope from the dock to the boat. "Not exactly," he said. "Some of the buildings in town are different. You will see."

We took the road to town, and it looked the same as the road on World 2A. But as we came nearer, I saw churches, and temples, and mosques.

"So you allow worship here on World 2B?" I asked.

"Worship is not forbidden on World 2A *or* World 2B," he said. "But it seems the people here are more inclined to build places of worship than those on World 2A. It's really a function of the kind of people who come here, compared to there."

"Aya told me not many Christians come to World 2A." I said. "And that most of the people there are atheists or agnostics."

"Yes, that is true," he said. "But here, 80 percent of the population *says* they are religious, which is consistent with the general population of Earth. But we've had to limit the number of buildings that each of the major religions can build. There are four Hindu temples, one for each of their four main denominations, two Muslim mosques, one for the Sunni and one for the Shia, three Jewish temples, one for the Reform branch, one for the Orthodox, and one for the Conservative, three Buddhist temples, and three Christian churches."

"Why only three Christian churches?" I asked, knowing there were many more Christian denominations than that.

"Did you know there are forty-five thousand Christian denominations on Earth, Cynthia?"

"Seriously?" I knew there were a lot Christian faiths, but I would have guessed there were at most maybe several dozen of them.

"I have no reason to lie to you Cynthia. And that is why we held the line here at three. It was that, or forty-five thousand."

"So what *are* the three Christian churches?"

"Catholic, Protestant, and Eastern Orthodox."

"Oh my," I said. "You're packing quite a number of different faiths into that Protestant church, aren't you?"

"Indeed," he said. "Many people aren't happy about it, but there are limits to what can be done. The good news is that while most of these people fiercely resist coming together in church or temple or mosque, they find common ground in the building over there to your right."

I looked that way and saw a large red brick building with white columns out front. Sprawled out behind it and on both sides was, of all things, a golf course. I could see golf buggies buzzing around out there and people swinging clubs.

"Is that a country club?" I asked, baffled.

"I'm afraid it is," said the Teacher.

"Well, this World 2B is very different indeed, isn't it?"

"Yes." He nodded. "By the way, are you hungry, Cynthia?"

"Why yes, Teacher, I am, come to think of it. I forgot to eat on the way here."

"What would you like to eat?" he asked.

"Fish and vegetables would be nice," I said.

"Restaurant 2 then," he said.

"So they eat the same foods as we do on World 2A?" I asked.

"Yes, and no," he said. "The restaurants in town are the same, but the country club has a greater selection of foods."

"Do they have beef and pork?" I asked.

"Of a fashion, yes," he said. "They've developed meat substitutes made from the local farm products. Soy beans are a critical ingredient in those, I'm told. I haven't tried them."

We entered the restaurant, sat down, and ordered our meals from an Imprint. Both of us had fish and vegetables, and it was delivered quickly. There was no one else inside.

"Why is no one here?" I asked. "Are they all working?"

"Some, probably," he said. "The work routine is different here."

"How so?"

"It's managed by the World 2B government," he said. "I'm not really involved in it."

"They have their own government? How did that happen?"

"It's been that way for a long time," he said. "They seem to manage things fairly well."

"So the work gets done on the farms, and the fish are processed when they're delivered, no problem?"

"Actually, Imprints staff those facilities," he confessed.

"What about the Imprint House? Are there any humans there?"

"There is no Imprint House here on World 2B," he said.

"Why?"

"It wouldn't work here."

"Why?" I asked again.

"In time you will understand more," he said. "There are some things I can clear up for you, though."

"Thank you," I said, relieved. I was actually beginning to feel a bit discriminated against over on World 2A, although from what I'd seen so far, I thought World 2A was a better place to live, by far.

"The Makers are a purely intellectual species," said the Teacher. "They have existed throughout the ages with only one desire—to learn more about the Megaverse and all of its inhabitants. But when they encountered human beings, they marveled, intellectually speaking, at the vast and complex set of emotions displayed by your species. I've already told you that, but here is the rest of it. A theory was submitted for consideration that the Makers might improve as a species if they could learn more about human emotions. Two emotional traits were identified that were responsible for most of the advancement of the human species—empathy and narcissism."

Now I could fill in the blanks. World 2A was full of empaths. World 2B was full of narcissists.

"So why do you need me here, on World 2B?" I asked. "How can I help you, Teacher?"

"Please explain to me why the people here on World 2B can hate one another when it comes to differences in religion, yet put religion aside when pursuing other matters of self-interest."

Chapter 25

I was surprised when the Teacher was presented with a bill at the restaurant.

"They use money here?" I asked.

"Yes," he said, shrugging his shoulders. "The 'take what you need' philosophy of World 2A was a non-starter here. These people just take and take and take until there is nothing left for anyone else."

"There are definitely people like that on Earth," I said. "What I don't understand is why the Makers would find that kind of person to be of interest."

"Many of the people here on World 2B built vast business empires. Some were leaders of nations. They could not be ignored by the Makers. Please try to understand, Cynthia, from the perspective of a species that has only one ambition—to learn. The Makers are the most skilled observers of all time. And while there are many characteristics of these narcissistic people you may find repulsive, the Makers have no emotional reaction because they possess no emotions. They simply observe and learn, and what they see is that this kind of person has advanced the human species as much or more than any other. Their only rival are the empaths, whose sole motivation is to help others, and throughout the ages, they have succeeded."

"You've asked me a question, Teacher, and I think I have an answer for you, but can we see more before I give it?"

"Of course," he said. "What would you like to see?"

We were back out on the street now. Everything in the center of town looked the same as in World 2A. There were the three restaurants, the grocery store, the clothing store, the bookstore, the wine bar and—what was that? There was another building, right next to the bookstore, which I didn't recognize.

"What is that building for?" I asked.

"That is the sex brothel," he said.

"What?" I asked, both confused and offended. "I thought our sex drive had been deactivated?"

"On World 2A, yes," he said. "But not here on 2B. It was determined by our analysts that the sex drive is an important component in the psychological structure of the narcissist."

I shook my head, failing to understand how this world could produce anything worth keeping for the Makers. The Teacher was obviously following my thoughts. His mind reading seemed instantaneous in nature, whereas Maddie could read thoughts only after they'd been stored as memories.

"First, let me be clear that our purpose is not to indulge these people," he said. "Our purpose is to elevate them, to purify their most predominant characteristic, just as it is on the world of the empaths."

"So you build them a whorehouse?" I asked, disheartened that the Makers would allow this.

"We have observed a direct correlation between achievement and sexual drive in these individuals," said the Teacher. "A sexual release is needed, from time to time, or achievement begins to decline."

"And just who goes into this den of iniquity? You said that 80 percent of the people here are religious. I'm not sure about Muslims, and Hindus and Buddhists, but I doubt whether a place like this is tolerated by their faiths. And I know for certain there are no good Christians, of any denomination, who would come here."

I was surprised at how emotionally I was responding to what I was seeing here on World 2B. It just made no sense at all. There was nothing here that was any different from the worst of what Earth had to offer. So why were the Makers so intrigued by it all? Then, the Teacher made an interesting observation.

"Not everyone goes into the brothel, Cynthia. Many take care of their sexual needs on their own. But religion has nothing to do with who partakes from this house or not, nor does gender. And while 80 percent of the people here on World 2B are men, women also go in there. Moreover, our methods for classifying a person have nothing to with religion, or gender. We go deeper than that, to the core of the person. They are either empathic, or not. They are either self-obsessed, or not. At their core."

"But the truly faithful are *faithful* at their core!" I exclaimed.

"And thus, you have answered my question," he said.

"What?" I asked, but then I thought about the Teacher's original question again. He'd asked why people of different religions could hate one another, but then put religion aside when self-interest was served. I was beginning to understand why he felt I'd answered it, so I summarized my opinion to see if he agreed.

"These people, the ones here on World 2B," I said. "They are not *truly* faithful. They use religion for selfish reasons, not for the reasons the faith prescribes."

The Teacher was nodding his head, but my mind was whirling. I thought of some of the people at my own local church, just a handful really, who would make curious comments. At the socials, or the bake sales or other get-togethers, I would sometimes overhear them gossiping about individuals from outside our faith—how they were unworthy of God's love and completely despicable. I never understood why they would spend their time tearing down others simply because they had chosen another faith, or had no faith at all. And then a piece of scripture came to mind that I remembered well. It was from the book of Matthew, Chapter 7, verses 21 to 23:

Not everyone who says to me, "Lord, Lord," will enter the kingdom of heaven, but only the one who does the will of my Father who is in heaven. Many will say to me on that day, "Lord, Lord, did we not prophesy in your name and in your name drive out demons and in your name perform many miracles?" Then I will tell them plainly, "I never knew you. Away from me, you evildoers!"

What this meant was that many people think they're following Christ but are self-deceived, because they are living for their own selfish desires rather than for God. I could give full voice to my answer to his question now, and even though I was aware that he understood, I felt the need to say it out loud for my own benefit.

"These people love no one except themselves," I said. "They use their religion to lift themselves above others, to help them feel superior. But they love no one, inside or outside of the church, except themselves. The best they can do is to accept a few people into their lives based on their affiliations. Church membership or country club membership are completely acceptable to them, but neither love of God nor love of others has anything to do with it."

"Thank you, Cynthia," said the Teacher. "I think we can leave World 2B now."

On the way back to World 2A, the Teacher taught me how to sail. It was a basic sailboat, with only one sail and a handle for steering, and as soon as I learned how to tie a few knots and read the wind, it was easy to operate. I was so happy to be away from World 2B. I hadn't met a single person there, but I'd seen enough about their way of life to realize it was not a place for me. I was glad to be returning to World 2A, and even though my hand felt steady on the rudder handle, I still felt unsettled about what the future would bring.

But the Teacher wasn't finished with me. He had one more thing to put in front of me.

"Cynthia, there is a reason I am teaching you to sail."

"Why?" I asked.

"Because one day, you will sail this boat to World 3."

"What is World 3?"

"It is the World of the Makers."

Chapter 26

Life continued on World 2A. I went to work when the Teacher told me to, and I left when he told me leave. Work in Department 5 was mostly rewarding. I loved caring for the infants, and I tried to convince myself that I was helping them get started in life, even though it would be difficult for most of them, as it had been for my Maddie. For isn't it better to live and suffer than not live at all? I wasn't sure, and each time one of us handed a baby to the Teacher and he entered the Transfer Station to take them to Earth, my doubt and my pain escalated as I recalled the turmoil of my own child's life. But then more babies came, and I nurtured them to the best of my abilities, until their time to leave arrived.

My personal challenge of wanting to go through the door to the Transfer Station was resolved, for now. I understood, from my conversations with the Teacher, that it would be futile to go back to Earth by myself, but I still hoped to one day convince him to take me there with him. I realized that if I was thinking this, he would know it, but that didn't bother me. I would have told him the truth about what I wanted if he'd asked, but he didn't need me to because he already knew the truth.

One day, I noticed I hadn't seen Wang Li for quite some time. We'd become friends and spent time together outside of work. Aya and Wang Li and I often did things together. But many sessions in Department 5 had passed by without me seeing her. We didn't always work at the same time, but we often did, and when her absence continued, I began to wonder if her status had changed. I asked one of the other women who worked in our department if she had seen Wang Li lately, and she told me Wang Li had "moved on."

"Moved on to where?" I asked, concern rising in my gut. "Was she transferred to another work area?"

"No," said the woman. "She's moved on from World 2A."

"To the World of the Makers?" I asked, hopeful for her.

"I don't know," she said. "We never know where someone goes when they leave."

"But we can ask the Teacher, right?" I asked. "He will certainly know."

"The Teacher will not answer that question," said the woman. "It is not for us to know."

In spite of what she said, I believed that if *I* asked him, he would tell me. He'd already revealed things to me that no one else here knew, but I never discussed that privileged information with anyone. I understood intuitively that these revelations came with a vow of secrecy. So there would be no harm in asking him what had happened to my friend Wang Li. I would never tell anyone. I made a mental note to ask him when the opportunity presented itself.

During the times when I wasn't working, I kept myself busy in several ways. I'd acquainted myself with the bookstore early on and found it a very different place than a bookstore on Earth. Inside the store was a single kiosk. To get a book, you simply spoke to the kiosk, telling it the title you wanted. The first book I had asked for was the King James Version of the New Testament. The kiosk took about twenty minutes to prepare it for me. Then a door opened in the front of the kiosk, and there it was. I read from it often, and spent a considerable amount of time searching for passages about heaven and what it would be like. The conclusion I reached was that the Bible left a lot about heaven up for interpretation, but I took solace in the fact that I believed fully that I would eventually get there. I believed in my heart that my time here on World 2A was part of my path, and if I went to World 3, that would be too. And I had no fear of "continuing on." For me, that would be a direct path to the Promised Land. Well, that's not really true. I didn't want to go there until after I knew Maddie was going to be okay, and I didn't know that. My greatest fear was that I might never know.

I also started writing. There was an Imprint who worked at the bookstore who didn't have much to do, so I asked her one day if she could get me paper and pencil. She went into the back and came out with a pad of paper and a few pencils. She even had one of those little manual pencil sharpeners, so I was off the races. I did most of my writing at the wine bar, and usually had a glass of wine sitting beside me while I wrote, which I rarely finished. I wrote about my life, of course, which didn't really get interesting until I adopted Maddie, so I started there. And then it went from interesting to frightening, moved on to devastating, and finally settled in with confusion. The confusion part was mostly after I arrived on World 2A. There was so much I didn't know about this place still, and the questions just piled up in my head. The Teacher would answer some of them, and Aya would also try to help when she could, but overall, I really didn't understand why I was there, because the Lord had yet to help me understand.

I still lived in the dwelling where I'd started, near the Human House, where Aya lived and worked. She and I had become best friends. Aya no longer had any responsibilities for my well-being and adjustment to World 2A, but she enjoyed being with me, as I did with her, and we sought each other out when we weren't working. Aya had permission from the Teacher to tell me anything she knew, and that included the nature of her work at the Human House, although I wasn't permitted entry there. Aya had explained that the "preparation process" she'd referred to on the day of my arrival was the process of growing the human bodies before their Essence was transferred to them. The first few stages were very much like what occurred at the Imprint House, although it was much less of a production line, because the quantity of humans being processed was much less than the quantity of Imprints. We talked about why that was, and while I'm certain the Teacher would have explained it to me if I'd asked, we concluded that more Imprints were needed for two primary reasons: first, many of them very likely didn't survive long, considering most of the Earth was still quite primitive, with poor living conditions and famine rampant throughout much of the world; and second, many of the humans the Imprints marked would never make it to World 2A. This was because when a *marked* individual died, they could only come to World 2A if there was an opening, and while we couldn't measure time there, it seemed that people didn't leave that often.

I wasn't alone in my dwelling much, except to eat, although I sometimes read when I was there. Most of the time when I was in that area, I sailed. The Teacher had left his boat tied up at the dock down below where I lived and had encouraged me to take it out into the bay as often as I liked, and I found myself going quite a bit. There was something about the mechanics of sailing that appealed to me, although I never fancied myself as a mechanical person. No, actually, it was more than that. It was the blending of a mechanical device with the natural environment that felt so perfect when I was sailing. The feeling to me was like slicing into nature and becoming part of it. It felt so good. So pure.

I liked to bring Aya sailing with me when she was free. The first time I asked her to go, she refused, because she said no human on the island, except me, was permitted to sail. I thought I sensed, once again, a tiny pulse of envy from her during that first discussion, but it passed quickly and I let it slip out of my mind. To put her mind at rest, I spoke to the Teacher, asking his permission to take Aya sailing with me, and he readily agreed. I asked him to please send her a thought message letting her know it was okay, and he did.

After that, we sailed together often. Aya enjoyed it very much, and I liked having her with me. I also took pleasure in bringing joy to my best friend, and if I am very honest, a tinge of pride in being able to do something others were not allowed to. I resolved myself to purge my mind of this sinful pride, for it was not the way of our Lord, and I was certain the Teacher would agree it was best to be rid of it.

One day, Aya and I were up at Mountain Lake, the place she'd taken me early in my time on World 2A, which had become a favorite of mine, as it had been for her for a long time. We were lounging on the beach, watching the young men and women dive off the cliff where the waterfall tumbled down. None of them dove from the top, which would have been suicide, since it had to be at least a three-hundred-foot drop. But Jimmy, the young man with Down syndrome, would go the highest of all of them.

At that very moment, he was nearly halfway up the cliff. The other cliff divers had stopped about a third of the way up and were waiting for him to dive. For me, watching the climb alone was nerve wracking. And then, when Jimmy launched himself out from the cliff wall, his hands reaching out together in a double fist, his body slowly turning into a vertical position as he plummeted down, piercing the water with hardly a splash, I was terrified for him, but also exhilarated when his head popped up onto the surface of the water, a loud cheer erupting from all of us, including the people still up above on the cliff. The smile on his face was so broad, so *true*, that it made the anxiety his climb and dive produced in me, well, worth it, I suppose I would say. But I really wished he wouldn't climb so high. He was the most perfect empath on World 2A, and it would be a harsh blow, to all of us, to lose him in a needless tragedy.

Later that day, Aya and I were still on the beach. Both of us were reading. I heard footsteps coming down the hill and wondered who it would be. I knew most of the people on World 2A by then, and each and every one of them was a joy to be with. The saying "not a mean bone in their body" applied to all of us here, and I had to admit, it truly was a wonderful thing. The only sadness was when someone left. Not only did I miss them, I worried for them. So few of the people on World 2A had the same beliefs as me, and it saddened me they might not receive the same consideration as I would when the time to "continue on" arrived. For me, it wasn't a question, like it was for the agnostics among us. For me, it was knowledge. But I digress. What I want to tell here is the story of who came down the hill to Mountain Lake, not long after Jimmy's dive.

A lanky man with a bald head emerged from the forest that day. He was muscular, but thin, as if he worked out a lot, perhaps running long distances. Aya tapped me on the arm and tilted her head toward him, whispering to me.

"He came through Human House recently," she said. "I wasn't assigned to him, but I found him to be a very handsome man when I saw him lying there, his body waiting for the Essence Transfer. What is your opinion about the way he looks?"

It was interesting that Aya was speaking at all about the way a person looked, but as I thought about it, I often did the same thing. As I've said before, it was an intellectual endeavor as opposed to one laced with sexual feelings, as it would have been on Earth. But these considerations actually became quite secondary to me at that moment, because as the man came closer, I realized I knew him. It was Dr. Tom Branch.

My jaw dropped, and I stood, but my legs were too weak to walk. I just waited there until he came onto the beach and walked up to me. He extended his hand to shake, but I was so filled with emotion that I launched myself at him and hugged him tightly. Here was a person from Earth I had known while I was there, the first such person I'd encountered here on World 2A. Until the doctor came down that hill, I hadn't realized how much I missed my life on Earth. Tears filled my eyes, not only from my grief over what I had lost, but because I knew that he was here because he'd died.

We separated, but I still held both his hands in mine, and I could see he also had tears in his eyes.

"How did it happen?" I asked.

"I was out on a training ride on my bike and got hit by a truck," he said. "Those narrow mountain passes finally were the end of me."

"I'm sorry, Dr. Branch," I said.

"I'll make a deal with you, okay?" he said.

"What?" I asked.

"If you call me Tom, I'll call you Cynthia. Deal?"

"Deal," I said. "I have so many questions to ask you, Tom, I don't know where to begin. But first, have you met my friend Aya?"

"Absolutely," he said. "She's my neighbor!"

"Well guess what. That means I'm your neighbor too! I live right next door to Human House."

"How could you be my neighbor and neither of us know that?" he asked.

"Well, I don't know about you, but I'm not there much. With work, and all the fun things to do on World 2A, I don't get home too often."

"Same with me, I guess. I don't know where the time goes."

"I don't think it goes anywhere," I said. "Because I don't think it's here at all!"

We laughed together, and Tom got the conversation back on track.

"Where would you like to start?" he asked. "What can I tell you about things on Earth since you left?"

"Well, to be polite, maybe you should ask questions of me first, about World 2A," I said, finally regaining some semblance of manners after the shock of seeing him.

"I know enough about how things work here to wait a few minutes to find out more," he said. "And frankly, I'm glad to be here. I'm one of those agnostics, you know."

We shared another laugh, and then I asked the question that was foremost in my mind. Eventually, I would get around to asking Tom about Amy and how she was doing, but my focus at the time was to try to add pieces to the puzzle that would help me figure out some practical matters.

"What year did you die, Tom?"

"March of 2004," he said.

"So I've been here for nearly six years!" I exclaimed. "I had no idea!"

"Yes," he said. "It appears so. We never knew what happened to either you or Maddie. It was like you disappeared and never came back. Please tell me. Did Maddie meet the same fate as you, or is she still on Earth?"

"I don't know for sure," I said. "I think she's still there, but she's been hidden by her captors, according to the Teacher."

"Oh, that's interesting," he said, nodding his head as if things made more sense to him now.

"Why? I asked.

"I work at the Monitoring Station, and I know there are three Imprints unaccounted for on Earth. Once I got here and learned about the Imprints, I wondered if Maddie might be one of them. I always liked her, but now I truly love her, because she gave me the gift of eternal life. She had to be the one who marked me, right?"

I wondered if Tom knew that people didn't stay here on World 2A forever, but I didn't say anything because I wanted to keep the conversation on track, and it wasn't my place to tell him anyway. So I just responded to his question about Maddie.

"It's very likely she was," I said, trying to smile but struggling to. Talking about my daughter had brought on a surge of grief, and a dash of hope, but I needed to put that aside for now, because standing in front of me was a man who might be able to help me reunite with her, somewhere down the line.

"So you work at the Monitoring Station," I said. "Well then, please tell me more."

Chapter 27

"How did you manage to get assigned to the Monitoring Station?" I asked. "That's the most prestigious posting on World 2A."

The three of us were walking back to town after our day at Mountain Lake, following the gravel road. The sky was blue, and a few white clouds ambled along on the light breeze, as always. Aya and I were holding hands, something we did often, a custom that was common among women where she was from, which I had grown to very much enjoy. Aya and I gave comfort to one another, and holding hands only increased the experience. Tom was walking with his hands free, beside us.

"The Teacher knew all about me," he said. "That I had treated Maddie, and of course that I also knew you, and he told me you were here. I knew it was only a matter of time until I ran into you. Anyway, the Teacher was well aware of my quantitative abilities, which he felt would be wasted on a fishing boat or growing soy beans. So he put me in the Monitoring Station."

Tom was obviously quite happy to be on World 2A, and it helped me to better understand how people who weren't religious felt about life after death. To them, it was a surprise. An unexpected gift. And if I was honest, I felt lucky to be here too, even though I knew it was not my ultimate destination. And while it was exhilarating to have someone I knew from Earth here on World 2A, my priority at the moment was to learn as much as I could about the Monitoring Station.

"What's it like working there?" I asked. "Is it highly technical?"

"Not really," he said. "The technology behind it is a complete mystery. But all we have to do is keep an eye on things. I'll admit there's a lot of bodies to track, but there are five of us working there at any given time, so the work's not that taxing."

"So what are you keeping an eye on?" I asked, trying to sound casual.

"We watch the Imprints on Earth, primarily," he said. "It's not like we have a video of them or anything. It's just a lighted dot on a map, for each one. If the dot goes out, we alert the Teacher, and I guess he arranges for a replacement Imprint."

From my time working at Imprint House, I was well aware of how the replacement process worked, but I didn't want to divert Tom away from his discussion of the Monitoring Station, so I simply nodded my head, encouraging him to continue.

"We also monitor all the marked humans on Earth," he said. "There's a lot of them, and there's a screen that automatically ranks them regarding their fit with regard to World 2A or World 2B. There's another screen that keeps track of all the humans on World 2A and World 2B that lets us know when a person leaves one of these worlds. At that point, we initiate the process to find a replacement from Earth. The technology that does this is beyond my understanding, but somehow, the Monitoring Station knows when a person that's been marked is about to die, and if they're high enough on the list, the station sends out a capture signal that hovers near them until just before the moment of death, and then it grabs their Essence, microseconds before death takes them."

I had a general idea about most of what Tom was telling me from my discussions with the Teacher, but not this much detail. It wasn't surprising to me that the Monitoring Station on World 2A also managed the supply of humans for World 2B. If the Teacher couldn't trust them to go fishing, he certainly couldn't trust them to manage the process of who was brought to their world. But none of this was the kind of information I was looking for.

"So what about Maddie?" I asked. "What are you people at the Monitoring Station doing to find her, and the other missing Imprints?"

"Frankly, nothing," he said. "We've been given no instructions regarding them other than to leave their switches off."

"What switches?" I asked, beginning to get nervous.

"Each Imprint on Earth has an on/off switch," he said. "Sometimes, we receive instructions from the Teacher to turn one of their switches off."

"And then what happens?" I asked.

"I don't know," he said. "I assume they're brought back here, for reprogramming or something."

I wasn't aware of any reprogramming department at the Imprint House, or anywhere else on World 2A. We mostly made babies, but we also made adults every now and then, if they were needed for posts on World 2A or 2B. But I never saw any Imprints brought in for reprogramming.

"Interesting," I said, still trying to remain casual but struggling to do so. "But what does the 'on' setting mean?"

"It just means the Imprint is to remain in place."

"Kind of like, they just keep on doing what they're doing, right?" I asked.

"Sure," he said, realization dawning on his face.

I took the logic to its obvious conclusion, so Tom wouldn't have to say it.

"So 'off' could mean that they just stop doing what they're doing," I said. "As in, they're turned off."

"You mean, like, dead?" he asked. "You think Maddie is dead?"

"I don't think so," I said.

"What does it mean then?" he asked.

"I think it means the Teacher *wants* her dead," I said, anger and fear boiling together inside me.

Chapter 28

For the first time, I asked for a meeting with the Teacher, rather than the other way around. The way I did it was to think it, over and over again. Eventually, I heard his voice. *Meet me at the dock.*

When I arrived, the Teacher was standing there, his arms folded together in front of him. I said hello and moved to get on the boat, but he stopped me by speaking aloud.

"We'll talk here today," he said.

"So we aren't going for a sail?" I asked, wondering why not.

"The sailing will happen later," he said. "We'll talk here, first."

I stood and faced him, knowing that I could keep no secrets.

"I'm sure you know why I'm here," I said.

"Ask your questions." His voice was firm, and he wasn't smiling.

"Are you going to kill Maddie?"

"You mean Imprint 17035, I take it," he said. "And the answer is yes. She was discovered, captured, and hidden from us, her mission compromised. She is of no further use to us."

"But she has usefulness to *me*!" I said, a pleading tone in my voice.

"That's irrelevant," he said. "You are here to serve us, not the other way around."

"Yes, I'm your slave, as are all the others here. You don't indulge us the way you do those on World 2B, do you?"

"How do you mean?" he asked.

"They ask you for churches and temples, and their wish is granted. They want a country club, and voila. They have it. And they don't even have to ask for sexual services! You provided that to them on your own."

I watched the Teacher for a reaction, but as always, he was stoic. He wasn't talking, so he must have been thinking, or communicating with the Makers, and I took that as a good sign. I waited for quite some time, and then he spoke.

"What are you asking for?" he said.

"I'm asking you, first, to turn Maddie's switch back on. And second, I'm asking you to take me with you to Earth, so we can find her and bring her back here."

This time, he didn't hesitate.

"The second request is out of the question," he said. "The first, however, I am in a position to grant, on one condition."

I wasn't a skilled negotiator, but I could tell, just from his willingness to consider granting my request to save Maddie's life, that I had some kind of leverage over him. I didn't know what it was yet, but I wasn't going to let him off that easily.

"I want to go to Earth to save my daughter," I said. "I don't care what you want."

Again he went silent, his expression unreadable. Then he spoke.

"You will go to the Makers," he said. "Now."

"I don't want to go to the Makers!" I said. "I refuse to be helpful to those who will not help me!"

But he was undeterred.

"There are two ways you can go to the Makers, Cynthia. One is for us to transfer your Essence to them, as we do with all other humans who go there. Two, which is a rare privilege for a human, you can sail to them."

I was frightened and confused, not for myself, but for my poor Maddie. I believed in my heart that if my Essence went to the Makers, she would be lost to me forever, but I sensed some kind of opening in the second option, sailing to World 3. There had to be some advantage I could gain by doing that.

"What is the benefit of sailing there, to *me*?" I asked.

"If you sail there, and things go well, you might be allowed to come back to World 2A, unharmed and unchanged."

"Teacher, you know I don't care about my own well-being. God will protect my soul, and bring me to Him when he deems me ready. But it seems I'm the only being in the universe, in any universe, who cares about Maddie enough to give my life to help her. To you and the Makers, she's just a number. But not to me! She's my reason for being alive, and I will not have her harmed. Take my life if you wish, but I will not cooperate with you until I have your word she will not be harmed."

"Sail to World 3, and I promise you her switch will be turned back on, and it will remain so until such time that we learn she is either dead or alive. If we find her alive, we will not harm her, as long as you remain useful to us here."

"Turn the switch on, now!" I commanded.

The Teacher was silent, just for a moment. I sensed he was communicating with someone, and then he spoke.

"It is done," he said. "Now go to your dwelling and bring food and water. Bring all that you can carry. It's a long journey to World 3."

I was relieved, but not completely satisfied.

"I don't know what will happen on World 3, and I know you won't tell me. But I ask you this, Teacher. If I return, will you help me find Maddie?"

This time, he didn't hesitate.

"If you return, I promise to inform you of all that is being done to find her," he said. "If upon learning this, you have practical ideas that can aid in the search, we will consider them."

I thought about what I had accomplished so far in this meeting. The Teacher had commanded someone in the Monitoring Station to turn Maddie's switch back on. He had also promised to work with me upon my return to World 2A to try to find her. Not necessarily in the way I had envisioned, but maybe there was a better way, and the more knowledge I had, the more likely I could help formulate a plan that would work. Yes, it wasn't certain that I'd return at all, but I'm an optimistic person and preferred to think that I would be, somehow.

"I'll go and pack my things," I said, then turned and climbed the hill to my dwelling.

Chapter 29

I was soon back on the sailboat, ready to cast off, but the Teacher had a few more things to say.

"It is a long way to World 3," he said. "Much further than World 2B."

"How will I find it?" I asked.

"Sail directly out of the bay," he said. "Do your best to keep that heading as long as you can. If you feel you are lost, help will come to you."

"What kind of help?" I asked.

"It does not matter," he said. "You will make it to World 3. In time."

"Are there sharks out there?" I asked.

"No. But there are other creatures. None will harm you."

"What about rough seas? Will I encounter any?"

"No," he said. "But the water is very deep, in places. Now go."

"Teacher, I have one more question, and it's important. Why do the Makers want to see me? Why me?"

"You have something they want," he said. "Or at least some of them do."

"What?" I asked.

"It is not for me to say at this time. I hope you receive the answers you desire on World 3, and that you return safely to World 2A."

He turned away and walked down the dock. I cast off and raised the sail of my tiny boat, pointing it straight out to sea. When I turned back to see if the Teacher was watching, he was already gone. I wondered how he did that. It didn't matter, though. Either way, I was on my own now, heading to meet the most powerful beings in the universe. Except for one, and I prayed He was watching over me now.

I held my course and sailed away from World 2A. Every now and then I looked back, and of course, it got smaller and smaller until it was gone altogether. The water was calm, but I could see nothing in front of me except a vast ocean. With the disappearance of World 2A, and the absence of celestial objects in the sky, I had no way to get my bearings. I saw nothing but endless spans of water in every direction.

I sailed on, and the only thing that gave me any sense of time were the hunger pains in my belly. I ate some fruit and drank from my water bottle, wondering if I'd brought enough to see me through. Time passed, although how much I had no idea, as was always the case on this strange planet. One thing I became certain of was that I was utterly lost. Lost at sea.

Suddenly, up ahead, I saw a huge head break the surface of the water, followed by a massive body. The whale rose up and out the sea, then flopped over onto its side. It was close enough to me that the splash spilled onto my boat, filling it with several inches of water, the waves rocking the boat precariously. Then a large, eel-like creature slithered up over the side of the boat and came into it. I was terrified, but the eel seemed to have no interest in me. I noticed the water level inside the boat was dropping, and it became clear the eel was sucking in the water, its body expanding like a balloon filling with air. When the water level had receded to just a tiny amount, the bloated eel flopped itself up over the side and disappeared into the sea.

I looked up and saw the huge whale swimming beside my boat. It was looking at me with one of its eyes, an orb that was at least six inches in diameter when the lid was fully opened. The pupil of the eye turned forward, sending me a message, it seemed, to go the way the whale went. Then it moved out ahead of me, adjusting its speed to my boat. And there it stayed, presumably showing me the way.

I followed the whale for ages and ages, eating all of my food as immeasurable time slipped by. I had only one water bottle left and it was nearly empty, but I drank from it anyway as I was terribly thirsty. When I looked up ahead, my heart skipped a beat because the whale was gone—perhaps diving for food, I hoped, but it did not return. I worried that I would become lost again, but then I spotted something on the horizon. It looked like the peak of a high mountain, and as I continued sailing toward it, I saw that is *was* indeed a mountain, a lone peak rising out of the sea that surrounded it. Hopefully this was World 3.

As I sailed closer, I saw that the mountain was in the center of the island and was surrounded by a forest that grew on the otherwise low-lying and relatively flat land. I saw no modern cities or monorails or anything that one might expect when entering the domain of a highly advanced species. There was an enclave at the base of the mountain composed of several dozen of the white cottages like the one I lived in, but not much more than that.

Soon, the outline of a large docking area came into view. It was much larger and more complex than the tiny wooden dock on my bay on World 2A. In fact, it resembled a marina on Earth. At least a dozen large yachts had berths, and several cigar-shaped speed boats. There were fishing boats as well, but these were more like sports fishing boats as opposed to the small commercial vessels of World 2A. There were also some large sailboats. Off to one side was a shorter length of dock, one with a few unimposing sailboats nestled up against it, so I went there, pulling down my sail when I knew I had enough momentum to make it to the dock.

As I came up beside the dock and reached for a rope to tie my boat down, I noticed a tall man with long, blond hair coming down the dock toward me. He wore a white robe and looked very much like the Teacher back on World 2A. In fact, as he got closer, I confirmed it was the Teacher himself who had come to greet me.

"Hello, Cynthia," he said. "How was your trip?"

Chapter 30

"Why didn't you just bring me with you?" I asked.

"I have my reasons," he said. "But it was interesting, wasn't it? I think you particularly liked the whale."

"I did," I admitted. "The eel was a little frightening, but helpful. Are there other creatures living out there?"

"Oh yes," he said. "Many different species."

"Perhaps I'll see some of them on my trip back."

"I'm sure you will," he said. "Assuming you go back."

"What do I need to do to ensure that?" I asked.

"You need to convince the Council it's the right thing to do, with regard to you."

We had left the marina and were now walking along a surfaced road, which rose slowly but resolutely up from the waterside. We were surrounded by forest, so I couldn't see anything other than trees and the road ahead.

"Where are we going?" I asked.

"To the top of the mountain," he said.

"Why?"

"That is where the Council meets."

"So are you going to give me any background on what this Council wants from me?"

"Of course," he said. "I think I've mentioned that the Makers are very interested in empathy and narcissism. These two traits are polar opposites, yet each has helped your species to advance more than any other. World 2A, World 2B, and World 3 are a controlled experiment. The Makers are trying to determine if incorporating either or both of these two traits into their own Essence can help us to improve as a species."

"So this whole planet is just an experiment?" I asked, not knowing how I felt about that.

"Yes," he said. "We are experimenting with several things here, but the one in which you are involved is the investigation into empathy and narcissism. And this 'planet,' as you call it, is really a space station, and was built entirely by the Makers. We call it Earth Station, because its purpose is to harvest things from Earth that might help us."

It was hard for me to accept that this whole place was just an experiment. I guess I'd wanted to believe it was more than that. Perhaps a stepping stone to greater enlightenment, especially for people like me who were seeking eternal salvation in the company of our Lord. And as I thought further, trying to stretch my feelings as far as they could go, I realized that maybe this whole place, this Earth Station, could still serve that purpose for me. As always, the positive road was the one I chose to take.

"Wow," I said. "These Makers really are advanced, aren't they?"

"Well, they don't think in terms like that, but I can see how you would draw that conclusion, Cynthia. The Makers place stations like this near planets that interest them, all across the universe. They create bodies that replicate the appearance of the species they are studying, which is why I myself look human, and why the Imprints look human. That way, we can come and go as we please from your planet without being noticed—with a few exceptions, of course, one of whom is the Imprint you know as Maddie. She got noticed."

"Why can't we see this, uh, station, from Earth?"

"This is complicated, Cynthia, so I will give you an analogy. Have you ever seen an ant farm?"

"Yes, of course," I said. "I remember having one as a child."

"Did the ants ever notice you when you were walking around their farm, or looking in at them?"

"I don't think so, no."

"And if you wanted to open the top of the ant farm and put food into it, you could do that, right?"

"Yes."

"Did the ants see you do it? Or did they just see the food after it arrived?"

"I think the latter," I said.

The analogy was a helpful foundation for what came next.

"The Makers exist in space which is outside of your universe," he said. "Even though your universe is tremendously large, it is not infinite. There is a boundary. The Makers live beyond that boundary, but they can cross it any time they choose. But back to the ant farm. In the same way you can look at the ants in their farm, the Makers can look at you, on Earth. And just as the ants cannot see you, so it is that you cannot see the Makers. I will explain more of the science at a later time, but we should talk about the upcoming meeting right now."

"I understand the analogy," I said. "Thank you. And I'm sure the science of it is beyond my understanding anyway, so I'm fine with the answer. Please, tell me about this meeting."

We were out of the forest now, winding our way up a switchback path to the top of the mountain. I felt certain the Teacher could have just snapped his fingers and both of us would have appeared up there at the top, but we needed this time—more specifically, *I* needed this time—to try to figure out what was going on.

"Let me tell you about the composition of the Council," the Teacher said. "There are 150 members. Fifty beings on the Council are pure Maker. They are in bodies that look human, but their Essence was drawn 100 percent from an original Maker. That is why they are known as 'Originals' in Council terminology. There are also fifty beings who have been carefully selected from World 2A. They are also in bodies that look human, but their Essence is a hybrid. Half of it comes from the human Essence and the other half comes from pure Maker Essence. We call these beings 'Empaths.' The final 50 are drawn from World 2B and are also hybrids—50 percent Maker and 50 percent a World 2B human. These Council members are called 'Selfs.'"

"All right," I said, noticing the path was beginning to flatten out. I looked down to the right and saw something amazing. It was a network of great mansions along the flank of the mountain, looking out at the ocean. I knew enough of World 2A and World 2B to know that this must be the dwelling place of the Selfs, while the other side of the mountain, which I had seen as I sailed in, was the village of the Empaths. Why the Selfs needed so much and the Empaths needed so little was a question for another day, however, since what I needed to get a handle on, and quickly, was my own fate. "And this Council is going to decide what to do with me?"

"Yes," said the Teacher.

"Well, don't they already know what they want to do with me? I mean, why do I need to be here at all?"

"There is no consensus on what to do with you," he said.

"What options are being discussed?"

"There is a group that wants to be rid of you, immediately. There is another group that is fine with you going back to World 2A and continuing to evolve. And there is another group that wants what you want."

I didn't have any clue what he was talking about. "And what is it they want that I also want, if I may be so bold?"

"They want to meet God."

Chapter 31

We arrived at the meeting place of the Council of the Makers. It was flat ground at the top of the mountain, paved in some kind of material that resembled concrete in color but had the feel of hard rubber under the feet. The shape was circular, and there was a large ring of chairs near the edge. Many of the chairs were occupied, and every single person looked like the Teacher, with one exception: some of them were female. But I'd seen enough to confirm something I had wondered about from time to time.

"You're one of the Makers, aren't you?" I asked the Teacher.

"Yes," he said. "I hold one of the fifty Originals seats on the Council."

"Why didn't you tell me?"

"It would have changed nothing," he said. "But now you know, so we can move on."

The Teacher was right. It made no difference to me that he was one of the Makers. I had always viewed him as a very powerful being, and I still viewed him that way. I suppose the only thing I had gained was that I now knew something of his background, since he had revealed bits and pieces about the Makers since my arrival on World 2A. But I did foresee one problem.

"How will I know it's you anymore, since there are so many of you?"

"That is an excellent question," he said. "Believe it or not, each of us is an individual, although we share a hive mind."

"That's like a collective consciousness, isn't it?"

"Yes. Each of our thoughts, our knowledge, is known by all the members of our race. Not just the ones here, but everywhere. I should also remind you that the bodies we occupy here on this station are not our original bodies. This station is dedicated to the cultivation of human Essence, so we take on the appearance of humans while we are here."

"What do you look like in your original form?" I asked.

"Another excellent question, but one I'm afraid I have no good answer for, Cynthia, because the Makers have no physical form when were are not working at one of the stations. We are pure Essence, invisible to all beings except ourselves. At any rate, in regard to your last question, you will know who I am by your connection to my mind. There will always be a familiarity between us because we have shared specific thoughts and experiences together."

"If you say so, Teacher. I suppose I'll soon find out."

"Indeed you will," he said.

I looked around once more at the circle of Makers and noticed one of the females stand and approach us. She was tall, and dressed in the same kind of white robe they all wore, tied at the waist and flowing down, nearly touching her sandaled feet. Her features were similar to those of the males, sharp and distinct. She had high cheek bones and pale blue eyes, also like the males, but her skin was smoother, more delicate. A small waist and the swell of her breasts completed her femininity. She came and stood in front of us, a beaming smile on her face, as if she knew me and was glad to see me.

"May I introduce you to the newest member of the Council?" said the Teacher. "This is Aya."

My heart skipped a beat. Why would one of the Makers take the same name as my best friend? And why was this woman smiling so intensely at me? But the woman approached me and hugged me tightly, and my questions were answered.

"Why?" was the only word I could muster, because a feeling of great loss was cascading through me.

"My time finally arrived," she said, but it was not her voice. It was a new voice, no accent, not the Aya I knew. The Teacher stepped in to help me with my confusion.

"Aya faced a challenge similar to the one you face," he said. "She had all the empathic purity she needed to become a Maker, save for one flaw. Envy. Of course, you must realize that the envy coursing through her Essence was but a fraction of what most humans feel, but still it was too much to qualify her to pass through to us. So we gave her one final chance to meet the challenge. You."

"How was I involved?" I asked. "I had no idea about any of this."

"That is true, but it is also true that you sensed a tiny pulse of envy coming from Aya when I heaped privilege upon privilege on you, privileges which she did not enjoy. But in the end, Aya was able to turn her envy into love. Love for you, Cynthia. Do you deny this?"

"No, of course not!" I exclaimed. "I love her too, and it hurts me deeply that you've taken her from me! She's the best friend I've ever had. In either of my lives."

I was crying now, the feeling of loss surging out of me in waves of tears. Then Aya took my hand, just as she had from the beginning of my time on World 2A and throughout our friendship. I began to settle down as she spoke to me.

"The Teacher did not take me from you, Cynthia," she said. "It was my choice. It was what I wanted. And it is what I want for you. To join us."

The Teacher interrupted before she could say another word.

"Don't mistake Aya's yearning to have you by her side once again as an invitation, Cynthia," he said. "The possibility of you becoming a Maker exists, certainly, but the road you must travel to get here would be a long one, should you even get that opportunity. You have much anger and pride to overcome for that possibility to become reality."

I was so confused at that moment, I didn't know what to say. I was being brought before this Council for them to render a judgment on my fate, but how was I to plead my case when doubt and indecision ruled my mind? As I recalled from my conversation with the Teacher on the way up the mountain, three possibilities were being considered for me by the Council: immediate expulsion, which I assumed meant death; a return to World 2A to continue my advancement toward purity so I could become a Maker; or somehow introducing the Makers to God. But none of these options included what I wanted to happen most before I departed for heaven. I wanted to know my Maddie was safe and would remain so.

And with that thought, my confusion passed, and I knew what I had to do.

Chapter 32

We took our seats and waited for the meeting to begin. The Teacher was to my right, Aya to my left. Some of the seats were still empty, but every now and then a Maker would simply appear in a chair, from nowhere it seemed.

"Where are they coming from?" I asked.

"They come from missions across the Megaverse," said the Teacher. "Let me explain further. Those of us who are Originals work on a variety of projects. I myself am tied to this station and the Earth, so I do not leave. But the other forty-nine have assignments elsewhere, along with the rest of our race. They come here only for meetings of great importance."

"What about the Selfs and Empaths?" I asked. "Do they travel?"

Aya provided the answer. "We are not pure Makers. We are a hybrid of an original Maker and the Essence of our human self. We are an experiment, Cynthia, and until we prove our value, we are not permitted to do the work of the Makers, other than the work on this station. So we do not travel. On the other hand, we see and know all that is taking place throughout the Megaverse because we are part of the hive mind. And I must tell you, I have seen and learned so much that is beyond the comprehension of a human mind. If I may be so bold, it is as if I were a god."

I looked at the Teacher when Aya said that. The part about being a god—I was trying to see if he acknowledged that statement or not. Because from what I'd learned over the past hours, or days, or however long I'd been here on World 3, the Makers were very much like God in that they seemed to see and know everything. I had to ask myself the question, were they God? Was the God of the Bible, my God, just an illusion? Or no, perhaps the correct word was allusion? Did the Bible simply allude to God, metaphorically, so that I could actually be sitting with the real God at that very moment?

But no, that was not the case. For these beings, other than the hybrid Empaths, lacked one thing that was the essence of God. Love. They were trying, in their highly advanced yet methodical manner, to elevate themselves to the level of God. And that must be why some of them wanted me to help them.

The Teacher sent a thought into my mind at that moment that brought my contemplations to an end.

The meeting will begin now. All of us will use our spoken voices so as not to inundate you with too much information at one time. I will lead the meeting because I am your mentor on this station. Be silent, and speak only when asked a question.

The Teacher stood and addressed the gathering.

"Thank you all for coming," he said. "This meeting has been called to make a decision on the direction of one our most promising human Essences. She sits beside me and is called by the name Cynthia, as you all know. I speak in the slow voice so that she can understand, as will all of us during this meeting. Cynthia has been told we will decide on one of three paths for her today. She will either continue the journey which began with her death on Earth, she will return to World 2A for further purification, or she will introduce us to the one she calls God. Who will speak first?"

A male on the far side of the circle stood up and looked at me.

"Hello, Cynthia," he said. "I am known as Gabriele. I am a Self, meaning I spent time on World 2B before coming here. While on Earth, I was the leader of a country whose name will not be said, because it is irrelevant. What you should know is that I am the one who has raised the motion for you to introduce us to your God. My question is, can you do that?"

I didn't know if I should stand, as Gabriele had, or remain in my seat, but I supposed if I was going to introduce these beings to God, I should at least be standing. So I did. I had wanted to ask the Teacher one more question before the start of the meeting, but that time had passed, so I asked it here.

"Before I answer, please tell me, Gabriele, why am I the one you're asking to do this? What is so special about me? There must have been many true believers who came before me who could have provided this service for you."

"Less than you might think," he said. "But yes, others like you have come before us, and tried to show us God. All have failed."

So I wasn't the first. They must really have wanted to find God if they had tried before, and were still trying. And before I say anything else about what transpired at the meeting, I'll just mention that I didn't figure out the motivation behind the Makers' desire to find God until after the meeting ended. It certainly didn't make complete sense to me, at that point, why they even cared about finding God. Later, the Teacher would tell me something that made it all fit into place. I should also let you know that I was never one to "spread the Word," as they say. My faith was personal, and I'd never tried to convert anyone, not even Maddie.

But now I found myself in this meeting, surrounded by all these powerful beings who supposedly wanted me to help them find God, and it was a bit intimidating, especially since it appeared that my life might depend on it. I assumed the others before me, having failed to introduce the Makers to God, had long since moved on to the Kingdom of Heaven, as I soon would, so it seemed, because I had no answers that would be different from those of any other true Christian. The problem for me was that I had unfinished business on Earth, but I dared not even think of that now. The Teacher must have known where my mind was going, because he spoke to help me get back on track.

"To help Cynthia understand why humans like her have been brought before the Council before, let me explain further," he said. "We are creatures who seek all knowledge, Cynthia. Others like yourself, including those from other faiths, Muslim and Hindu, for example, whose faith is so firm that it is no longer faith at all, but knowledge itself, have earned our attention. Why? Because we want to know what you know. It is as simple as that."

That made sense. And the time it took for the Teacher to speak those words allowed me to clear my mind and proceed. I had been asked to show them God, so I would tell them how.

"Thank you, Teacher, for that enlightenment. And the answer to Gabriele's question is yes, I can do that," I said. "All we will need is 150 copies of the King James Version of the New Testament."

I looked straight at Gabriele and awaited his response. He was smiling.

"All of us here can recite the Bible—both the Old and New Testaments—word for word," he said. "So that approach is a waste of time."

"And yet you have not met God?" I asked.

"I admit that I have not," he said. "Can you help me?" He was still smiling. What was unclear was his level of sincerity. After all, he was a Self, and the human part of him could be very deceptive.

"The only help I can offer is that you continue to pray for God to come to you, Gabriele. And if you open your heart to Him, he will hear you."

"Actually, that's not what I had in mind," he said. "I am proposing a blending of your Essence with the Essence of an Original, and then a trip to the Kingdom of Heaven."

I found it interesting that Gabriele wasn't volunteering himself for this journey to heaven. Very likely he was quite content with his current status. I also wondered how his charade wasn't obvious to the entire group of these all-knowing beings. But then I considered where each of them came from. The Original Makers were beings with no emotions, no beliefs other than the value of the attainment of knowledge. As the Teacher had explained, they viewed my belief in God as just one more journey in the attainment of knowledge, one they had not yet been able to take. The Empath group was undoubtedly composed of atheists, like Aya, and agnostics. The atheists would argue this proposition was absurd, a waste of time, and life. The agnostics, on the other hand, might be intrigued, because never in their lives had the possibility of actually getting an answer to the question of God's existence been plausible, until now. And the Selfs were probably a mixed bag. If they were part of the non-religious population of World 2B, they would side with the atheists. If they had religion in their lives while on Earth, it was for self-serving reasons, not because they were true believers. By definition, it was impossible for a true believer to end up on World 2B. What I didn't know was whether or not the purification process on World 2B involved a renunciation of God, or not. But it hardly mattered—I felt I had a basis for putting Gabriele's proposition to rest, once and for all.

"That is fine," I said. "But if I am blended with an Essence that is not already a true believer in God, the resulting hybrid will be incapable of reaching the Kingdom of Heaven, because this hybrid will no longer have pure faith in God."

The smile left Gabriele's face.

"Motion withdrawn," he said, and sat down.

I sat down as well, and the Teacher, who had remained standing throughout the proceeding, took over.

"We are left, then, with two options," said the Teacher. "Return Cynthia to World 2A to resume her purification, or allow her to continue on. Are there any comments or questions regarding either of these?"

To my chagrin, the Self known as Gabriele stood up again.

"I say to the Council, here is a human who believes firmly in a God which none of us have met, to the core of her being. She will gladly continue on because she is 100 percent certain she will end up in the Kingdom of Heaven. I admit, to my shame, that I never attained this certainty. It was this admission that gained me entrance to this esteemed Council. I should also point out there is not a single member of this Council who believes in this God of Cynthia's in the way she believes. Many of us sincerely want to know this God, but after many attempts, continue to be disappointed. The conclusion we must reach is that people such as Cynthia are self-deceived. It is not *knowledge* of God they possess, it is only fantasy. The question in my mind is how can someone like this ever be a productive addition to the Council, when her sense of self is entirely wrapped up in this God that none of us will ever see?"

I nearly jumped out of my seat to answer his question.

"Excuse me, Gabriele," I said. "Was the question for me, or for the Council?"

"It was for anyone who wants to address it, including you," he said.

"Very well then, I will address it, if I may." I looked at the Teacher for permission to speak, and he nodded.

"First, I agree with much of what Gabriele has said. I don't know how someone like me could add value to a Council of nonbelievers, like you. And yes, for me, my final destination *will* be the Kingdom of Heaven, most definitely. But I ask you this—what if I could work with one of you, one of the Originals, and teach them how to see and feel God? And what if I succeeded? Would I have value then?"

"Absolutely," said Gabriele. "But none of the Originals will submit to such rudimentary teachings as reading from the Bible."

"I can understand that, Gabriele, since you've already made clear that the Makers know what the Bible *says*," I said. "What I can teach you, sir, is what it *means*. And there is one pure Maker I see regularly. Please allow me to return to World 2A, and I will work with the Teacher to help him know God."

"Teacher," said Gabriele. "What say you? If the Council voted to have Cynthia return to World 2A for further purification, would you submit to being taught by her about her God?"

The Teacher didn't hesitate.

"Of course," he said. "To learn all there is to be learned is the purpose of the Makers, Gabriele. Please, never forget that. We do not judge others based on a comparison of them against ourselves. We learn where we can learn, and if I can learn more from Cynthia than I already know, I am more than willing to try. Can we put this to a vote? The resolution is that Cynthia be returned to World 2A for further purification, with the additional responsibility of teaching myself how to know God."

Aya leaned over and whispered in my ear. "A consensus within the Council is attained when 80 percent of the members vote in favor of a resolution. The vote is happening now."

I sat down and waited. All of the Makers were still in their seats. A memory from my time on Earth came back to me just then—the day of the bad man, when Maddie was only four years old. I had wondered during that incident if *that* would be the time when I would go to heaven. As I waited for the results of the vote to be revealed to me, the same thought came to me. Had the day for my ascension finally arrived? The truth be told, I hoped now was not the time, because I desperately wanted to help my daughter. And to do that, I needed to return to World 2A. I also needed the help of the Teacher, who just then announced the results of the vote.

"The Council has voted, 141 to 9, to allow Cynthia to return to World 2A, to continue her purification and to help me know her God as she knows him."

Chapter 33

The Teacher rode with me in the boat back to World 2A. He let me sail, and I hoped it was because he was telling me, without telling me, that I was the teacher now. So as World 3 faded into the distance behind us, I started by gathering background information that might help me in the intimidating task I'd been assigned.

"Teacher, were the Makers culling souls from Earth during the time of Jesus?" I asked.

"Culling Essences? Yes, we were. We discovered Earth around ten thousand of your years ago, and began our work there around the time of the building of the Great Pyramids, nearly five thousand years ago."

"So was Jesus one of the people you marked for World 2A?"

"Yes, he was. We knew all about Jesus and his time on Earth, and we found him very interesting. He had one of the highest empathic ratings ever, and we were anxious to work with him when his time on Earth was over."

As I listened to the Teacher speaking about Jesus, I marveled that I was standing here, speaking with someone who'd actually been alive during the time of Christ. And while the Teacher remained as intellectually detached as ever, excitement boiled inside me to hear more.

"So what happened?" I asked. "Did he come to World 2A?"

"Actually, no," said the Teacher. "We initiated the capture protocol just before he died, but it failed. It was the only failure we have ever experienced during all the millennia of human Essence captures, and it is the reason we continue to search for a way to go wherever it is Jesus may have gone, which all who follow him, including you, say is the Kingdom of Heaven."

This was an amazing revelation to me, and it was the key to me fully understanding the "why" of all this searching for God by these godlike beings, because, obviously, the power of God had prevailed over the power of the Makers to ensure that Jesus's soul went where it was supposed to go. I was somewhat disappointed that He had not done the same with me, but also aware that God's plan for me would be unique, and that I should accept it, and follow it, until my time to go to Him arrived. I now realized that my mission to convert the Teacher was very likely part of God's design, and this inspired me to try harder to achieve the seemingly unachievable.

"Teacher," I said. "Can you feel love?"

The Teacher sat back and pondered this question, something he rarely did. He always seemed to know the answers to my questions before I even asked them, but he took more time than normal before responding to this one.

"I've told you before that the one you call Maddie, known to us as Imprint 17035, was similar to me, but lacked some of my abilities. In fact, Maddie's form became a favorite of ours when we discovered it in the northern reaches of Europe around a thousand years ago, and we've adopted it for use as our own human form. The only thing Maddie lacks, compared to us, is some of the more advanced capabilities of our race, such as pure mind-reading and teleportation—and of course, she was given no knowledge whatsoever during her programming. So everything she has learned during her time on Earth has been from her memory reading, her studies, and from you. Most of her emotions came from you. She literally learned how to feel from you, Cynthia. And she learned how to love from you."

"Why do you speak of Maddie, Teacher, when it's *your* ability to feel love I have asked about?"

"I use Maddie because she's a reference point you can relate to. I've told you she is like me, and I've told you she learned emotions from you. But the difference between Maddie and me is a vast amount of knowledge about nearly everything in the Megaverse. In order to hold and retain such a vast amount of information, which includes knowledge of the emotions of every species we've ever encountered, the Makers must be able to stand back from it, to observe it, but not live it. This 'firewall' is an inherent part of who we are, but it was not included in Maddie's programming, so she was able to learn emotions from you. She feels them as a human feels them. I myself, being a pure Original, cannot do that, although I must admit that after thousands of your years working on Earth Station, with humans such as yourself, I feel I have a very good understanding of all human emotions. I suppose I can even feel some of them, a little, but not as strongly and purely as you do."

We were far out to sea now, and I had no idea where I was going. My expectation was that my friend, the whale, would appear soon to show us the way, but instead, a school of dolphins popped up above the surface of the water. I counted six of them, but there could have been more, or less. They were in front of us, leading us forward, and as I watched them launch themselves completely out of the water, only to plunge back in and disappear a second or so later, I wished I could see them more clearly and be closer to them. Suddenly, I saw only five of them jumping, and moments later one of them popped up right beside the boat, emitted a high-pitched note as if to say hello, then settled down right up against the hull. I reached down and touched it, petting its undulating body and feeling the spark of another living thing come into me. I felt exhilarated, but the disappointment of learning that the Teacher could not feel pure love was still with me.

"That's a pity," I said. "For if you cannot feel love, fully, you can never know God."

"I assumed as much," he said.

"So why did you agree to try?"

He looked at me. "Because I made promises to you that I would like to honor."

"You mean telling me what's being done to find Maddie, and letting me share my ideas about how we might save her, and maybe going with me to Earth to try and find her?"

"Yes, partly," he said.

"Why just partly?"

"Because I never promised to take you to Earth."

"Fine, I'll just go by myself then," I said, trying to push him to agree to take me.

"Are you thinking of going to the Transfer Station in the Imprint House again?" he asked.

"Yes, if I have to."

He shook his head. "What you will find there is an empty room."

"What? I thought you said I could go to Earth if I went in there, but I probably didn't want to until we found out where Maddie is, and then you would go with me, maybe."

"I said you *might* be able to go to Earth on your own," he responded.

"But now you're telling me you deceived me?" I asked, a spike of anger rising within me.

"'Might' doesn't mean definitely," he said. "You must learn to listen more carefully."

"So I can't go unless you take me?" I asked.

"Yes, but that's not likely to happen, I'm afraid."

"But why, Teacher? You've basically said you want to honor your promise to help me. Why can't you help me fulfill my greatest desire?"

"Please don't forget that you were given permission to return to World 2A to continue your purification, and to help me find God."

"But it seems so unlikely I will succeed in helping you see God. Why would the Council agree to something that's all but impossible?"

"There are no secrets between me and the Council. We all knew there would be no finding your God for me."

"So why did they vote to let me come?" I asked.

"Because *I* wanted it," he said.

"But why?" I asked again. "Was it sympathy for me that led you to lobby for my return?"

The Teacher pressed his lips together, the only sign of emotion I'd ever seen in him.

"Perhaps," he said. "But it is what I wanted. I am the Master of Earth Station, and the Station Masters' requests are always given special consideration on all our projects throughout the Megaverse."

"Well, there must have been some kind of emotion behind your request, Teacher, because the logic itself is questionable. Your actions demonstrated that you have integrity, and to have that, there has to be some emotion behind it. So I suppose there's still hope, because it shows you have some level of feeling inside you. Perhaps not enough to feel pure love, but maybe in time you actually can, if you allow yourself to."

"I'm not sure what I feel right now, or what I might learn to feel in the future," he said, the first sign of confusion I'd ever witnessed in him. "But I know that by helping you, I might also be able to help my species. If we succeed."

"As you say," I said, "we've had our first 'session' during this sail, so when we get back to World 2A, you'll bring me up to date on what's being done to find Maddie, right?"

"Yes," he said. "I can do that."

Part 3

Maddie

Chapter 34

2006

"He did it," I said. "And I know where the bodies are buried. He wasn't careful, so his DNA will be on them. And in them, unfortunately."

My partner and I were sitting in the interview room at the jail in Anchorage, Alaska, where Randy Morris was being held. He'd been arrested for murder and was a suspected serial killer, but the evidence was sparse. Until now. We'd met with him and his attorney, and it was a simple matter of me removing my glasses, placing them on the conference table, and looking at him while Terry asked innocuous questions. It didn't matter what he asked. We just needed Randy Morris to be there, and for me to look at him.

My partner, Terry Ross, was a twenty-nine-year-old FBI agent. He'd been an agent for six years and was good at his job. He had that FBI persona: all business, no emotion, dress like a clone of his brethren, drive a blue Ford Taurus, the whole enchilada. He was medium height, maybe five foot ten, had brown hair, and was in reasonably good shape. He didn't have a potbelly or any extra body fat. And he'd been getting a lot of attention from his superiors since I'd been loaned to the FBI by the DOD, not long after the old woman and the boy died. We were solving cases at an unprecedented rate, and while it was common knowledge in the higher circles of the FBI that it was because of me, Terry still shared in the fruits of our success. He got me where we needed to be and protected me when necessary. Not all cases were as open and shut, and as risk-free, as this one.

"How many bodies are there?" he asked.

"Nine," I said.

"That's three more than he's suspected of," he said. "Nothing new there."

It was almost always the case, when I "viewed" a guilty subject, that I uncovered more crimes than they were suspected of. One time we'd gone undercover, posing as poker aficionados at the high-stakes table at a Las Vegas casino. I was all dressed up in expensive clothes, wearing makeup and with my hair done up in sexy bun, and I wasn't wearing the collar they used to keep me from running away, because I had on this low-cut dress that showed off my, well, you know, which I'd been told was a good way to distract men at the poker table. I must say, I was definitely getting some stares. I was no longer the ugly duckling I'd been as a twelve-year-old. Once my period came, I started to fill out and get some shape, and now I was a twenty-year-old, six-foot-tall blond with a thin waist and, well, you get the picture. Not that it made any difference in my life, and why should it? I still lived in my glass house back on the secret military base when I wasn't working, and Terry had been instructed to shoot me if I tried to escape while I wasn't wearing my collar. I don't know if he would have done it, because he'd developed a soft spot for me during our two years working together. A crush, if you must know.

Anyway, back to the Vegas story. We'd been assigned to one of the guys who was playing at the table. He was a suspected arms dealer, and while most of his activity was outside of the US, there was some flimsy evidence that he'd begun bringing illegal arms into the US and selling them to white nationalist groups. The jerk was wearing a tuxedo, like he was someone important, and he'd been winning a lot of money—until I sat down.

It looked like he had around a million dollars of chips stacked up in front of him, and he was gloating and posturing over it like he was the king of the world. But no one in this world could beat me at poker when I had my glasses off, which was the case here. I knew every card that every player was holding, so it was like taking candy from a baby. All I had to do was look at them and access their short-term memories, and their cards were in my head.

Terry had agreed to let me win all the guy's money before we arrested him, and I took my time doing it. I also gathered both his short- and long-term memories, and the criminal activity he'd been involved in was immense and broad sweeping. He sold arms to nearly every rogue regime around the world, and was definitely expanding into the US, but it turned out he also had a thing for torture and murder. He had just murdered a prostitute earlier in the evening. He'd paid a large sum of money to her pimp before she came to his room, telling him he wanted to keep her, so the pimp was out of the picture from that point forward. The body had not yet been disposed of. It was still in his suite, stuffed in a closet by his bodyguards while they went out to buy the chemicals to make it go away.

Terry wasn't playing, but he was watching, pretending he was my boyfriend, which he wasn't. He should be so lucky. I waved him over and whispered into his ear, giving him the scoop on what was in the guy's suite. He told me to hurry up and finish winning the guy's money, because he was going to be arrested right here at the table within an hour or so. Then he went to call for backup and to make arrangements with the hotel staff to let him and the backup team into the guy's suite.

Anyway, I started winning faster, suckering the arms dealer into betting big when he felt he had the sure thing. I had purposely lost a few hands, pretending to bluff with a tell. I'd picked up from the others at the table that they were trying to determine what my tell was, so I gave it to them. I would look down at my cards when I was bluffing, not raising my eyes up until the other people had made their bets. The rest of the time, my head was up, looking people directly in the eye, which was how, of course, I learned the cards they were holding, among other things.

The arms dealer was holding four kings and had just placed a $75,000 bet on the table. I had a straight flush, so I knew I would beat him, but I wanted to wipe him out. So I matched his bet, then went all in and looked down at my cards. I was sure he was looking at me, and I was certain he knew my tell was to look down at my cards when I was bluffing. So he went all in, and I won it all.

But that wasn't the worst news of the evening for the arms dealer. Terry arrived at that moment with two other agents, and they arrested the guy right there. Terry stayed with me while the others took the guy into custody, and I gave him all my chips, which amounted to over $2 million. He said he'd turn it in at the agency the next day, and I had no doubt that was what he'd do. Terry was a very dependable and loyal agent. They ended up getting a confession from the arms dealer regarding all of his activities and contacts in the illegal arms business, in exchange for waiving the death penalty, which was still alive and well in the state of Nevada. But he was put away for life, where he belonged.

Randy Morris, the serial killer, would be going away for life as well. There was no death penalty in Alaska, where all the murders had been committed. Our work was done here, so we flew back to Nevada, and Terry drove me to the base where I lived. We said our goodbyes, and I was escorted by the polo shirts to my glass house. I changed out of my work clothes and put on my orange jumpsuit, then lay down and tried to sleep. But sleep evaded me.

For some reason, I was thinking about myself. I don't mean in a vain way, like how I looked or how much smarter I was than the people I worked with, or how I deserved a better fate than the one I was living. I was thinking about *who* I was. What I was becoming.

You see, I'm a sponge, not just of information, but of everything, especially emotions. When I was growing up with my mom, I learned how to be honest, and kind, and how to love. But now I'd been away from her for eight years, and my life had been spent mostly with professional people like Dr. Lemare and the polo shirts, whose job was to keep me confined and learn all they could about me, with as little emotion as possible. And for two years, I'd been working with the FBI, people like Terry Ross and other crime professionals at the Las Vegas field office, and they were as dispassionate about what they did as Dr. Lemare. They were all motivated by a desire to do good, don't get me wrong, but because they saw so much bad, they built a veneer of detachment around what they did. Otherwise, they wouldn't be able to continue doing it.

And you know what a sponge does when placed in water, right? It sucks it up. Can't help itself. That's how it was with me. I was becoming more jaded about life, not only because I was a prisoner, but because of the people I was surrounded by. And thinking about this, knowing what I was becoming and definitely not happy about, I brooded and got angry, then sad, then frustrated. I couldn't sleep, and I was so alone. I longed to have my mama come to me and sing me a song that settled me down while she rubbed my back, quieting my restless mind and pouting heart and helping me fall asleep, knowing I was loved.

Chapter 35

The old woman, whose name on Earth had been Abagail, and the boy, who was named Tommy, had died two years ago, in the summer of 2004. At that point, I'd been in custody for six years and was eighteen years old. By the way, I forgot to tell you what else happened when I went through puberty, other than me blooming into a beautiful young woman. Anyway, I got my period, and along with the blood and pain came this release of information about where I'd come from and what my mission was. I already knew all of it, from years of living with Abagail, but it was interesting that my period was the time the Makers had chosen to let *me* know what was going on. It would have been a lot better to do it sooner.

But back to Abagail and Tommy. I'd gotten to know both of them very well during the four years we lived together in the glass houses. I hadn't been allowed to communicate with them when I first arrived, as you know, but it didn't take long for me to convince Dr. Lemare that it was in everyone's best interests to let the three of us interact. The first thing I suggested was that they put some kind of device on us that would stop us if we tried to escape or to hurt anyone. They came up with a collar that could send an electric shock into us that was powerful enough to kill us, or they could just send enough of a surge to knock us out. At least, that's what they told us. I didn't really know, because they'd never had to use it on us.

Anyway, after we all got the shock collars, Dr. Lemare felt more comfortable letting the three of us communicate. I had agreed to tell the doctor what was being said, in private meetings between her and myself, when the three of us were communicating telepathically. They set up a little table in between our glass houses where we would meet. Once I got the "conversations" going with the other two, one of the first things I told them was that I would be reporting on our talks to Dr. Lemare, so if there was anything they didn't want to disclose, they didn't have to.

I mostly found out stuff that Dr. Lemare probably already knew anyway, but hadn't mentioned to me. For example, Abagail had spent most her time on Earth in Bakersfield, California, an agricultural and oil town in the southern part of the Central Valley. She'd worked as a nurse in one of the local hospitals until she'd retired at the age of sixty-five. It was after her retirement that she'd begun to experience lapses in her ability to control her emotions. She had no idea why it was happening, but it was definitely getting out of control by the time she was identified and captured.

The boy, Tommy, had been adopted by a family in Grand Rapids that had done it only for the adoption assistance benefits it yielded. They were poor, not only financially, but as role models. He'd grown up fending for himself, always in trouble, with no guidance whatsoever on how to deal with his "abilities." He didn't seem to be the tattletale that I'd been as a young girl, but after being sent to reform school and evaluated by a psychiatrist, his abilities had been discovered, and he'd ended up as a prisoner at the military facility in Nevada.

Anyway, after about six months of the three of us communicating telepathically, Dr. Lemare granted my request to allow us to begin eating together at the table. We had lunch to start, and then we added breakfast and dinner. It was like we were a little family, although the other two were still somewhat suspicious of me, since I was the one who'd been granted so many privileges, and since they knew I would be reporting our conversations to Dr. Lemare. But I talked to her about letting those two have some things in their houses that would give them pleasure and help them pass the time, like the books did for me.

Abagail requested live plants, lots of them, and it amazed me that someone who was reputedly so violent could show so much love and caring for another living thing. Tommy requested video games, which he played endlessly. I was worried that Dr. Lemare and her team would deny that request because of the electronics, but she explained that since there was no Wi-Fi in the building that housed us, and since the building itself was shielded to prevent electronic eavesdropping, even if Tommy figured out a way to turn the video games into an electronic signaling device, the signals would never escape. But Tommy had no ambition to create such a device. He just wanted to play the games.

I myself was content to read my books to pass the time. I'd been a big reader even before my capture. It gave me something to do in a world where friends were few and far between, but the speed of my reading had been a problem for my mom, because it was expensive to buy so many books. I could read a book almost as fast as I could turn the pages, so there was no such thing for me as staying up all night to finish one. I could read three average-length novels in one evening, and did so when the books were there, for lack of anything better to do. I truly did enjoy it. The love of gaining more knowledge was deeply seeded in me, and sometimes I wondered if it was part of my programming.

Anyway, even though I was in captivity, the problem of keeping me in a supply of books was now Dr. Lemare's problem, since she'd agreed to it and truly wanted me to have something to do, but it was difficult for her. The Kindle eBook reader wasn't introduced until 2007, but I'm not sure I would have been allowed to have one anyway as it relied on Wi-Fi to work. So I had to read paperbacks. I'd give Dr. Lemare a list of twenty-five books and she'd order them from somewhere, but that would keep me busy for only a few weeks. Money wasn't the issue, it was the inconvenience of it. Still, I usually had a book to read, and if the supply was running low, I'd force myself to read slower.

I'd taken to reading science fiction, since I knew my mom was out there somewhere, either in some alternate universe or so far away in the galaxy that only a wormhole could take you there. The sci-fi books helped me to dream of what might be possible, and I suppose they gave me some vague hope that I might one day see her again.

But back to Abagail and Tommy. We became good friends over the years, and I think my values, which I'd learned from my mom, kind of rubbed off on them. They became polite, and they started to think of others before thinking just of themselves, and I took pride in that. I felt lucky to have been taught about life by a caring person rather than some uneducated, insensitive parents like Tommy had. I always knew she was a good person, and I guess I assumed that was because of her religion, you know, how they always taught you to "do unto others" and stuff like that, but now I realized it was more than that.

It was ironic that it took losing my mom to get to know who she truly was, and it made me sad to think of her out there, somewhere, in a place that wasn't where her religion told her she would go. I wondered sometimes if she was strong enough to cope with that, and if she was still surviving, wherever she was, in spite of it not being where she wanted to be. I made myself believe that she was, and you know what? I think believing she could do it helped me to carry on in the place I found myself living, against my will. But it wasn't long after I had these thoughts that a new idea entered my mind, one that would alter the course of my life.

Chapter 36

Now I need to tell you about how Abagail and Tommy died. It was the summer of the year 2004 when I convinced Dr. Lemare we should be allowed outside for walks in the fresh air. And believe me, it was no easy task. I remember our first meeting on the subject, there in the divided conference room, which we still used even though I could have just worn the glasses. I think there was still some trepidation on the part of my captors—not so much Dr. Lemare, but the people above her—that I might end up getting information from her that I wasn't supposed to have, or maybe harming her, but it didn't matter. I was fine with meeting like that, as long as I got what I wanted. In this case, that wasn't as easy as I had hoped because there were some things I didn't know.

"Dr. Lemare," I said. "I've been wondering if the three of us Imprints could start going outside from time to time."

The doctor's mouth closed, and her lips turned down in a frown. She didn't say anything, so I assumed she was thinking.

"Did I say something I shouldn't have?" I asked. "I mean, I've been stuck inside for six years, and it's even longer for Abagail and Tommy. All of us are now completely cooperative, telling you absolutely everything we know. How could we do any harm by going outside? Are you afraid we have some way of communicating with the beings on World 2A if we get outside of this protected facility?"

Dr. Lemare took a deep breath and let the air out in a rush. It was as if she'd made up her mind to tell me something she might get in trouble for. I leaned forward, doing what I could with my body language to encourage her to proceed.

Then she told me why we were being kept inside.

"Maddie, our experience in tracking and capturing your kind is extensive. Before Abagail, Tommy, and yourself, we identified many Imprints, and brought all of them into custody. And in each case, the same thing happened. Sometimes it happened in a few hours, other times it happened in a day or two, but it was always the same."

"What?"

"They died," she said. "Complete brain failure."

"Why?"

"We assumed it was a failsafe to keep them from telling us anything. It was suggested that a signal of some kind might be causing it. Eventually, after many deaths, we began experimenting with ways to block the signal that might be killing them, and we finally figured it out. We built vehicles lined with lead and other materials, and we built this facility, and in so doing we were able to block the signal, as proven by Abagail, who was our first captured Imprint who didn't die. We learned a lot from her. Then we brought Tommy in, then you."

"So you're saying the reason we're kept in here is to keep us from being killed by some signal from World 2A?"

"That about sums it up," she said, a look of regret on her face. "I'm sorry, Maddie."

I sat back and thought about this new revelation. Before this, I'd been thinking these beings from World 2A might be benevolent. I mean, they were giving people life after death, which was a pretty big deal in my mind. I was hoping they wanted to eventually help all humans live forever, and we, the Imprints, were the boots on the ground to help them achieve that. But I never thought of these beings as killers. That's what they were, though, and they were killing their own. It was as if the Imprints were just tools that were completely expendable, of no value to them, while the humans were the gold they were mining.

I had to put that aside. What I needed to figure out was if I wanted to spend the rest of my life in a cage, and it didn't take very long to do that.

I remembered my mom telling me, just before we fell, that she'd rather die than be separated from me, and that was what had happened. And so here I was, six years later, alive but separated from the one person who had loved me unconditionally and for whom I felt the same kind of love. The life I was leading wasn't life, and I decided right then and there that I didn't want it to go on this way. I even convinced myself that if I died, I probably would end up back on World 2A anyway, just like my mom had. And if not, at least I wouldn't be a living corpse, with no purpose whatsoever.

What I'm telling you is that I decided I still wanted to go outside. As such, I had to convince Dr. Lemare why it could help her organization too.

"I think you're missing a few things," I said.

"Oh really," she said, raising her eyebrows in feigned surprise. "Such as?"

"For one thing, I've been here six years, Tommy a little longer, and Abagail much longer than that. Don't you think these beings on World 2A understand that you've long since obtained all the information you could possibly get from us?"

"Well, certainly," she said. "Why is that relevant?"

"First, there's no reason for them to kill us anymore. They know we've spilled the beans!"

"Okay," she said, leaning forward, suggesting she might be getting a little more interested in my line of thought. "What else?"

"Doesn't it seem more likely they'd simply want to find us, communicate with us, maybe bring us back?"

"I suppose it's possible," she said. "But how does that help me?"

And that was the point. Dr. Lemare and her group had nothing more to learn from me and the other Imprints. But what if I could help them establish first contact with these alien beings?

"Dr. Lemare," I said, "what is your group doing here? I mean, what is your goal?"

"Our primary mission is to protect our country," she said. "But there are a variety of other goals, especially for those of us who are civilians. I myself am fascinated that I've been able to meet and converse with beings like yourself."

I interrupted her then, redirecting her to where I needed her to go. "Have you ever talked to other kinds of aliens? You've implied in other conversations that you might have."

"That information is confidential," she said.

"Who am I going to tell?" I asked. "But okay, you can't tell me. I'm assuming you haven't talked to them, either because there's no basis for communicating or because they were just plain dead when you found them. They can't live in our atmosphere or something like that. Am I on the right track?"

"Again," she said, "I can't really discuss that." I could tell from her facial and body language that I was basically right, so I decided to go for it.

"I think I'm in a position to offer you the chance to have first contact with the beings who created me," I said.

"How so?" she said, trying to hide her excitement.

"Put me outside," I said. "If I die, you don't lose anything, because you still have the other two, and you've learned all you can from me anyway. But even if I do, they will have figured out where we are. And they might be inclined to pay you a visit. I'm sure you and your team have already concluded these beings don't mean us—mean humans any harm, right? But if you're worried about that, just post soldiers and weapons or whatever when I'm out there. You can also bring out all of your instruments and tracking equipment and try to glean some insight into what kind of signal they're sending, if any, and where it originated."

"I can't believe you would risk this," she said.

"That's because I don't believe I'm going to die, Dr. Lemare. I think I'm going to be able to establish a direct line of communication with these beings. Look, I don't know if they'll ever be willing to come and sit down at a table with you, but perhaps I can ask them questions for you, and maybe get some answers. In the end, what matters is that I'm willing to do it, and I think you should consider it."

I admit that I really didn't believe I'd be able to establish a direct line of communication with the beings from World 2A, but I guess I was hoping that I could, and in so doing maybe get to see my mom again somehow, get them to bring me back there so Mom and I could be together again. Deep down, though, my motivation went back to Mom's words to me before she fell. After six years in captivity, I was definitely willing, wanting actually, to die if I couldn't be with her again.

"I'll speak to my superiors," said Dr. Lemare.

Chapter 37

It was kind of a big deal when they let me go outside for the first time. Abagail and Tommy were kept in their glass houses, but I had explained all of it to them—the reason we were kept inside, my theory that the Makers wouldn't want to kill us anymore. Still, it was quite clear to everyone that my life would be at risk when I stepped through the doors. Dr. Lemare said she'd convinced her superiors that the risk of losing me was offset by the chance of a first contact opportunity. It was also common knowledge that our value to the US government had declined precipitously since they'd gathered all the information they could from us long ago. We were now just prisoners being held, at great expense, so the chance for a return on that investment, no matter how small, must have been appealing to the administrators of our imprisonment, because my trip outside was approved.

Once Abagail and Tommy and I had said our goodbyes, they were put back into their houses, and I was escorted out of the big room, down the hallway to the door that had been selected for my exit to the outside world. The polo shirts were with me, and one of them opened the door. I peered out and saw that a lot of equipment had been set up out there, with the objective of identifying and tracking whatever kind of transmissions came to me when I stepped out. The polos both wished me luck. I stepped outside, alone, and the door closed shut behind me. I was honestly pretty scared.

Dr. Lemare had explained prior to my exit that there was a fenced-in area surrounding the building, but because we were in the desert, it wasn't very pleasant outside most of the time. Most of the area around the building was paved, but there were a few patches of land with local plants growing, like cacti and stuff. She said it would be very hot since it was summer and that I should be prepared for it. When I went out, it was like stepping into a sauna. I started perspiring immediately, but that was good news, because I was still alive. My heart rate slowed a bit, and I took a few more steps. There were no humans operating the equipment, and I assumed they must have stayed inside, not wanting to expose themselves to whatever transmissions might be beaming in from the heavens.

When I looked farther out into the area around our building, though, I saw hundreds of soldiers, all dressed from head to toe in protective gear, lining the outside perimeter of the fence. Most of them held guns of various shapes and sizes, and some of them sat behind larger weapons. There were even a few tanks out there. It all seemed way overdone, in my opinion, and the longer I was outside, the more foolish it seemed.

I felt nothing, other than the extreme heat. There were no messages coming to me inside my brain, no instructions to do this or do that, but I was alive. There was a chair out there for me to sit in, and I did so, hoping something might happen, but nothing did. I just sat there sweating up a storm.

While I waited, I tried to figure out what I was going to say to Dr. Lemare. Should I make up a story about what the Makers wanted my captors to do and what the consequences would be if they didn't comply? No, that wasn't me. After everything was said and done, I decided my best option was to start small. I would lobby for Abagail and Tommy to be let out with me next time, arguing that if there were three of us out there, it tripled our chances for some kind of contact to transpire. It was obvious that I'd been right about the Makers no longer wanting to kill us—I mean, they weren't stupid, right? They understood there was nothing to be gained by doing that, just as I'd predicted.

As it turned out, Dr. Lemare was more than willing to let the three of us out next time. She even promised that if we behaved, she'd put a picnic table out there where we could eat lunch on days when it wasn't so hot, and that sounded great. Small pleasures were a way of life for all of us, and this was a nice one to look forward to. I asked if we could go out in the early morning, before it got too hot, and she agreed to that as well.

On the day that was to be our first journey outside together, all of us were very excited—Abagail and Tommy because it was their first time outside in years, and me because I was proud and happy to be the one who had made this happen for them. Abagail and Tommy were pressed up against my back as we waited for the polo shirts to open the door, pushing me forward like a crowd waiting to get into a concert of some famous rock band. When the door opened, they literally pushed me out. I stumbled forward a few steps, and the shock of the bright sun hitting my eyes caused me to squeeze them shut.

After getting my eyes back open and adjusting to the brightness, I turned around to get the sun out of my eyes, and when I looked back, I saw Abagail and Tommy lying on the ground. The polo shirts were kneeling down, feeling for their pulse. The men looked up and shook their heads, telling me they were dead.

Chapter 38

Did you kill them?" I asked, sitting in the divided conference room, facing Dr. Lemare on the other side of the glass. "With the shock collars?"

"Absolutely not," she said. "They died of complete brain shutdown, not heart failure. It was just like what happened to all the others, before we secluded you. We had nothing to do with it."

Dr. Lemare's hair had become grayer over the years I'd been incarcerated. As time went by, and there was less and less for her to do with us, I wondered why she was still working here. Once, I had asked her why no more of us had been brought in, and she said the trail had gone cold; there were no more leads to track. And now, two of us were dead.

"I'm very sorry about this," she said. "I know you were very close with Abagail and Tommy."

Yes, I was. And it was my fault they'd died. Well, not really. They'd wanted to go outside as much as I had, and I knew for certain they hadn't cared if they lived or died, same as me. The lives we'd been leading were meaningless, to all of us, especially knowing that we weren't from this world anyway.

Now, though, I knew I didn't want to die. Part of me had known that since I walked out that door the first time.

"I wonder why they want me alive but didn't care if the others died?" I asked.

"You tell me," she said. "Did you receive any messages from them while you were out there?"

No, there'd been no messages. But as I was lying awake that night, alone in my single bed in my glass house, I couldn't help thinking that my mom was involved. After all, if the beings who made us were on World 2A, and she was on World 2A, and my friends were dead but I was alive, was that because of my mom in some way? There was no way to confirm it, but in my heart I knew it was true. My mom was still looking out for me, I just knew she was. Her last words to me were "I'll watch over you from heaven," and while she wasn't in heaven, I knew darn well she was watching over me. Perhaps she was closer by than I thought.

While I was lying there that night, restless and agitated, I realized my life was going to be terribly lonely without Abagail and Tommy to share it with. That was when I hatched the idea of asking Dr. Lemare to use me to help *them* do some good in the world.

I told her I'd go crazy living here twenty-four seven with no one to talk to and no sense of purpose in my life. I argued that I had no desire to escape, and while this wasn't exactly true, I had that urge fully under control. I also pointed out the obvious—that with the shock collar, I wouldn't be a flight risk, even if I wanted to run. There was an initial concern that the same thing that happened to Abagail and Tommy would happen to me, but I convinced Dr. Lemare to test that proposition by allowing me outside again. They let me go out, reluctantly, and I was fine. They kept taking me out every day, at different times, for weeks. While this was going on, I pointed out that there was nothing more for them to learn from me here on the inside, but they could expand their knowledge of my capabilities by sending me on missions on the outside, missions that could help put criminals behind bars.

Eventually, Dr. Lemare got my request approved, and I was loaned out to the FBI. The agreement with the Bureau specified that they could have no information on my background and would not question me, in any way, about my abilities. What they would get in return for their compliance with these rules was a guaranteed case solver, and after one trial run, where I proved the guilt of a bank robber, telling them where he'd hidden the money, I was hired.

The FBI was so impressed with my work they wanted me full time, but that was more than DOD would allow. They only let me handle one case per week, and since I solved every case within five minutes of seeing the accused, my main time away from the base was travel time. Every now and then, I got an exciting assignment, like the one in Las Vegas at the casino, but for every ten cases I was assigned, nine were handled in boring conference rooms and courtrooms. I was sometimes able to cajole Terry into taking me to a nice diner, if it wouldn't affect his own schedule or in any way impugn his reputation with the agency. But after two years working with the FBI, even though I was doing a good service for them, and for people in general, I wanted more in my life, but I felt powerless to do anything about it. And then, on the Monday following the week when I had solved the Randy Morris case, something changed.

Chapter 39

On Monday morning, I was escorted outside by the polo shirts to the pickup spot for my next assignment. It was 6 a.m. The blue Ford Taurus pulled up, but Terry Ross wasn't behind the wheel. A man got out who seemed to be a very different kind than Terry. For starters, he was taller than me, whereas Terry had been shorter. He was well built, like some kind of retired athlete, and he had a strong chin, a full mouth, and a solid nose, with a slight curve from top to bottom. His dark hair was combed back with some kind of hair gel, which I didn't like, but his overall appearance was an improvement from Terry's. He even dressed better. He was wearing an expensive, dark gray, tailored suit with nearly invisible pinstripes running up and down it, a fine white shirt, and a red silk tie. He extended his hand to introduce himself while reaching for my bag.

"Hello, Ms. Pace, I'm Gino Morelli. Please, let me take your bag."

His voice was very pleasant. A salesman's voice. The kind you get comfortable with if you aren't too careful. I shook his hand, which had thick, strong fingers, but he didn't squeeze too hard. That would have been a mistake for him to try on me. I felt certain I could crush it if I wanted to, but I *didn't* want to. So far, I liked him. I let him take my bag, then went around to the passenger's side and got in. He put my bag in the trunk and came around to the driver's side, sliding gracefully into the car. He put it in drive and weaved his way out of the base, showing his credentials as he exited.

"What happened to Terry?" I asked.

"He got promoted," said Gino. "On his way to DC as we speak. I'm his replacement."

"Are you from the Las Vegas field office?" I asked.

"I am now," he said. "I worked as an attaché in Europe for my first three years, then was assigned to the NYC field office for the past five years, but my family's from Vegas, so I jumped at the opportunity to come back."

I wondered why he'd used the word "assigned" rather than "posted" or simply "worked out of," but I didn't want to sound too forward by asking. I was wearing my glasses, standard protocol for my work at the FBI, and the agents had been briefed to make me wear them at all times, until my abilities were needed in a case. They knew why I was wearing them, specifically for the protection of their privacy, especially their FBI secrets. No one cared that wearing the glasses also helped me.

"What kind of work did you do in NYC?" I asked.

"Strictly undercover," he said. "Which is what I'll be doing here as well."

"What about me?"

"You too."

Technically, all of my work was undercover, since my purpose was never revealed to the subject. But it sounded like things were about to change, and frankly, I was kind of happy to hear that.

"Any particular kind of undercover work?" I asked.

"Organized crime," he said.

My excitement about a change of pace took a hit when I heard that, but I suppose I shouldn't have been surprised. Gino Morelli had the look of a mobster and the name to go with it. Now I understood why he'd used the word "assigned" when he spoke of the NYC field office. He very likely never even went into the office, to keep his cover intact.

"Well, that's a new one," I said, trying to make light of it. "I think I can guess, but where will our work take us? This week, for example."

"This week we're going to Europe," he said. "If you actually are as fast a learner as I'm told you are."

Europe? Well, that wasn't what I'd expected. I thought we'd be working the casinos and Vegas in general, since it was a known hotbed of activity for organized crime. But hey, I was happy to run with it.

"What will I be learning?" I asked.

"To speak Russian fluently, and know its history and geography thoroughly," he said.

"That won't take very long," I said. "A day at most, if you have the right reading materials for me."

"We'll see," he said. "And by the way, if you want to take off those glasses, it's no problem. It might be easier to get to know me that way."

Another twist I'd never experienced before, but I kept the glasses on for the moment.

"Before I do, may I inquire as to why you think that's a good idea?" I asked.

"If we're going to be partners, especially on undercover assignments like the ones I'm involved in, we need to know each other as well as possible."

"That certainly *would* allow me to get to know you," I said. "But I'm not sure how much I can tell you about me. I'm pretty top secret, or so I'm told."

"I figure you're some kind of captured Russian spy," he said, and he looked serious. "I mean, you look Russian, you know, tall and blonde, with Slavic features. And you've got these 'abilities,' probably some kind of implant in your brain or something that lets you do that stuff. Am I close?"

"You're not supposed to ask questions like that," I said.

"Yeah, and you're not supposed to take off those glasses, either," he retorted.

"So I won't take them off," I shot back. "And for what it's worth, no, I'm not a Russian spy. I've never even been to Russia. I've never left the country as a matter of fact. Don't even have a passport."

I wasn't supposed to tell him any of that, but his offer to let me take off the glasses had affected me, I suppose, just the way he'd wanted it to. My frame of mind going into this assignment was probably a factor as well. I wanted someone other than Dr. Lemare to simply *know* me. Whether it would be Gino Morelli or not was to be determined, but so far he was pushing all the right buttons.

"It's good to know I'm working with someone who's completely unprepared for the assignment," he said. "Thanks."

"How do you mean?"

"We won't be dealing with your basic mafiosi thugs on this assignment, Ms. Pace. We're going for bigger fish, even bigger than the mafia bosses. The kind of people we'll be dealing with are highly sophisticated international bosses, of the clandestine sort. Not the mafia."

"So why is the FBI sending a guy who looks like a mobster on this assignment?" I countered, but Gino wasn't offended, or deterred.

"Because I'm good at what I do," he said. "So you gonna take off those glasses, or what?"

Chapter 40

Gino Morelli had been born in Brooklyn, New York, and lived there until he was eight years old. He was raised in a good Italian family and was the oldest of four children, with two younger brothers and a younger sister. His dad worked as a chef in an Italian restaurant and had been offered a better job in Vegas when Gino was eight. The family had been based in Vegas since that time.

He was a star athlete and had gone to Stanford on a football scholarship. A knee injury during his sophomore year ended his athletic career, but Gino continued on at Stanford through a combination of financial aid, student loans, and working twenty hours a week at a local restaurant. He'd had a steady girlfriend who was also a student at Stanford, but she'd broken up with him in the last semester of their senior year. He took it hard and hadn't had a serious relationship since.

Gino graduated with a degree in business and got a job in New York in the financial industry. After two years, he concluded the world of business was not his destiny, so at the age of twenty-three, he applied for a job at the FBI and was accepted. The FBI assigned him to their attaché office in Luxembourg. The attaché offices around the world were there to help the FBI build relationships with foreign law enforcement agencies. This included local, national and international groups, including Interpol. During his three years overseas, Gino established a number of strong contacts with law enforcement officials in Luxembourg, the Netherlands, Belgium, Germany, and France. These contacts were an important part of his next assignment.

At the age of twenty-six, Gino was transferred to the NYC field office and given a job as an undercover agent, which he'd been doing for the past five years. Most of his assignments involved tracking and making contact with reputed high-level international criminals, with the ultimate goal of proving their guilt and capturing them. Gino was often invited by foreign governments, especially those in the places he'd worked while overseas, to handle cases on their soil. These invitations were essential for the FBI's direct involvement outside of the US. Otherwise, the work would fall into the jurisdiction of the CIA. But Gino's contacts were strong, and the trust in him was impressive. People wanted to work with him. He was more than a smooth talker. He was honest, and always did what he said he was going to do.

The opening in Las Vegas was a great opportunity for Gino, because his family was still based there. His father continued to work at the Italian restaurant, his mom was an active volunteer for the local Catholic church, and his younger sister was at graduate school at UNLV. His two brothers were working back east, but came to Vegas regularly. Apart from the family connection, Vegas was also a popular destination for many of the criminals on Gino's radar. He would still have to travel out of the country on cases, but he would also get the chance to work locally from time to time.

I didn't spend much time in Gino's short-term memories, just enough to gather the highlights of this week's assignment. Gino was posing as an independent businessman trying to make a substantial purchase of heroin from an international syndicate. The guy we'd be meeting was a Russian. I was supposed to be Gino's girlfriend, and in this case, his translator, if necessary. Hence the need for me to learn Russian, plus the country's history and geography. The meeting with one of the operatives from the syndicate was to take place in Amsterdam. I wondered how all of this could be done in time for me to get back to the base by the weekend, which was one of the very strictly enforced provisions of the DOD's agreement with the FBI. I wasn't aware of any restriction on me traveling internationally, but in retrospect, that might have been something the DOD should have insisted on.

Overall, Gino Morelli turned out to be an outstanding person of the highest integrity. I wasn't sure if my internal marking system was still functioning, but if it had been, he would probably be marked as a candidate for World 2A.

"Okay, I'm up to speed on you," I said.

"Everything check out?" he asked, grinning.

"Yeah, you're good. And I know the assignment for this week too. But I have a question."

"Shoot."

"So it's Monday," I said. "Are you going to be able to get me back where I belong by Friday?"

"Probably," he said.

"Won't it be a problem if we don't make it back? For you?"

"Probably."

"When is the meeting?"

"Wednesday evening, over there," he said. "Fly back Thursday, theoretically. Gives us a day to play with if there's a delay in the meeting."

"Where do we start?" I asked.

"I'll drop you off a block from the Vegas field office this morning. I never go in there. They know you're coming, and they've brought in some Russian language teacher to work with you."

"Okay," I said. "Where will I be staying tonight?"

"We've booked you into the Bellagio for tonight. Tomorrow we'll fly to Chicago, take a night flight to Amsterdam, and arrive there Wednesday morning. That'll give us all day to make the time adjustment before the meeting. But I have a question for you, okay?"

"Sure."

"I'm told all I have to do is get you in front of this guy and you'll know his whole life history, including all of the people he works with and the locations of where they keep the drugs. The whole spiel. Is that right?"

"Yeah, that's right," I said.

"How long will it take?"

"About five minutes, just like it did for you."

"Okay," he said. "That'll be great. Make my life a whole lot easier, that's for sure. Assuming we don't get killed, of course."

"It's pretty dangerous, isn't it?" I asked.

"Yeah, and since you have no training in this kind of thing, I figure it increases our risk. I'll do my best to get you up to speed. But first things first. I'll drop you off here, and maybe meet you tonight at the Bellagio for dinner to continue briefing you. That okay with you?"

"Sure," I said as he brought the car to a stop on a side street.

"You need the address?" he asked.

"No thanks. I've been there before."

"Okay. Later alligator."

"Bye," I said. I stepped out of the car and went to the field office to learn Russian.

Chapter 41

I'd taught myself how to read in some of the Romance languages during my time living in the glass house—French, Spanish, and Italian—but my pronunciation was poor because I'd never heard the languages spoken. But picking up the meaning of the written language was easy. I just had to read a few books in those languages, and somehow, the meaning of the words just came to me. I figured Russian would be a little more challenging since it had a different alphabet, and I also needed to be able to speak it. It seemed likely that the memories of the guy I was going to be reading would be in Russian, so I really needed to know the language well from both a written and spoken perspective. I had a plan for accomplishing that, but I was certain it would be a different plan than that of the person who'd been assigned to teach me.

After my identity was confirmed and I'd gone through security at the field office, I was brought to a conference room stocked with high-tech gear, like a sophisticated sound system, a video screen, and a few laptops on the conference table. An older man was sitting on the far side of the table, and he stood up when I entered. He was a typical FBI employee, wearing a dull gray suit, a white shirt, and a paisley tie, with neatly combed gray hair. He introduced himself as Dr. Ivanov, and while his English was good, it was clearly a second language for him, maybe even a third or fourth. He had obviously been born in Russia. As protocol demanded, I had my glasses on, which would make the learning process more difficult, but not impossible, if I could talk Dr. Ivanov into my approach.

"Dr. Ivanov," I said. "Have you been briefed on my 'abilities?'"

"Yes, I have," he said, his Russian accent clearly present. "But I must admit, Ms. Pace, I am not exactly sure how to proceed. It seems highly unlikely, to me, you will be reading, and speaking Russian by the end of the day."

"I have an idea for an approach that should work," I said, confidence in my voice.

He brightened at this statement, almost as if my success learning Russian would somehow enhance his own career, which was hard to understand since he was already well past retirement age from what I could see. It was clear he was going to cooperate, though, which was a big first step.

"The first thing I need to see is a book on the Russian alphabet," I said. "Do you have one of those?"

"Why yes, I do," he said. "Here it is, right here."

He pushed the book across the table, and I picked it up. It was more of a pamphlet, perhaps twenty-five pages long.

"Would you like me to stay here while you study, Ms. Pace, in case you have any questions?"

"Oh, this won't take long," I said. "But I would love a cup of black coffee, if it's convenient."

"Yes, of course," he said. "I will have some myself, as well. I'll be right back."

I picked up the pamphlet and read it. I learned that the modern Russian alphabet contained thirty-three letters—twenty consonants, ten vowels, one semivowel and two modifiers that altered the pronunciation of a preceding consonant or following vowels. There were some signs, called Hard signs and Soft signs, that indicated certain letters were not to be vocalized, and some rules on how to spell and pronounce words that were not native to the language. I read the book again, committing everything to memory, and placed it on the table. Dr. Ivanov returned with the coffee.

"How are we doing?" he asked, his tone jovial as he placed my cup in front of me and returned to his side of the table. I wondered if he was preparing himself for the worst or just happy he wouldn't have to work too hard that day.

"Thank you for the coffee," I said. "It's going fine, Doctor. I was wondering if you could run through the pronunciation of the letters in the book for me, once or twice."

"Of course," he said, and he didn't need the book to do it.

When he'd run through the pronunciation of the letters twice, I held up my hand.

"Too much information, eh?" he asked.

"No, sir. I can repeat the pronunciations back to you now, and please let me know if I make a mistake." I recited the alphabet sounds to him and watched his eyebrows go up.

"Oh my," he said, his eyes wide. "That was perfect!"

"Thank you, Doctor. Now, may I ask for a book written in Russian? I've read most of Dostoevsky's books in English, and I really like *Crime and Punishment*, if you have it."

"We have no hard copies of books, but I can pull up the Russian version of *Crime and Punishment*, and you can read it on the laptop that is in front of you."

"I'm not sure about that, Doctor," I said. "I've never used a computer."

He sat back in his chair.

"Oh, I see," he said. "Well then, perhaps I can show you how to use the mouse, which is what you use to scroll from one page to the next."

"Okay," I said. "I'm sure I'll get the hang of it."

"First, I will find the document and load it onto your machine."

Dr. Ivanov fiddled with his computer. Then I saw my screen come to life, and the title page of *Crime and Punishment,* in Russian, appeared. I noticed it also had appeared on the video screen that was mounted to the wall of the conference room. The doctor came over and gave me a quick lesson on how to use the mouse, and I began reading the book. I had successfully learned to read other languages by simply reading books, but all of these languages used the same Roman alphabet as English. Because of this, my reading of *Crime and Punishment* started out very slow. I'd say it took me nearly a full minute to read the first page. Then I started to get the hang of the way this language worked, and my speed picked up. By the time I was about halfway through, around page three hundred, I was reading a page in about ten seconds, and by the end, I was under five seconds a page. Dr. Ivanov sat patiently, for nearly two hours, until I finished. I closed the book and looked up at him.

"So, you are finished?" he asked, his tone incredulous.

I nodded my head.

"Amazing," he said. "And you understood it all?"

"Well, yes," I said. "But I had the advantage of having read the book in English previously, but that was actually the key to me understanding certain words. I have a photographic memory, you see."

"Yes, one would have to in order to do what you have done," he said. "What do we do now?"

"I was thinking you could read the first chapter aloud to me, and then if we could begin speaking, only in Russian, I should be able to pick it up."

Dr. Ivanov read the first chapter of *Crime and Punishment* to me, and after that, we spoke only in Russian, for the rest of the day. The first thing he said to me in Russian was, "Are you hungry? It's nearly lunchtime."

Chapter 42

It was an understatement to say the Bellagio was a lot nicer than any hotel I'd ever stayed in. My mom and I had gone to the Outer Banks a few times and stayed in basic hotels, and when I was on assignment with Terry, he usually booked us into Hampton Inns or Marriott Courtyards. Even those were much nicer than anywhere I'd ever stayed, and they put my glass house at the base to shame. But the Bellagio was a whole different animal.

The room was on the tenth floor and overlooked the lake and fountains I'd seen on the way in. The bedroom had a massive, king-size bed, and there was a well-stocked mini bar and a large desk with all of the electronic accessories, none of which I needed. The bathroom was large and fabulously appointed. The vanities were made of marble, and there were even lighted makeup mirrors in there. But the huge soaking tub was what drew my attention. It had been so long since I'd soaked in a tub I couldn't resist it, so I got the tub filling, then found some bubble bath and poured it in. I stripped off my clothes and lay down in the luxurious, bubbly water. It was heaven. When I finally got out, I put on one of the Bellagio robes that was hanging on the back of the bathroom door, dried my hair with the hair dryer, then put on some makeup. Unfortunately, I had to put my dull gray business suit back on, for lack of anything better, but what can you do when you're a pauper in a palace?

When I left the room and went back to the main floor of the hotel, I had time before dinner to walk around, trying to get a feel for the place, but it was too immense to take in at one time. The lake and fountains outside were amazing. And inside, in addition to the casino, there was a luxury shopping mall called the Shops at Bellagio that had all the high-end brands like Gucci, Hermes, Louis Vuitton, etc. I knew about these brands from all the reading I'd done, but I'd never owned anything that expensive. To be honest, I really didn't understand what the fuss was all about, but people with money seemed to keep these places in business, so who was I to argue? I also stumbled into the Conservatory and Botanical Gardens, and the place was so sprawling and so filled with exotic plants that it was easy to get lost. Unfortunately, I had to leave sooner than I wanted to, because I was meeting Gino for dinner at seven.

I found the restaurant, a place called Picasso, and it became apparent that I was slightly underdressed. The boring gray pantsuit the FBI had given me was no match for most of the other diners. The other women were in evening gowns and sexy dresses, and the men wore fancy suits—some even had on tuxedos. It was clear I would be dining over my head, just as I would be sleeping over my head, later. I was never a big sleeper, so it was comforting to know the casino would be open all night if I was bored. I didn't intend to gamble, even though I knew I could walk away rich, but there was nothing for a person like me to do with money. I was a prisoner out on work release, nothing more, and the shock collar was there to stop me, hidden under my fully buttoned blouse, should I decide to make a run for it. While I'd been having thoughts about trying to escape recently, from sheer boredom more than a desire to "make a new life," this new assignment had sparked my interest, and I wanted to see it through.

Gino arrived at 7 p.m. sharp. He was wearing the same fancy suit he'd been wearing when he picked me up thirteen hours earlier, with a fresh shirt and a different tie, so he fit right in. We were escorted to a table for two that would give us some privacy. As we walked toward our table, Gino pointed out that much of the art on the walls was by Picasso himself. Frankly, I was getting a little annoyed that everything in the Bellagio shouted "Money, Money, Money," but I guess that was what casinos were all about. It certainly was a change of pace for me, so I stopped short of actually complaining to Gino. That would have been extremely disingenuous. On the contrary, I wondered why he'd booked me in here at all, and I asked him as much.

"I don't understand how I went from Hampton Inns to the Bellagio," I said. "What gives?"

Gino chuckled.

"Look," he said. "I don't want to disparage Terry and the job he's done for the agency. He's a real pro, and whatever job he's ever been assigned, he's done it impeccably well. And he's been recognized for it, and now he'll have a desk job in DC as his reward. My pay grade is no different than his, but the type of work I do is very different. I work at the upper end of the spectrum in terms of wealth and power, and the agency feels I need to live that way as well, in order to play my role to the best of my abilities. I don't always have a partner working with me, but when I do, they get the same treatment I receive."

"Okay," I said.

"Why are you still wearing those glasses?" he asked. "I told you it wasn't necessary when you're around me."

"To be honest, it helps me, sometimes," I said. "I need to concentrate on what you're going to tell me about the assignment, and having memories from you, or the waiter, or whoever happens to be sitting near us is a big distraction."

"Thanks for telling me that," he said. "That's useful information."

We ordered wine and appetizers, and Gino asked me how my Russian lessons went. I told him I'd become a fluent reader and speaker in the morning, then studied Russian history and geography in the afternoon. Dr. Ivanov said I was ready, so that part of my training was complete. Gino said he'd been briefed by Dr. Ivanov, who was dumbfounded by my ability to learn the language so quickly, having never seen anything like it throughout his long career. Then Gino said something that threw me off a little.

"So I'm told you have some kind of a shock collar on, and they gave me this little remote to use in the event you disappear, or try to disappear."

He pulled the remote out from a hidden pocket inside his lapel, and while he was doing that I caught sight of the shoulder holster and gun he was wearing. Nothing new there.

"Yep," I said. "Terry had that as well. And they have a master control back at the base, in the event that I were to overpower you before you could use yours."

Gino seemed to find this amusing, even though I was certain he'd been briefed on my extraordinary strength, which had nearly doubled since I'd grown into adulthood. It didn't matter to me. I had no intention of escaping, at least not until this assignment was over, and maybe not even then, depending on how it went. Suddenly, Gino pushed a button on the remote. I heard a click on the collar and realized that he'd unlocked it.

"If you want to go to the lady's room and take that off, it's fine with me," he said. "And if you don't come back, I guess I'm fired, but hey, it just doesn't feel right to me. We're either going to trust each other, or this case does not move forward."

"I'll take it off when I get back to my room," I said. "And thank you. I've already decided I want to see this assignment through. It seems a lot more interesting than most of my gigs with Terry. There were a few that were pretty cool, like the one with the arms dealer, but most of them were quite boring."

"I read the file on that case," he said. "You won over two million bucks that night. And I'm pretty sure the agency cashed in those chips and kept the money. So as far as I'm concerned, you've paid your way and then some. Staying here at the Bellagio is the least the agency can do for you."

"Thank you," I said. "And about the collar. That means a lot to me, Gino. May I call you Gino, or is Agent Morelli what it's going to be?"

"Gino is good for now," he said. "If I can call you Maddie. Is that okay?"

"Sure," I said.

"But when we get on that plane tomorrow afternoon, both of us will have completely different names. Capisce?"

"Capisco, signore," I responded.

"So you speak Italian too?"

"I read it better than I speak it," I said. "Same with my French and Spanish. I haven't had much chance to hear those languages spoken. But my spoken Russian is good, I promise."

"Amazing," he said. "This is going to be fun!"

"I'm excited too," I said. "But a little nervous. Are you going to brief me in greater detail on this case?"

"Indeed. Let's order our main course, and then we can go over a few things."

Chapter 43

Gino explained that the Russian man we'd be meeting in Amsterdam was not part of the traditional Russian organized crime groups like the Odessa Mafia. In fact, this man didn't even live in Russia; he hadn't been seen inside the country for the past ten years. Unfortunately, his place of residence was completely unknown. He owned a large yacht that he stayed on quite a bit, and it came into port all around the world at various times. But the boat never stayed long in any given port of call, and neither did he.

His name was Boris Volkov, which when translated into English meant Fighting Wolf. It was undoubtedly an alias, one of many used by this notorious criminal. He was a high-level executive in a crime syndicate that specialized in anything opium-related. This included the opium poppy itself, which they sold by the container load, as well as the many drugs that were made from it, including morphine, codeine, and of course, the most well-known—heroin.

Volkov was in his mid-forties, was known to be ruthless, and never stayed with a woman for more than a month.

There was always one by his side, though, and undoubtedly there would be one accompanying him during the dinner meeting as well. It was unclear how much business he would discuss in front of his date, or in front of me, so Gino warned me in advance to take advantage of any time I had in Volkov's presence to access and record both short-term and long-term memories, with special emphasis on his criminal activities.

Gino told me the place we'd be dining was called Café Loetje, a steakhouse not far from the Museumplein, which was where the famous Rijksmuseum and Van Gogh museum were located. It was frequented mostly by locals, but international visitors who were "in the know" also went there. According to Gino, it had the best steak in Amsterdam, by far.

"Do they have other items on the menu?" I asked. "I don't eat beef or pork, or chicken for that matter."

"I believe they have one vegetarian offering and one fish offering," he said. "And they have a great salad selection. But Loetje isn't as fancy as say, this place here, so we'll have to dress you appropriately."

"You mean the dress I wore the night we took down the arms dealer won't be coming out of mothballs?" I asked.

"I heard about that dress," he said, grinning.

"From who?"

"Terry, of course. He said you were a knockout in that dress."

"He never said anything like that to me. Would have been nice to get at least one compliment from the guy."

"Well, he's by the book," said Gino. "I'm a little more of a freelancer. Have to be, really. And that's why I'll tell you in advance that your looks could be a problem, for both of us."

I wondered if Gino was hitting on me, which had never happened to me before. I mean, I knew Terry liked me, but he'd never done anything forward with me. I'd read about men making advances in books, but never experienced it, due to my limited contact with other human beings since I'd become an adult. And while I thought Gino was a very handsome man (although I hated the way he wore his hair), it seemed premature, and inappropriate, for him to be so forward. Nevertheless, I could feel my cheeks reddening. He quickly clarified what he meant.

"What I mean is that this guy Volkov is a real womanizer. He takes pride in always having a beauty by his side. But with you there, it's not likely his date will be the best-looking one at the table, and that could be a problem."

My blush continued to blossom as I heard this, but I needed to understand more fully what Gino was getting at.

"How would that be a problem, if it were true?" I asked.

"Jealousy, number one. Jealousy of me. That's not a good foundation for the consummation of a business deal."

"And number two?"

"He might want *you*, to be blunt," said Gino, and now I saw a little red appear on his own cheeks. "And guys like this usually get what they want."

"So what do we do about this? I mean, why would the FBI even assign me to this case if they knew it would be an issue?"

"Because I asked for you," he said.

"Why?"

"I need the intel that you, and only you, can get from this guy. Meets like this are not so easy to come by, so we have to maximize the opportunity."

"Okay, so what do we do?"

"There's only so much we *can* do, but I'm certainly not going to have you wearing a dress that shows off your body like the one you wore in the casino that night."

"Why don't I wear this then?" I asked.

"That's like announcing, 'Hi, I'm with a federal agency and I'm going to arrest you now.'"

"Okay, so when will we get something for me to wear? Doesn't our plane leave at noon tomorrow?"

"Yeah," he said. "We can just go over to the Shops at Bellagio when we finish dinner. They'll have something that'll work, I'm sure."

We finished eating and went shopping for an outfit. We found two at Jolie Paris that Gino thought would be fine, then bought a handbag at Prada, a watch at Cartier, and a pearl necklace and diamond bracelet at Tesorini. The total for all of these things came to over $15,000, but Gino didn't bat an eye. While I was trying on dresses, I had to remove the collar, and when I came out with it in my hand, he took it and put it into the pocket inside his vest.

"You won't be needing this anymore," he said. "At least until I take you back to the base on Friday."

I raised my eyebrows, knowing it meant I could walk away from all of this as soon as he left. But he knew that too. And then I realized that this "trust" thing he'd been referring to was real for him. We would soon be walking into a dangerous situation, and we needed to trust each other. He'd certainly earned mine, by allowing me to take off the glasses, and by removing the shock collar. Now I needed to earn his. I wouldn't run—not yet.

Chapter 44

Our plane touched down at Schiphol International Airport in the Netherlands at 8:59 a.m. on Wednesday. It had been Tuesday when we left, and technically, it still was in Vegas. I hadn't slept on the plane, but I wasn't tired. As I've mentioned before, I don't need much sleep. So I felt fine. Gino, on the other hand, looked a little haggard even though we'd had the luxury of flying First Class.

Before we left for the airport, Gino had given me a passport, a driver's license and a credit card in the name of Anna Zakarhov. It was an American passport; if it had been Russian, my last name would have been Zakarhova, to match my gender, but it didn't matter. I was an American. My story was that my parents had emigrated when I was a baby and settled in North Carolina, which would explain my Southern accent. It wasn't necessary for me to speak with a Russian accent when speaking English, but I was to say that my parents taught me Russian because their heritage was important to them. It was the political system that bothered them. They'd left before the fall of the Soviet Union, and even though democratic institutions had been installed not long after their departure, they had remained in the US, which was just as well, because the political system in Russia was still corrupt and still your basic dictatorship, in spite of the label of democracy.

Gino was now Dante Romano, an Italian-American whose grandparents had come over from Italy after World War II. He was an independent businessman of substantial means, and he had legitimate businesses to prove it, but the vast majority of his income came from his dealings in the illegal drug trade, specifically in heroin. The meeting was set up by an intermediary, who was actually an undercover agent working for a federal agency in the Netherlands. The agency had contacted the FBI and asked for Gino, whom they'd known well during his time as an attaché in the Luxembourg office.

After we came through immigration, we picked up our luggage and exited into the main area of the airport. Gino approached a kiosk and purchased two train tickets, and we went down some stairs to wait for the train. I had never known that some airports had train stations underneath, and I found it quite convenient. We took the train to Central Station in Amsterdam, and after we left the station, we walked across an area where trams were coming in and out, crossed a street, and went into the Victoria Hotel. Once again, convenient.

It was only around 11 a.m. at that point, but Gino had arranged for an early check-in. He asked me if I was hungry, and I said no. He said he wasn't either, and mentioned it would be wise for both of us to go to our rooms and take a nap. The meeting wasn't until eight that evening, and he said we could take a light meal around four, if that worked for me. It sounded fine.

When we met that afternoon in the hotel restaurant, Gino went over the details one more time. I was his girlfriend, which was why I was wearing expensive clothes and jewelry, but I also spoke Russian, which was the reason for me being there. Gino explained that normally he would attend a meeting like this by himself, but it would be reasonable to explain that I was there in the event Mr. Volkov didn't speak English. Background information on Volkov from the Dutch authorities, while sketchy, indicated that he *did* speak English, but if Gino were truly an independent businessman, he very likely wouldn't know that. Hence, my presence. Gino mentioned that it might be possible Volkov would ask me to leave, once it was clear I wasn't needed to facilitate the meeting, but he felt that wasn't likely once Volkov got a look at me. According to Gino (and by the way, it's not me saying this, I'm just repeating what Gino said), yes, I would be dressed in an understated way, but there was no way to hide my natural beauty. He said that even if we shaved my head and dressed me in a potato sack, I would still be attractive to men. Anyway, let's move on from this. It makes me uncomfortable.

We both had a salad while we talked, and when we were done, Gino suggested we meet at six thirty for a drink in the hotel bar, then catch a tram over to Café Loetje. Apparently, Gino went there every time he came to Amsterdam, so he knew the easiest way to get there. I went back to my room, showered, put on some makeup, and dressed.

The dress I chose was the one I was most comfortable in. It was a full-length sweater dress that exposed none of my long legs or anything up top, but it did leave room for the string of pearls to be seen. It was dark gray, almost black, and made from some kind of material that was soft and warm. In

October there it could get a little nippy at night, according to Gino, and even though I had a shawl to help keep me warm, I was happy to be wearing that dress. The only negative was that I needed to wear heels to keep the dress from touching the ground, and even though they were medium height and had a block heel design, they still made me taller than I really wanted to be.

After putting on my Cartier watch and diamond bracelet, I dabbed on just a touch of light perfume, grabbed my shawl, and headed down to meet Gino at the bar. He was sitting right up at the bar itself and beckoned me to join him on the barstool next to him. I was surprised to see he had actually dressed down a bit from what I was used to seeing him wear. He wore khaki pants, a blue button-down shirt, and a blue blazer, but no tie. I mean, he and I looked fine together as a couple, but I didn't understand why he had ditched his fancy suits for this.

"What happened to your suit?" I asked.

"The guy has done his research on me, and I'm sure he's already seen pictures of me dressed in tuxes and fine suits. Café Loetje is an eclectic place, so the way I'm dressed will probably be somewhere in the middle of where everyone else is dressed. Volkov has apparently been there before, because *he* requested the meeting to take place there, so my guess is he won't overdress either."

"But what about me? Am I overdressed?"

"Not at all," he said. "A lot of people go there to eat before going to a show at one of the theaters in town, so there'll be plenty of ladies more well-dressed than you. On the other hand, there'll be a lot of women dressed much more plainly. But everything goes at Loetje. It's an informal atmosphere, and everyone is welcome. By the way, you look beautiful, Anna."

He leaned over and kissed me lightly on the lips. I was stunned for a moment, first at being called Anna, and then by the kiss.

"Gino, what the heck!" I said, pulling back abruptly.

"Dante," he reminded me. "And look, if you're going to be my girlfriend, you need to get into the part a little more, okay? Seriously, Anna, you're a beautiful woman, and my goal is not to take advantage of you, now or ever. But you need to get comfortable with this, and quickly. A lot is at stake, including our lives."

"I understand," I said. "I'm sorry. But I've never had a boyfriend. In fact, that was my first kiss, ever!"

"Just relax," he said, pulling me closer to him. I tried to do as he asked but was still a little tense. He leaned closer to me, whispering. "Let's make your second kiss one that you'll remember," he said. And then he pressed his lips against mine. I was stiff for a minute, resisting, and then I just fell into it. His lips were moist, and I could smell his cologne, even the mouthwash he'd used. And then he opened his mouth slightly and I followed his lead, doing the same. And then our tongues met. I felt his strong arms behind me, pulling me tightly against him, and I raised my arms up and lightly held on. And just as I was starting to feel comfortable, actually enjoying it, he pulled away. "Okay, that was better," he said.

I felt the redness going to my cheeks, but Gino, I mean Dante, pretended not to notice. He left thirty Euros on the bar, stood up and took my hand, and pulled me toward the exit.

"Time to go to work," he said.

Chapter 45

We took the number 16 tram and rode it over to the area of town where Café Loetje was located. Dante pointed things out for me as we rode along—the Red Light District, the original Heineken Brewery, a park where he said he often walked—and then we got off at a stop that looked like it was in the middle of a quiet neighborhood. He pointed up ahead, and I saw the restaurant at the corner of the next intersection, but there were no other restaurants or shops in the area. It was a peaceful place, and Café Loetje seemed like an oasis in the brisk autumn evening.

There was a line of people out front waiting to be seated, but Gino took my hand and pulled me past them. We pressed against some people, forced our way through the door, and entered the bustling restaurant. As we continued slowly forward through the crowd, I took off my glasses and slipped them into my purse. There was a bar to the right as we pushed past other patrons and found the reception counter. We gave our name, and they took us through a door and into a room that bordered the street on two sides. Every table was occupied, but one in the center had two empty seats. A man and a woman sat at the table, presumably Volkov and his date. The man waved us over, then stood to shake our hands. He wasn't what I had expected.

Boris Volkov did not in any way resemble a "fighting wolf," as his name suggested. He was shorter than average, and quite thin, almost as if he were ill. His head wasn't bald, but his hair was thinning and gray. He was dressed casually, wearing khaki pants and a white collared shirt, similar to what Gino was wearing. The woman was beautiful. She was a Euro-Asian blend and had shimmering dark hair that flowed down over her bare back, and she hadn't taken the care I had to hide what was in front, what with the plunging neckline of her dress. Boris introduced her as Lydia, but that wasn't her real name. I had already done a quick read of her and learned that she was a high-end prostitute named Patricia Lee that Volkov had hired for the night. But I didn't need to waste any time on her. He was my job, so I looked him right in the eye.

He was already staring directly at me, and the look on his face was, unfortunately, one of desire. While the information the FBI wanted poured in, he addressed me, in Russian. He asked where I was from in the mother country, and I responded that I had been born in a village about an hour south of Moscow, but had left with my family for the US as a baby. I asked him how he knew I spoke Russian, and he said I was obviously of Russian decent, so he'd taken a chance. He wondered how I spoke so well, and I explained that Russian was the language of choice inside my household; English was reserved for the outside. I told him my parents put great value on the language and traditions of their homeland. He nodded and went silent, as if he were reminiscing about his own life in Russia, and his departure ten years ago.

I was a little concerned with the way Volkov had been looking at me, with lust in his eyes, but Gino, I mean Dante, saved me and inserted himself into the conversation, steering it toward the menu. He recommended the Biefstuk ossenenhaus, beef tenderloin, and Volkov nodded, speaking in English.

"Yes, I have been here many times, Dante. The beef is wonderful. And the salads are great too."

We ordered our meals. Dante and Volkov ordered the salad appetizer and the beef main course, while both Lydia and I ordered the vegetarian meal. Volkov ordered red wine for the table and began speaking mostly with Dante, asking questions about his background, while Lydia and I talked about Amsterdam. She told me all the nice places to go, and said she particularly enjoyed the casino in town, which was named Holland Casino Amsterdam. We finished the meal, then had a wonderful dessert called Dame Blanche, and then Volkov made an interesting request that sounded more like an order.

"Ladies, do you think you might find a seat at the bar for a few moments while Dante and I speak privately?" he asked.

Of course, we complied. But as I was about to stand up, I felt Gino's hand take mine. He leaned over and kissed me, not hard, but not lightly either. I must admit that it felt good, but when I glanced over at Volkov, he was glaring at us, as if he didn't approve.

By that time, the restaurant was less crowded—after all, it was a Wednesday night—and we found two seats at the bar and ordered wine. After about twenty minutes, the two men joined us, their coats on, obviously having paid the bill. We all chatted for a few minutes and said our goodbyes.

I was surprised that when we got outside, Gino walked to the left instead of straight across the street toward the tram stop where we'd gotten off, but he explained.

"I know a place over near the Museumplein where we can have a drink and talk. I assume you have what we need?"

"Oh yes," I said. "All of it."

"Good," he said. "Did you see those two goons he brought with him?"

"Yes, I saw them. I found out they were there when I was reading Volkov's memories."

"Typical Russian enforcer types. Big, strong and ruthless."

"I hope we don't see them again," I said, but my wish wasn't granted.

We walked down the quiet street, which was darker than I would have liked. There were a few streetlights, but they were separated by long distances. Suddenly, I heard a pop, then Gino collapsed onto the sidewalk. I saw blood coming from the back of his head. I leaned down to him and pushed on him, saying his name, but he didn't move. Suddenly I felt the press of metal against my head. A gun.

"Get up," came the deep voice, speaking in Russian. "Leave him! He's dead. And you will be too if you try anything."

Anger coursed through me as I raised my hands, feigning submission, but then I pivoted and knocked the gun away from his hand. I should explain further what happens to me when the anger comes over me like that. It's like time slows down. I'm sure the men were highly trained and knew how to fight, but their movements seemed so very slow during the seconds this altercation lasted. I kicked the first man in the groin and he went down, but then I felt the strong arms of the other grabbing me from behind. I twisted out of his grasp and slammed a fist into his head. He didn't go down, but he felt it. Then I kicked him in the knee with the heel of my shoe and he collapsed, holding his knee and screaming with pain. With both men down, I ran, leaning over and snatching my purse up off the sidewalk as I departed the scene.

The heels made it difficult, so I slipped them off and held them in one hand. I reached an intersection that was busy with cars and trams and buses. I saw a bus at a stop, getting ready to pull out, and jumped onto it just before the doors closed. The bus pulled away. I looked back and saw one of the Russian guys about fifty yards away. He'd seen me get on the bus, so I'd have to make some additional evasive moves to make sure they couldn't track me. I put on my heels while I decided what to do next. I would mourn Gino's horrible death later. For now, I had escaped. I was free. And I wanted to know what freedom really felt like, at least for a while.

Part 4

Conclusion

Chapter 46

Cynthia

What year is it on Earth?" I asked.

"2006," said the Teacher.

"Last I heard, it was 2004! And that certainly didn't feel like two years ago. It seems more like two weeks ago. I can't keep track of time up here."

"As I said," he replied, "time is different here on Earth Station. Things proceed in a different way. It is the reason beings in your universe cannot see us."

"Can you explain that to me further?" I asked.

"Yes, I believe I can," he said. "In your universe, space, time, energy and matter are inextricably woven together. In our universe, there is no matter, just space, time and energy. Our species is a pure energy field, and without the presence of matter, our energy never diminishes, making us immortal. Matter, however, changes our energy field, our Essence, in a way that causes us to slowly lose our energy, and we begin to age. When we are living in our space, we don't even notice the passage of time. It passes, but we do not change with its passage, so it is irrelevant to us. Here, in your universe, the presence of matter causes time to become very relevant to us, because it will kill us if we allow it to."

"But in your current form, you're made of matter," I said. "This station is made of matter. So how do you survive here?"

"That is simple," he said. "We make the station travel very, very fast. Close to the speed of light. And in so doing, time slows down here compared to its passage on Earth."

"But I thought Earth Station was very close to Earth. I got the impression it was just sitting there, right beside Earth, but invisible to the people there because it's in a different reality. I mean, how else could they not see it?"

"I remember that conversation," he said. "I believe it was one of the first ones we had. I remember quite clearly I told you at that time it was too soon to explain this to you. And now that I have explained it, you seem as if you don't want to believe me."

I'll admit that I had no understanding of how time slows down when an object approaches the speed of light, but I wasn't trying to deny the fact that we were traveling that fast. I was just confused about how other things I knew about could happen if we were traveling so fast, so I continued probing.

"Teacher, I believe you. But I don't understand how you can get to Earth if we are just traveling through space at the speed of light. It must be a long way away?"

"We are circling Earth," he replied. "To you, the distance of our orbit is great. We are farther away from Earth than the diameter of your entire solar system. But to us, that is a small distance, in comparison to the size of the Megaverse."

"So when you go to Earth, how do you get there?"

"All of the Imprints we have placed on Earth are beacons for us. We simply lock on to one that is close to where we want to go, and the transfer is facilitated. The Imprint we use as a beacon is not even aware of our presence when we arrive."

"And the reason people on Earth can't see this station is because it's so far away?" I asked.

"That, plus our speed. There is no instrument on Earth capable of seeing Earth Station."

I was surprised that I could actually understand everything the Teacher was telling me. I'm sure the actual science, the equations and such, was far beyond anything I could ever absorb, but his explanation was easy to follow, so much so that I began to wonder how this station was affecting me. Was it making me like them, which would mean I actually could never return to Earth?

"What about me?" I asked. "As I am now. Could my Essence withstand the passage of time on Earth now that I have come here?"

"Yes, it could, because your Essence was formed there. It can return with no ill effect."

"And this body? How can it survive there?"

"It will begin to age there, whereas here it will age so slowly it is nearly imperceptible."

We were approaching the bay below my house on World 2A, and a wave of disappointment hit me as I remembered that Aya wouldn't be there to greet us, ever again. I wondered how my life on World 2A would go now that she was gone.

"Teacher?" I asked.

"Yes?"

"I will be very lonely on World 2A without Aya. She was my best friend, and I miss her. I had another close friend at work who is also gone. Can you tell me what happened to Wang Li?"

"She continued on," he said, with no emotion in his voice or on his face.

"Why?" I asked. "She was a good person."

"She was never going to take the next step. She had insecurities in her own being that she masked with humor, but they were too deep to qualify her to move on to the World of the Makers."

"But this 'continuing on,' what is it, Teacher?"

"To us, it isn't a place. It is the existence of the Essence without a material body to hold it. In our space, outside of your universe, that is our primary form. But in your universe, we do not know what happens to the Essence when the body is no longer with it. We can capture the Essence when it is still in the body, but we cannot follow it when it is free to travel on its own."

"Why?" I asked, not understanding how these supposedly all-powerful beings, who were pure Essence in their native state, couldn't follow the path of other beings' Essence. "Why can't you see where Wang Li's Essence has gone?"

"Perhaps it is because she has gone to the place where God sends people like her."

"You mean Hell," I replied. "After all, Wang Li was not a believer."

"Yes, that is what I mean," he said.

"My faith teaches that all of us are sinners, and that only those who admit this, and put their faith in God, will end up in Heaven. The rest end up in Hell."

"And do you believe that your friend Wang Li ended up in Hell?" he asked.

I paused, searching my heart for the answer to this question, and then it came to me.

"Actually, I don't believe she'll go there," I said. "She's a good person. Otherwise, she would never have been brought here to World 2A."

"But this is inconsistent with the teachings of your faith, is it not?" he asked.

"Yes, it is," I admitted. "But it's what I believe. The Bible is inconclusive on the matter of Hell, as far as I'm concerned."

"But you still believe in God, and Heaven?" he asked.

After asking his question, the Teacher pulled down the sail, and I maneuvered the sailboat up alongside the dock. He reached out and grabbed the rope, tying it to the cleat. Then he stood up, turned, and looked directly at me. I gazed up at him and saw that he was waiting for me to either acknowledge or deny his last statement.

"Yes," I said, but a sliver of doubt had crept into my being. I wondered how I could ever be the one to show the Teacher the way to God if I wasn't even sure about all the teachings of the Bible. Was I just choosing the things I wanted to believe while ignoring the others? For the first time since I was a child, a thread of uncertainty about my faith had weaved its way inside me. It was only a tiny amount of skepticism, but it was affecting me in a profound way. I knew I would have to spend time praying, alone, to see where it led me, but now was not that time. I stood up and joined the Teacher on the dock.

"Come, let us go to the Monitoring Station," he said. "I have some things to show you. Your friend Tom can help us."

Chapter 47

Maddie

I got off the bus at the next stop and ran to catch a tram that was pulling to a stop nearby. I had no idea where it was going, but it didn't matter, since my only objective was to lose the thugs who were after me. I spent a few moments looking at the map on the inside of the tram to see where it was going. It looked like it would stop at Central Station, but I wanted to be sure, so I walked up toward the driver and asked him a question. I spoke English because I didn't know Dutch, but Gino had told me that most Dutch speak English very well.

"Excuse me, sir," I said. "Do you know which tram I take to get to the Victoria hotel?"

"This tram stops at Central Station," he said. "That is where you should get off."

"Thank you, sir."

I waited until the tram arrived at Central Station and got off when it stopped. I went to the Victoria Hotel, wary that Volkov's thugs might already be there, waiting, but I didn't see them. I hurried to my room, packed my things, then made to leave, just as I realized I had no money. I'd actually ridden the bus and the tram without paying, but neither driver had said anything to me. I wouldn't get far without it. I had a credit card, but I'd read enough spy novels to know they could be traced. I sat down on the bed to think things through, and suddenly, I knew what I should do.

I left my bag in the hotel room and went down to the concierge to ask him how far away the Holland Casino was. He said it was a few kilometers and could be reached by tram or taxi. I asked how long of a walk it was, and he said that would be easy as well, only around thirty minutes. He opened up a map and drew on it with a pen, showing me the way to get there. I thanked him, wishing I had money for a tip, but promising myself to give him one if I returned.

I made the walk in twenty minutes and entered the casino. They asked for my ID, and I showed them my passport and entered. I located the poker tables and realized, of course, that I had no money. But as I thought it through, if I was going to be using the credit card, this would be the time and place to do it. As of now, no one at the FBI knew about what had happened, so they wouldn't be tracing the card in real time. By the time they started tracing and found I'd used it at the Holland Casino, I would be long gone, hopefully.

I used my credit card to buy a thousand euros worth of chips and sat down at the table with that buy-in. I was in a hurry, so as soon as I had won ten thousand, I left the table and cashed out. They gave me twenty 500-euro bills. I handed back two of the bills and asked the cashier if she could give me ten of the one-hundred denomination instead. She nodded, counted it out, and handed it to me. I stuffed all of it into my purse and left.

I walked back to the hotel and went to my room. I sat down at the desk and removed a piece of hotel stationary and an envelope from the drawer, quickly writing down all the important details of Volkov's illegal activities, also explaining that Volkov's men had killed Gino and attempted to abduct me. When I'd finished, I folded the stationary, inserted it into the envelope, wrote the address and phone number of the FBI's Las Vegas Field Office on it, and sealed it. I grabbed my bag and left the room. When I arrived at the main floor, I rushed over to the Concierge desk. The same man who had given me directions to the Holland Casino was behind the desk.

"Excuse me, sir," I said. "I was wondering if the hotel can help me send a letter to the U.S. by an international courier service?"

"Why yes, we certainly can. We primarily use DHL, but they deliver everywhere in the world."

He estimated the cost to be around 80 euros. I gave him the letter, along with two 100 Euro notes, and asked him to take care of it, urgently, and to keep the change. He promised to handle it that very moment.

"Thank you," I said, turning around and leaving the hotel. I walked across the square to Central Station and bought a first-class ticket to Paris, went to the track, and waited for the train. The train pulled into the station, the passengers disembarked, and about twenty minutes later, I was allowed to board. The train didn't leave for another thirty, but once it was moving, I relaxed.

Then I began to cry. I wept quietly to myself for a long, long time, and my tears were a mix of sorrow and horror over what had just happened to Gino. But after the train was well out of Amsterdam and speeding along toward Paris through the night, a tinge of excitement for what lay ahead crept slowly into my consciousness.

Chapter 48

Cynthia

The Monitoring Station was far away from everything else I'd ever seen on World 2A. It was near a huge complex in a hidden valley in a section of the mountain range I had never visited before. The Teacher had brought me there via his way of travel, whatever it was. While we were standing on the dock together, he took hold of my arm, and poof—we were outside a building that looked like a sprawling warehouse, surrounded on three sides by mountains, with the other side open to a flattened area that was full of building supplies like cinderblocks, sand and gravel, as well as various kinds of machinery like tractors and bulldozers, and a variety of other things, like grain and cotton.

"What is this place?" I asked.

"This is where all the things from your universe are brought in, and also some of the crops that are grown here, for processing, so the finished products can be used throughout Worlds 2A and 2B," he said.

"That's the biggest building I've ever seen," I said. "What's inside?"

"Various manufacturing, processing, and assembly areas," he said. "Things are made in there that are needed here. Grain is processed here into foodstuffs, fish are cleaned and filleted, fruit is cleaned and trimmed. Glass for windows is made in there, as are the window frames and doors. Fusion engines are assembled and tested here. There's also a sophisticated laboratory and production area where the Imprint mixes are made, the ones that end up in Department 1 of the Imprint House. The list goes on and on."

"And the workers are Imprints?"

"In this facility, yes," he said.

"I've been wondering, Teacher, about the Imprints?"

"Yes, I know," he said. "You wonder if they have feelings, as your daughter does. And the answer is no. The Imprints who work here on World 2A are more like what you call robots. They are programmed to do a job, and they do it. Shall we proceed?"

I felt the Teacher was cutting off the discussion about Imprints prematurely. I had more questions, but clearly he didn't want to discuss them at this time, so I would save them for later.

"Where are we going now?" I asked.

"To the Monitoring Station, which is at the top of that rise over there."

I followed the Teacher's gaze to a different kind of building sitting on top of one of the mountains. Equipment that resembled satellite dishes and antennas sprouted from the flat roof. The Teacher took me by the arm again and we arrived at the station. He opened a door and beckoned me to follow him in. The room we entered was about twenty feet square and ten feet high. All four walls were floor-to-ceiling screens, with hundreds of blinking lights of various colors. On one wall, most of the lights showed green, but a few were red. The only human in the room was Tom Branch. He smiled and waved when we came into the room from outside.

"Hello," he said. "I was wondering why I was the only one working right now. Where are the others?" he asked, directing his question to the Teacher.

"They'll be along momentarily," he said. "I wanted you here because Cynthia knows you and will be comfortable with you explaining how things work here. Our focus, Tom, will be on Imprint 17035."

"You mean Maddie Pace, right?" he asked, looking a little nervous.

"Yes," replied the Teacher.

"How much am I at liberty to say?"

"Everything."

Tom's eyebrows raised, but he didn't hesitate to launch into his recital of what was going on.

"Well then," he said. "Since the last time I saw you, Cynthia, at Mountain Lake, there've been some developments. First, I was instructed to turn Maddie's switch back on, which I did, but I left the other two switches off."

I already knew this, because I was the one who had forced the Teacher to make this concession while we negotiated on the details of my trip to World 3. It was immediately after I had learned from Tom about the switches in the Monitoring Station, and while it didn't feel like it, that was more than two years ago, in Earth time—the spring of 2004. But Tom didn't know I was the one who had forced the change, just as I hadn't known that Tom was the one who'd been here to receive the instruction from the Teacher, until now.

"Where are the switches?" I asked.

"There are no physical switches," said Tom. "We've been trained how to transmit instructions using telepathy."

That bit of information got my attention, and I directed my next question directly to the Teacher.

"Teacher, do the humans here have the same kind of brain that Imprints have?"

"Why yes, they do," he said. "For the sake of efficiency in production."

"So Tom is actually using his brain within a brain then, when he communicates telepathically with the instruments in here?"

"Yes," he said. "And to answer your next question, no, that part of your brain has not been activated. It's inert. But if you ever come to work here at the Monitoring Station, we will turn it on for you."

I didn't know whether to be jealous of Tom, or happy that I wasn't burdened with all the baggage that came with the brain within a brain, but the Teacher corrected my thinking before I went too far with it.

"Tom can communicate with the machinery in here, but not with humans, or Imprints," he said. "We activate only those functions which are needed, you see."

"But the brain all humans here have is capable of all the functions Imprints have, if the need arose, right?"

"Yes, but there is no need for that," he said. "We want the humans here to be human, not Imprints. Tom's enhancement is just for the sake of …"

"Efficiency," I said, completing the sentence for the Teacher.

He nodded his head, and I looked back at Tom, but I was sure the Teacher knew I had logged this new knowledge away for potential future use.

"Please, Tom, proceed," I said. "I'm sorry for the interruption."

"Not a problem," he replied. "Anyway, it's easy work, here at the Monitoring Station, but it's essential to be absolutely accurate. If you look at this panel here, you can see lights in green, and a few in red. Above each light is a number, which indicates which Imprint we're talking about. You see the one here that's labeled 17035 has a green light below it. That's Maddie."

"And where are the other two?" I asked. "The ones that remain red? Is that them over there?" I pointed at two red lights that were close to one another in another section of the panel.

"No, that's not them," he said, looking a little uncomfortable.

"Where are they?" I asked.

"They're no longer on the board," he said, gazing down at the floor.

"They're dead," said the Teacher. "They came out of the place they were hidden and immediately suffered complete brain failure, meaning the signal from here reached them."

"But why?" I asked. "Why was that necessary?"

"I explained before that their function on Earth was completed," said the Teacher.

"But you could have brought them back here, couldn't you?" I asked.

"That's not the way things work, Cynthia," he said, his tone quite firm. But I just couldn't let it go, not without explaining what was in my heart.

"I'm just saying that the Imprints on Earth aren't like the ones up here," I said. "They have emotions. They are truly sentient beings, and shouldn't be treated as robots, to be turned on and off because they might be a slight inconvenience to you. Teacher, do you understand what I'm saying?"

"Yes, of course," he said. "Tom, can you give us a moment please? If you'll step outside, I'll call you back in when we're ready to continue."

Tom left the room, and the Teacher spoke.

"The Empath Makers on World 3 have brought up this very subject, Cynthia. Their arguments have been considered, but a consensus could not be reached as to how to change the policy that has been in place from the beginning regarding the Imprints on Earth. Only one exception has ever been made to this policy."

"And that was Maddie," I said. "Her switch is on, and her number is still on the board. But do we know, for certain, whether or not she's alive?"

"Yes," he said. "Do you see the number 17035 above her on/off switch?" asked the Teacher.

"I do."

"It's green, which means she's alive. If she was dead, it would be red. If she was out of reach of our signals, it would be yellow."

"So where is she?" I asked.

The Teacher took me by the arm and escorted me to the wall directly opposite the one we'd been looking at. It was a map of Earth, which covered nearly the entire wall. It was flattened out, like what you sometimes see in books and magazines, and it was spattered with glowing lights of various colors.

"She *was* in Nevada," said the Teacher. "At a secret military base. That was where she was being hidden from us. But not long ago, she started to appear on the screens for several Earth days each week, and then disappear again, like she'd been going in and out of the protected facility. She traveled around the country while she was out, but always returned. Now, though, she's in Paris, and she appears to be staying there. We think she might have escaped."

Chapter 49

Maddie

I found a basic hotel on Île Saint-Louis that accepted cash, and I paid for two weeks in advance. Île Saint-Louis was an island on the river—the Seine—that cut through the heart of Paris. The island was right next to Île de la Cité, which was where the Notre Dame Cathedral was located, giving me great access to both the Left and Right Banks, which was highly convenient.

The first thing I did after unpacking was go for dinner at a special restaurant called La Mouftelle that I had read about once in a newspaper. It was hidden away on the Left Bank down a bunch of tiny cobblestone streets, but I found it. There were only six tables in the entire place and the food was heavenly.

First, I ordered a white table wine that seemed better than any white wine I'd ever had. I admit my experience at drinking wine was quite limited, but I'm telling you, it was good. I had fresh mussels for an appetizer, and I couldn't decide if the mussels themselves or dipping my fresh bread into the broth was the more delicious experience. For the main course, I had sea bass sauteed in butter, with lemon and some other spices on it that I couldn't name, but it was fantastic. After crème brûlée for desert, I was full—of the food. My thirst to enjoy my freedom to the maximum, on the other hand, had barely been dented, although I was off to a great start.

The next day, I found a place to get my hair changed. I had them cut most of it off and dye it black. It curled forward nicely, just covering my ears. Very French. Next, I went shopping and bought some jeans and casual flannel shirts, some undergarments, a pair of sturdy walking shoes, and several pairs of socks. I realized my supply of money wouldn't hold out forever, so I asked around and I learned there were several casinos in Paris. This meant I had a source of income for the foreseeable future, unless the casinos started banning me for constantly winning.

I hadn't yet established a routine, but I wanted to. My spoken French was improving rapidly now that I'd been in Paris for a few days and could hear the people speaking the language. I could easily understand everything people were saying and was speaking more and more myself, and everyone seemed to understand me, more or less. It made sense for me to be out and about for that reason alone—to improve my grasp of the language—but Paris was such a vibrant city that it pulled me out into the street like a nail to a magnet.

I took a walk to the Montparnasse quarter and found the café that Hemingway, my favorite author, had frequented regularly. It was named La Closerie des Lilas and was right beside le Jardin du Luxembourg, this cool park full of beautiful gardens and trees. I had a cup of coffee at the café, and while I could see it would be a good place to write if it weren't crowded, it was a little too touristy for my taste. It was also too fancy.

I walked back toward Île Saint-Louis, keeping away from the big boulevards, and when I got close, I happened upon a quaint little café and went inside. It was called Le Paradis, which means "heaven," and this reminded me of my mom. It was small and a little weathered, but it wasn't packed with tourists, and it had a nice, peaceful, slow-moving atmosphere. The best thing was it was only a five-minute walk from the hotel I was living in, so I decided to make this my place for morning coffee and breakfast. And while I had hoped the café where Hemingway had written *The Sun Also Rises* would inspire me to begin writing, it was Le Paradis that did the trick.

I went to a store and bought a writing pad and some pens and pencils, and would bring them with me each morning to Le Paradis, along with a book to read if I wasn't inspired to write. I began to write the story of my life, which was actually the story of two lives—mine, and my mom's. The ache of missing her had never left me, but writing about our lives together helped me cope with it. Sometimes, though, I still wondered exactly where this World 2A was and what her life was like there.

Chapter 50

Cynthia

The Teacher teleported me back to my dwelling above the bay and left me there, telling me he would be back soon to talk more about Maddie, and our assignment to find God. He told me I no longer had to work at the Imprint House, and I asked him what I should do to keep busy. He said I would be busy enough as soon as he returned, and disappeared.

I had time to think at that point, for the first time in a long time, and I really needed to do that. I remembered my prayer from back at Mountain Lake, the first time Aya had taken me there. I had asked God to give me a sign so I could better understand what I should do. But God had not answered me. It was the Teacher who had put my heart to rest, at least temporarily, about whether or not I should go through the door to the Transfer Station and try to get to Earth. He had explained it would be futile to do that, and later he'd told me there *was* no Transfer Station, that it was simply an empty room. There was only one way to get to Earth, and that was through the Teacher. It seemed that God wasn't going to help me at all. Not even a sign to help me figure out what I should do.

My first prayer had gone unanswered, and on the return trip on the sailboat, I had admitted that I did not believe everything that was written in the Bible. It was also becoming apparent that the Makers were as powerful, if not more powerful, than God as he'd been described by the Bible. The Makers roamed from galaxy to galaxy, from universe to universe, like it was all their own backyard. And they made life! Maddie and the other Imprints were proof of it. I myself was proof the Makers could even make life *after* death. Could my belief in God be wrong? Could it be that God was created in Man's image rather than the other way around?

Yet it seemed the Makers were looking for God too. My God. They seemed to be seeking an answer to the same question humans had asked since the dawn of time: Where did I come from? I was confused, but for the first time since I could remember, I felt like the answers to my most critical questions would not be found with God. They would come from the Teacher. So it was with great internal fortitude that I forced myself to pray, one more time.

Dear Lord. My faith is faltering. I had no answer to my last prayer, and I've admitted to myself I do not believe everything that has been written in the good book. I don't know if it was your will to send me here to this place or not, but I'm glad I came here. I've met some amazing creatures and learned that the universe is a very big place indeed. Beyond imagination. But my experiences here have caused me to question if you, Lord, are bigger than these beings, the Makers. They seem so powerful it's hard to conceive that anything could be more so. My remaining hope is that they are looking for answers too. They wonder if you *are the one that created them, I think, although they have not said this to me. But why else would such powerful beings try to use me to get to you?*

My other concern is Maddie. She's been located, and the suspicion is that she is free from her captors. But my worry for her has only grown stronger since I learned this. Please Lord, tell me what to do? Death took me from Earth, but I did not end up with you, in heaven. Does this mean I should try to return to Earth, if given the chance, or should I continue on here, trying to help the Teacher find you? But if I am to do that, Lord, I need to find you again myself, first! Please come to me, let me feel you once again, and I will remain steadfast in my quest to know you for all eternity. In the name of the Father, the Son, and the Holy Spirit, I seek your guidance. Amen.

Chapter 51

Maddie

I'd finally established a rhythm to help me pass the days. The mornings I would spend at Le Paradis, drinking coffee, eating pastries, reading and writing. They didn't mind me staying there hour after hour, and I felt very comfortable doing so. For lunch, I would wander around the Right Bank until I saw something that suited me, then dine there.

But I often skipped lunch, because I'd become so enthralled with the beauty and diversity of my surroundings that I would just keep walking. The wide, treelined boulevards were sometimes filled with cars—up to four lanes in each direction—but the sidewalks along these grand streets were also wide, allowing masses of tourists to easily negotiate them while they shopped and then dined in the endless array of outdoor cafés. And there were so many beautiful parks to choose from! You could get lost in some of them.

I remember once wandering into a park called le Bois de Vincennes and staying in there for hours. I passed by several lakes and many, many gardens, a hippodrome for horse racing and then a velodrome for bicycle racing, and even a huge zoo, where the animals were separated from the pedestrians by moats of water rather than cages. I was in there so long that it began to get dark, and by then I had lost all track of where I had entered and actually struggled a little bit to work my out. With the arrival of night, the prostitutes had descended on the park, and with them, their customers, who were not the kind of people I wanted to meet. Luckily, I found my way out and immediately took a taxi back to my hotel.

In the afternoons, I would normally return to Le Paradis and sit outside, drinking wine and watching the people go by. I didn't write in the afternoons, as the mornings were my best time for that, but I always had a book with me, and took solace in my never-ending quest to learn more. I had a habit of visiting the casinos at night, and had made a pledge to myself never to win more than a thousand euros at a time. There were eight casinos in Paris, so I could go to a different one each night, never going to the same one more than once a week. I would also lose a little money from time to time, on purpose. In this way, I was never put on the list of people who had been banned for winning too much. I had an income of five to six thousand a week, which was more than I could spend, no matter how hard I tried. The biggest issue I had with money was where to put it, so I got a safe deposit box at a bank, the largest one they had, and filled it with notes.

All in all, my life was good. Easy, and luxurious, two things I'd never experienced in large doses before. I admit I was a little lonely. I hadn't met anyone who intrigued me enough to pursue even a friendship with. I was friends with the employees at Le Paradis, but we never socialized, except when

I was a paying customer. Still, all of that was okay with me. For the first time in my life, I was truly free, and Paris was a wonderful place to experience freedom. The city had a tantalizing energy and an endless supply of interesting neighborhoods. Without too much trouble, I could find enclaves, right in the heart of the city, where children played football on the streets and the parents didn't worry about them being harmed.

In so many ways, I felt like a child again, learning about the world and its many wonders. I wore the glasses most of the time, and this allowed me to experience the world as a normal person, which I cherished. I wondered often if my mom would someday find a way to contact me, but days and weeks and months went by, and it didn't happen.

One brisk afternoon in the spring of 2007, I was sitting outside at Le Paradis, reading, or shall I say rereading, *The Old Man and the Sea*, when I looked up and saw a man I recognized walking down the sidewalk, heading in my direction. It was the man from the memory of the firefighter, Lieutenant Bradford. He was tall and thin, with long, straight blond hair. He had on jeans and a flannel shirt and could have been just anyone walking by, but the fluttering of my heart told me otherwise. As he approached my table, I could feel the rapid thumping against my chest.

"Hello, Maddie," he said, a peaceful smile on his clean-shaven, handsome face. He looked to be around forty years old, but he could have been fifty, or thirty. "My I join you?" he asked, his voice smooth and pleasant. I nodded, unable to form words at that moment, and as he sat down, a thought popped into my head.

We can speak this way, if you'd like.

"No thank you," I said. "I prefer to speak the way all people here speak."

Again, he smiled.

"Yes, of course. But you realize you are not one of them, don't you, Maddie?"

A waiter came up and asked him in French if he would like something to eat or drink.

"Une tasse de café, s'il vous plait," he responded.

The waiter left, and I had no choice but to answer his question.

"I have the emotions of a human," I said. "It's all I know."

"I can teach you more about who you are," he said.

"Why would you?" I asked. "Are you my father?"

"In a sense, yes."

Then I asked the question I had to ask.

"Do you know where my mother is?"

He didn't hesitate. "Yes. She is on World 2A, but I think you must know that already," he said.

"I certainly hoped she was. But where is it?"

"It is nearby," he said. "I can take you there, if you'd like."

"Why am I alive but the other two Imprints aren't?" I asked. "It doesn't seem fair."

The man sat back in his chair, thinking for a moment.

"Their deaths are the normal way of things, for Imprints that no longer have a function," he said. "But your mother made sure you were treated differently."

"I thought that was her," I said, a feeling of love and pride coursing through me. "What is your name, sir, if I might ask?"

"I am known on World 2A as the Teacher," he said.

"Are you like me?" I asked. "An Imprint?"

"I'm a lot like you, yes," he said. "But I am not an Imprint."

"What, then?"

"It's a long story, Maddie. I'm happy to tell it to you, but my time here will be short. I would like you to come with me to World 2A."

"And if I don't want to go?" I asked.

"You don't have to," he said. "You will not be harmed, by us. You must realize, however, that you cannot evade being captured again, forever. As we speak, powerful forces have been mustered to find you."

"I supposed as much," I said. "But I really love my life here. I'm lonely, but I believe that time will take care of that, eventually."

"Don't you want to be with your mother again?" he asked.

"More than anything on Earth," I responded.

"Then come with me." His voice was imploring.

"Why can't she come here, and be with me here?"

"She has responsibilities on World 2A," he said. "And more than that, she has the opportunity to become one of us, a being like me."

"What about me?" I asked. "Can I become like you?"

"I don't know, Maddie," he said. "It has never happened, but then again, it has never before even been considered. I won't rule out that possibility."

"Teacher," I said, "if I come with you, will I ever be able to return to Earth?"

"I don't think so," he said. "But you have nothing here. All that you care about is on World 2A."

"That's not true," I said. "The most important person in my life is on World 2A, no doubt. But what you don't seem to understand, sir, is that even though you call me an Imprint, I am human in more ways than I am *not* human. Yes, I have these 'abilities,' as people call them, but at my core, I'm human. And humans live on Earth."

"They also live on World 2A," he said. "As your mother does."

"I've never been to your World 2A, sir, but I doubt very much that life is lived there as it is here. Life here is so full of surprise, excitement, disappointment, anger, joy, et cetera, et cetera. You say you're in some way my father. Please Father, bring Mother to me, here. Let us live our lives as best we can. Here. On Earth. She deserves to live a full life, here, and so do I!"

The emotion of my words seemed to bring an end to our conversation. The Teacher stood up and gave a slight bow.

"Goodbye, Maddie," he said. "Until we meet again."

"Wait!" I said, urgency in my voice. "Are you going to bring my mother here?"

"No," he said. "But I will return, in time."

Then he simply disappeared. I looked around to see if anyone had noticed, but the staff was all inside. I was the only patron sitting outside, and there were no people nearby on the sidewalks. He was gone.

He knew my mother and was willing to bring me to her, but I had said no. Had I done the right thing? I felt that I had, but the pain of loss was so extreme it rivaled my pain at the moment of my mother's death. Had my own selfishness led to the loss of any chance of seeing her again? What would she think of me if she knew what I had done?

Chapter 52

Cynthia

For lack of anything better to do, I walked to town, had some fish and vegetables, and wandered into the wine bar. Aya and I had been there many times together. Aya didn't drink alcohol at all, and I rarely had more than one glass during any given visit, but now I found myself well into my second glass, and yet I still felt so alone. Aya and Wang Li were gone, I no longer had a job on World 2A, other than to introduce the Teacher to a God I couldn't even find myself anymore, and my daughter was known to be alive in Paris, but that was far, far away from where I was now. And the Teacher had simply disappeared.

I finished my wine and left, wandering aimlessly in the general direction of Mountain Lake. I suppose I felt being there might help me feel better. It was always uplifting to see Jimmy there, performing great feats of diving from high up on the cliffs, being so warmly received by whoever was around at the time. And in thinking of Jimmy, of the life he'd endured on Earth before coming here, I began to feel less sorry for myself. Then my mind and heart began finding each other. They were not yet aligned, but the semblance of a plan was taking shape, and I hoped that by the end of my walk, I would have closure on what I truly wanted to do with my life, and my soul.

My contemplation was interrupted when the Teacher appeared by my side and joined me in my walk to Mountain Lake. This did not deter me at all, though, because I very much needed to speak with him.

"Teacher," I said, "I'm so glad to see you."

"And I you, Cynthia," he replied, a nearly imperceptible smile appearing on his face.

"Really?" I asked. "Are you truly glad to see me?"

"Yes, of course," he said. "Why do you ask that?"

"I'm just confused, Teacher. You say the Makers have no emotions, but being happy is an emotion. How do I reconcile this?"

"We are a species dedicated to learning," he said. "We are learning about emotions from your species. We are learning, and ultimately, we begin to feel some of the things you feel. Not as purely as you do, but we feel *some*. And so I can say with confidence that I feel some happiness to see you."

"But you can't feel love, can you?"

"Not yet," he said. "But I understand it."

"Why do you want to know my God?" I asked.

"We seek to know all things. Your God is something we do not know."

"Do you know where your species came from?" I asked.

He paused before he responded, as if he were debating whether or not to answer me.

"No, we do not," he said. "Perhaps your God will know."

"Perhaps," I said. "But I must admit that doubt about God has crept into my heart. I've lost touch with Him, so I feel certain I cannot help you meet him."

"Yes," he said. "I know this, and therefore the Council knows this, and all Makers know this."

"I'm wondering, Teacher, did you place this doubt in me?"

"I'm afraid not," he said. "That would have defeated the purpose of what we were trying to achieve. But that experiment is over now. It failed more swiftly than we had hoped."

"What will happen to me?" I asked.

"I don't know," he said. "What do you want to happen?"

As we approached Mountain Lake, I knew this was the moment of truth for me. My mind and heart aligned, and I said what I felt was the truth.

"I want to be with my daughter again, on Earth." As I said the words, I realized this had always been the truth. I wanted more than simply to assure her safety and freedom. I wanted to finish what we had begun together. I wanted this far more than I wanted to be here, or on World 3 as a Maker, more even than I wanted to spend eternity in the Kingdom of Heaven in the presence of our Lord. I wanted life on Earth, with Maddie, for as long as we could have it, together.

The Teacher was quiet for a moment. We turned off the road and began the walk down the path to the lake. I could hear people down below, having fun together, laughing and swimming and diving, but I was no longer one of those people. My time on World 2A was over, and I had failed in my assignment to show the Teacher God. It seemed my fate now would be determined by the Teacher and his colleagues, but I was no longer confident where my soul would go if it was released into the void by a second death.

"As you have just thought," he said, "your time on World 2A is finished. Your desire to become a Maker is nonexistent. And you seem uncertain now about whether or not you will go to your God if your Essence is released. But Cynthia, no human who has been remade here on World 2A or World 2B has ever been returned to Earth."

"Why?" I asked.

"There has never been a reason to do so."

"But Teacher, the only reason I died at all was because of you. Because of your experiment with human emotions."

"Yes," he said. "Yet it was also the reason why Maddie came into your life."

"That is so true, Teacher—but our time together ended prematurely. Let us finish what we have started, on Earth, where we belong, please. If you've learned anything about human emotions, you know I feel this in my core. And you must also realize there *is* right and wrong in the universe, and this is so very much the right thing to do!"

I was crying now, pleading with all my being to be allowed to follow my heart. My love of God was not dead—at least I hoped it wasn't—but at that moment, it paled in comparison to my love for my daughter, my need to be with her again.

"You ask me to let you finish what you have started, but this confuses me," he said. "What is it you have started, Cynthia?"

"Life!" I said. "Life as a mother and a daughter."

"You would be more like sisters now," he said. "She's nearly the same age as you are."

"I'll always be her mother. Please, Teacher! Please, let me go to her!"

"I must meet with the Council. This request is unprecedented. And do not forget that Maddie is an Imprint. She was not born on your Earth and was never meant to live there for any purpose other than to gather the Essences of those who might help my race improve as a species. Please, Cynthia do not get your hopes up. The more logical choice, for us, is to release you so you can find out, once and for all, if your God is waiting for you."

"That's fine, Teacher. If I can't go to Maddie, it's better that I'm released. But it would give me great comfort to know my daughter will be allowed to live after I'm gone. You need to promise me her switch will remain on."

"I cannot do that, Cynthia. This is a matter for consideration by more minds than my own."

Chapter 53

Maddie

Fall 2010

I've been in Paris for four years now, and I still love being here. I'm twenty-four and a half years old, but only the last four of those have been lived as a real human being. I write now in present tense because the story of my life is up to date. I've said what needs saying, and now I simply live and write as if this were a journal happening in real time. I write chapters in my head and record them later.

I sit in Le Paradis, enjoying my morning coffee, a croissant sitting on a plate next to my laptop, waiting to be eaten. Yes, I've purchased a laptop, a MacBook Pro, and I own a cell phone too. I'm not worried about being discovered because of the phone, because I've changed my name from Anna Zakarhov to Juliette Allard. Yes, it's a French name. My passport now is also French, and I have a French driver's license and a credit card with my new name on it. You see, when one goes to the casinos nearly every night of one's life, the opportunity to meet people who can get you things like new names and passports is continuously present, and I befriended one of them, then asked for a favor.

That said, I don't actually go to the casinos every night any more. I have more money than I need sitting in safe deposit boxes around the city, and I've decided my next project will be to find the right charities to give it to, without the authorities finding out who the generous donor really is. My expenses are modest now that I've moved out of the hotel and rented a one-bedroom apartment in one of those quiet neighborhoods with the children out on the street playing football, so I go to the casinos just for fun now. I have friends who like to go with me, and I wear my glasses so I can lose money right along with them. I've been with a few men as well, another new adventure for me, one that I find quite interesting, and sometimes thrilling. No one has stuck yet, but I'm patient. What choice do I have?

My hair is still short and black, and while I wish I could have my real hair back, that long and straight straw of my youth, I dare not risk it. Freedom is too delicious. Life is too wonderful. Still, I wonder about my mother. The being known as the Teacher has not returned to me with any news of her or of my request for him to bring her here. I had thought at least he would come back to insist that I return with him or meet the same fate as Abagail and Tommy. But no, he hasn't come. So I sit here and write, waiting for nothing, and for everything.

And then suddenly, unexpectedly, I see him. The slender man with straight blond hair, strolling casually down the sidewalk just as he did three and a half years ago. He enters the outside seating area of Le Paradis, and this time he doesn't ask my permission to sit. He simply does. The waiter rushes out, and the Teacher orders a coffee, as before. Then he looks at me, his pale blue eyes the same color as my own.

"Bonjour, Juliette," he says, a subtle smile on his face.

"Bonjour, monsieur. Pourquoi es-tu venu?"

"Because I want to speak with you again," he says.

"About?"

"Your mother, of course. And you."

"Is my mother still alive?" I ask.

"Yes."

"Is she happy?"

"I would say she is very happy, yes."

"That's good." I really am glad for her, but a little confused as to how she managed to move on with her life. I must admit that while I've also moved on, and can honestly say I'm happy, I still miss her terribly.

"She misses you too," he says. "Very much."

The Teacher has obviously read my thoughts. I suppose the glasses don't work in both directions. Or perhaps he is simply so powerful there is no glass on Earth or anywhere else that can deter his powerful mind. My thoughts return to my mom. It's good she's happy, but I'm still perplexed.

Then I see a beautiful young woman with auburn hair coming down the sidewalk. She's wearing jeans and a flannel shirt, and she's about my age. I notice she's carrying a writing pad like the one I used to write on before I got my laptop, and she has a daypack on her back, and she's looking at me, and I see that she's crying. And then I know who she is.

My eyes open wide. I want to stand and run to her, but my legs are rubber. My jaw starts shaking, and my own tears now gush as if a faucet has been turned on. She rushes to me, pulls me up from my chair, and squeezes me so hard the air is pushed from my lungs. We embrace for such a long time that it seems we'll never let go of each other, but eventually, we are done, and we sit down, staring at one another. I dare to ask the question that must be asked.

"Is this just a quick visit, or can you stay?" I ask, my voice shaky, hopeful.

She smiles the smile I haven't seen in twelve years.

"I can stay," she says, and then she breaks down in tears again, and so do I.

I look at the Teacher for confirmation, and he gives a subtle nod. Now the smile on his own face comes, and it seems more full than I would have expected from a being such as him.

"How can this be true?" I ask. "How can any of this be true?"

"Let's just call it a controlled experiment," he says. He stands and reaches out with both of his long arms, touching each of us on the shoulder.

"Until me meet again," he says. "Thank you both for teaching us things we did not truly understand, until now."

His hand comes away from my shoulder, but his other remains firmly on my mom's. I notice she's placed her own hand on top of his. He's looking directly into her eyes, and she's returning his stare with an equally direct gaze of her own. His hand slowly comes away from her shoulder, and hers falls away from his and comes to rest down by her side, dangling there with no partner. Then he disappears, leaving us alone at the table, together.

Epilogue

Cynthia

I think he likes you," says Maddie.

I blush, but I don't deny it. I just sit there smiling, thinking, feeling. Then I realize I can give her some insight into the man who is the closest thing to a father she'll ever have.

"He's learning," I say. "His people don't understand emotions. But they're trying to learn."

"Well, I think he's making good progress!" she declares, and we both laugh together.

We're still at the wonderful little café called Le Paradis. Maddie tells me it means "heaven," and I find this ironic, and a little unsettling. I still have a lot of thinking to do about what heaven really is, and isn't. I also need to get used to the fact that I'm twenty-seven years old, only two and a half years older than my daughter. I'm too embarrassed to tell her that the Teacher told me my sex drive would return when I was back on Earth. I must admit that for the first time, I did notice what a perfectly handsome man the Teacher is. He's a male version of Maddie, or at least his physical appearance is, and she's drop-dead gorgeous. But I definitely felt a surge of attraction toward him, and something else that perhaps I was unwilling to admit while I was with him on Earth Station. I care for him, and I believe he cares for me. I'm also comforted that I will see him again. "Until we meet again," he said, and he is a man of his word. I know him well enough to trust in that.

"I wonder if he let you come back because he's sweet on you?" asks Maddie, apparently unwilling to give up this line of inquiry.

"I don't know," I say. "But he did a lot of favors for me, the most significant being allowing you to go on living."

"Yeah, I knew that was you."

"And him," I add.

"Yes, like any good father would!" she jokes, but I sense she wants it that way, for him to be her father. I want it too, but for now, he's gone.

"Where do we go from here, honey?" I ask.

"I don't know. But I really like it here in Paris. I was kind of hoping you'd give it a try. I can help you learn French, don't worry about that."

And now I know, the time has arrived to tell Maddie I'm not exactly the same person she knew before I left.

"Je connais déjà le français," I say.

Maddie's eyes widened. "How?" she asks.

"The Teacher taught me before we came."

"Oh wow, great!" she says. "Was it hard? How long did it take?"

"Well, we didn't really measure time on World 2A, but it probably took a few hours, at least."

"What?" she says, dumbfounded.

I have another idea on the spur of the moment.

"Honey, why don't you take off those glasses," I say.

She tilts her head, a questioning look on her face, but she does as I say, holding the glasses up beside her like she'll put them back on any second. Then I send her a message.

You see, dear, they build humans a little different on World 2A than they do on Earth.

She takes a minute, and then I let her into my mind and she understands everything. My brain is like hers, and my inner brain has been activated, so I can do all of the things she does. I don't have any of her other programming, the marking capability and such, but we're now equals on the memory reading and telepathy. I can see she loves it, not only because she's happy for me, but because she's happy to have someone like herself as a best friend. I wonder if she understands that I can keep her out of my mind if I choose to, an ability she also has but may not have ever used. Perhaps I will teach her how one day, and maybe then I'll also tell her about the deal I made with the Teacher in order to come here. But the time for that has not yet arrived and Maddie has one more question to ask my mind anyway.

Do you have glasses? she asks, and I reach into my daypack and pull out a pair.

I actually have several, I say. *In case one of us loses a pair or breaks them.*

Then it's time for us to take a break from the thought communication, and it's good to know we both prefer speaking out loud. We put our glasses on, and Maddie tells me a few more things, still trying to convince me that Paris is the place for us to be.

"I can get you a French passport and driver's license, and a credit card, just like I have. My apartment is small, but we can get a bigger one." She's very excited, babbling almost, and I am so happy to be with her.

"What about money?" I ask.

"Money is no problem," she says. "I still have all my abilities, right?"

"Yes," I tell her. "The Teacher said you'd have to come back to World 2A for reprogramming if we want to change that."

"No thank you," she says. "I like myself just the way I am."

"As do I," I say, a mother's pride shining through my words.

"Thanks, Mom. I love you too. Anyway, my abilities come in handy at the casinos, if you know what I mean."

"In another world, I would disapprove of that," I say.

"What world is that, Mom?"

I think about that question, and then it comes to me.

"It was a world where a woman named Cynthia Pace lived, along with her daughter Maddie Pace. But both of those people have passed on, haven't they? And now there's a beautiful young woman named Juliette Allard who lives in Paris with her best friend. I don't really know what the best friend's name is, not yet anyway. Any thoughts on that?"

"How about Lili?" she asks. "Lili Allard. I've always wanted a sister."

"I think that could work," I say, excited about the future for the first time in a long while.

Then we just sit and stare at each other, basking in the glow of being together again. My little Maddie has grown into a beautiful woman named Juliette. She's smart, kind, full of spunk and vinegar, and so full of love, not only for me, but for life itself. I don't know yet what kind of woman Lili Allard will be, but I have time to figure that out, and Juliette will help me. And we'll face whatever comes next, together.

Acknowledgments

Many thanks to Dylan Garity for his insight and improvements during the editing of the book. Also to Joshua Griffin, for a fabulous cover design. And thank you to Sabrina Milazzo for her wonderful work on the inside of the book. I am also grateful to Claire Rushbrook for her final polishing.

About the Author

Steven Decker lives and writes in a small town in Connecticut, although he spends a lot of time in other parts of the world, and these places often appear in his books. In addition to writing, he enjoys time with his family, his dogs, and taking long walks in the countryside. *Child of Another Kind* is his fourth novel.

Printed in Great Britain
by Amazon

40333423R10175